12

AMERICAN CRIME STORIES

Selected and introduced by

ROSEMARY HERBERT

Oxford   New York

OXFORD UNIVERSITY PRESS

1998

Oxford University Press, Great Clarendon Street, Oxford OX2 6DP

Oxford New York

Athens Auckland Bangkok Bogota Bombay
Buenos Aires Calcutta Cape Town Dar es Salaam
Delhi Florence Hong Kong Istanbul Karachi
Kuala Lumpur Madras Madrid Melbourne
Mexico City Nairobi Paris Singapore
Taipei Tokyo Toronto Warsaw

and associated companies in
Berlin Ibadan

Oxford is a trade mark of Oxford University Press

First published as an Oxford University Press paperback 1998

British Library Cataloguing in Publication Data
Data available

Library of Congress Cataloging in Publication Data
Twelve American crime stories / selected and introduced by Rosemary Herbert. p. cm.
Contents: The cask of Amontillado / Edgar Allan Poe—The silver protector / Ellis Parker
Butler—A jury of her peers / Susan Glaspell—The other hangman / John Dickson Carr—Murder at
the automat / Cornell Woolrich—Red Wind / Raymond Chandler—The couple next door / Margaret
Miller—So pale, so cold, so fair / Leigh Brackett—Take care of yourself / William Campbell
Gault—The sailing club / David Ely—The oblong room / Edward D. Hoch—First lead gasser.
  1. Detective and mystery stories, American. 2. Crime—Fiction. I. Herbert, Rosemary.
  PS374.D4T86 1998   813'.087208—dc21   97–43719   CIP
ISBN 0–19–288047–0 (acid-free paper)

1 3 5 7 9 10 8 6 4 2

Typeset by Jayvee, Trivandrum, India
Printed in Great Britain by
Cox & Wyman
Reading, England

For

R H M

et la méthode champenoise

ACKNOWLEDGEMENTS

The editor would like to thank Edward D. Hoch for sharing his expertise and friendship. The magnificent resources of the Harry Elkins Widener Memorial Library at Harvard University were invaluable to the editor in her researches for this volume.

CONTENTS

Introduction xi

1

EDGAR ALLAN POE (1809–49)
The Cask of Amontillado (1846)
1

2

ELLIS PARKER BUTLER (1869–1937)
The Silver Protector (1909)
8

3

SUSAN GLASPELL (1882–1948)
A Jury of Her Peers (1917)
15

4

CARTER DICKSON (1906–77)
The Other Hangman (1935)
37

5

CORNELL WOOLRICH (1903–68)
Murder at the Automat (1937)
51

6

RAYMOND CHANDLER (1888–1959)
Red Wind (1938)
71

Contents

7

MARGARET MILLAR (1915–94)

The Couple Next Door (1954)

118

8

LEIGH BRACKETT (1915–78)

So Pale, So Cold, So Fair (1957)

134

9

WILLIAM CAMPBELL GAULT (1910–1985)

Take Care of Yourself (1957)

163

10

DAVID ELY (1927–)

The Sailing Club (1962)

184

11

EDWARD D. HOCH (1930–)

The Oblong Room (1967)

196

12

TONY HILLERMAN (1925–)

First Lead Gasser (1993)

206

Biographical Notes 217

Source Acknowledgements 221

INTRODUCTION

If detective fiction is a step-by-step account of the procedure undertaken by a person in the position to solve a crime, crime fiction is based upon much less predictable footing. While the gumshoes and other sleuths in detective stories proceed methodically through time and place to arrive at logical solutions, the protagonists who populate the pages of crime fiction may stray from such linear paths to discover psychological truths. Crime fiction's heroes and antiheroes may slide along snakes-and-ladders conduits from present to past in flashbacks, or search along circuitous routes into the psychology of crime.

The *Twelve American Crime Stories* assembled here are selected to show how crime writers use twists of characterization rather than plot twists to drive their fiction. The stories are also chosen to illuminate very American approaches to the dark deeds that are at the heart of crime writing, for it is fair to say that in a popular form anchored in everyday detail and the vernacular of the ordinary citizen, crime writing inevitably wears a national—even a regional—identity.

The volume begins with a work by Edgar Allan Poe that demonstrates his preoccupation with the psychology of criminal and victim alike. Poe, who laid the groundwork for so many traditional elements of detective fiction, here mortars a psychological foundation upon which conventions of crime writing have been built. In 'The Cask of Amontillado', Poe causes the reader to share the victim's mix of disbelief and horror at the actions of a criminal whose remorselessness anticipates many depictions of a similar criminal psychology, particularly in recent crime novels centred around serial killers.

Much crime writing is as dark as the crypt in which Poe's evil Montresor purports to place his cask of amontillado. It is therefore a rare treat to indulge in a crime story as effervescent as Ellis Parker Butler's 'The Silver Protector'. In a style that could be termed *la méthode champenoise* of crime writing, Butler lets loose a corker of a story. Here a homeowner's burglar phobia leads him to build a burglar trap *à la*

Rube Goldberg, complete with a glowing case of silver that tantalizes the intruder to death.

On a more serious note, Susan Glaspell, who hailed from the American heartland, was a woman ahead of her time when she wrote 'A Jury of Her Peers' in 1917. Based on an actual crime that she had covered as a journalist, this story is an important progenitor of today's issue-oriented crime writing set in a distinctly regional scene. It takes the country-wife peers of an apparent murderess to understand the dark motivation in this whydunit where every character experiences guilt on some level.

Carter Dickson, who is better known for piecing together the most impossible of puzzles under the Dickson pseudonym and his own name, John Dickson Carr, turns his talents to an exemplary tale of crime and punishment in 'The Other Hangman'. In this brown study on the psychology of bringing a neighbour to justice, the law becomes the means to the execution of both a murderer and of a perfectly legal murder. The redneck community here could only be found in America.

Cornell Woolrich, master of *fiction noir*, proves that even the brightly lit environment of an automated New York City eaterie can be the scene of dark doings, in his 'Murder at the Automat'. On the opposite coast, Raymond Chandler, the intellectual of the hardboiled genre, uses the hot California 'Red Wind' to heat up the action as gumshoe Philip Marlowe uncovers the psychological grit around which layers of language and mystery are coated in a case of stolen pearls and lost love.

Margaret Millar's uneasy attitude toward love is evident in 'The Couple Next Door', a prime example of the crime story's capacity to make readers question even everyday institutions like marriage. An outsider here learns that appearances are deceiving when the workings of the human heart do not match the impression a couple display to their neighbour. Leigh Brackett's protagonist, too, must re-evaluate his assumptions about the marriage of the love of his life to another man, when the lady is laid out dead on his doorstep, looking 'So Pale, So Cold, So Fair'.

Another lady is described as 'transparently fair' by Joe Puma, William Campbell Gault's wry but thoroughly decent private eye. In

'Take Care of Yourself' Puma proves that his powers of observation cannot be dazzled by the considerable beauty of Angela Ladugo, a 'civilized drunk on the brink of a pit'. Well-chosen wisecracks shatter this *femme fatale*'s flawless façade, revealing both Angela's inborn deceit and the author's essential wisdom.

While Puma will not be lead into temptation, David Ely's protagonist courts danger willingly in 'The Sailing Club', a tale that plunges the reader into the chilling world of corporate thrill-seeking. Here the male drive for success compels the aptly named businessman, Goforth, to pursue membership in an exclusive club open only to men who possess cut-throat qualities of competitiveness.

The versatile Edward D. Hoch, who has turned out short stories in almost every subgenre of mystery writing, provides a mesmerizing insight into the psychology of youths cooped up in a college dormitory in 'The Oblong Room'. It turns out that the case is no more open and shut than the big brown eyes of the suspect, the victim's roommate who had inexplicably remained in the room with the corpse for some twenty hours before the arrival of the police.

Tony Hillerman's 'First Lead Gasser' is a breathtaking example of the crime story's preoccupation with whydunit. The identity of criminal is never in question in this account of an American journalist covering a gas chamber execution; rather it is the truth at the heart of the crime that demands identification here. Hillerman, a former journalist who is best known for his police procedurals featuring Native American sleuths, based this story on 'one of those memories a reporter can't shake'.

While the detective story may be memorable for its appeal to the intellect, the crime story stirs the soul. Preoccupied with the emotional truth underlying human behaviour, crime fiction seeks to leave readers with memories that they cannot shake.

1

EDGAR ALLAN POE

The Cask of Amontillado

The thousand injuries of Fortunato I had borne as I best could; but when he ventured upon insult, I vowed revenge. You, who so well know the nature of my soul, will not suppose, however, that I gave utterance to a threat. At length I would be avenged; this was a point definitely settled; but the very definitiveness with which it was resolved precluded the idea of risk. I must not only punish, but punish with impunity. A wrong is unredressed when the avenger fails to make himself felt as such to him who has done the wrong.

It must be understood that neither by word nor deed had I given Fortunato cause to doubt my good will. I continued, as was my wont, to smile in his face, and he did not perceive that my smile now was at the thought of his immolation.

He had a weak point, this Fortunato, although in other regards he was a man to be respected and even feared. He prided himself on his connoisseurship in wine. Few Italians have the true virtuoso spirit. For the most part their enthusiasm is adopted to suit the time and opportunity, to practise imposture upon the British and Austrian millionaires. In painting and gemmary Fortunato, like his countrymen, was a quack; but in the matter of old wines he was sincere. In this respect I did not differ from him materially: I was skilful in the Italian vintages myself, and bought largely whenever I could.

It was about dusk one evening, during the supreme madness of the carnival season, that I encountered my friend. He accosted me with excessive warmth, for he had been drinking much. The man wore motley. He had on a tight-fitting parti-striped dress, and his head was surmounted by the conical cap and bells. I was so pleased to see him that I thought I should never have done wringing his hand.

I said to him: 'My dear Fortunato, you are luckily met. How remarkably well you are looking today! But I have received a pipe of what passes for Amontillado, and I have my doubts.'

'How?' said he. 'Amontillado? A pipe? Impossible! And in the middle of the carnival!'

'I have my doubts,' I replied; 'and I was silly enough to pay the full Amontillado price without consulting you in the matter. You were not to be found, and I was fearful of losing a bargain.'

'Amontillado!'

'I have my doubts.'

'Amontillado!'

'And I must satisfy them.'

'Amontillado!'

'As you are engaged, I am on my way to Luchesi. If any one has a critical turn, it is he. He will tell me——'

'Luchesi cannot tell Amontillado from sherry.'

'And yet some fools will have it that his taste is a match for your own.'

'Come, let us go.'

'Whither?'

'To your vaults.'

'My friend, no; I will not impose upon your good nature. I perceive you have an engagement. Luchesi——'

'I have no engagement; come.'

'My friend, no. It is not the engagement, but the severe cold with which I perceive you are afflicted. The vaults are insufferably damp. They are encrusted with nitre.'

'Let us go, nevertheless. The cold is merely nothing. Amontillado! You have been imposed upon. And as for Luchesi, he cannot distinguish sherry from Amontillado.'

Thus speaking, Fortunato possessed himself of my arm. Putting on a mask of black silk, and drawing a *roquelaire* closely about my person, I suffered him to hurry me to my palazzo.

There were no attendants at home; they had absconded to make merry in honor of the time. I had told them that I should not return until the morning, and had given them explicit orders not to stir from the house. These orders were sufficient, I well knew, to ensure their immediate disappearance, one and all, as soon as my back was turned.

I took from their sconces two flambeaux, and, giving one to Fortunato, bowed him through several suites of rooms to the archway that led into the vaults. I passed down a long and winding staircase, requesting him to be cautious as he followed. We came at length to the foot of the descent, and stood together on the damp ground of the catacombs of the Montresors.

The gait of my friend was unsteady, and the bells upon his cap jingled as he strode.

'The pipe?' said he.

'It is further on,' said I; 'but observe the white webwork which gleams from these cavern walls.'

He turned toward me, and looked into my eyes with two filmy orbs that distilled the rheum of intoxication.

'Nitre?' he asked at length.

'Nitre,' I replied. 'How long have you had that cough?'

'Ugh! ugh! ugh!—ugh! ugh! ugh!—ugh! ugh! ugh!—ugh! ugh! ugh!—ugh! ugh! ugh!'

My poor friend found it impossible to reply for many minutes.

'It is nothing,' he said, at last.

'Come,' I said, with decision, 'we will go back; your health is precious. You are rich, respected, admired, beloved; you are happy, as once I was. You are a man to be missed. For me it is no matter. We will go back; you will be ill, and I cannot be responsible. Besides, there is Luchesi——'

'Enough,' he said; 'the cough is a mere nothing; it will not kill me. I shall not die of a cough.'

'True—true,' I replied; 'and, indeed, I had no intention of alarming you unnecessarily; but you should use all proper caution. A draught of this Medoc will defend us from the damps.'

Here I knocked off the neck of a bottle which I drew from a long row of its fellows that lay upon the mould.

'Drink,' I said, presenting him the wine.

He raised it to his lips with a leer. He paused and nodded to me familiarly, while his bells jingled.

'I drink,' he said, 'to the buried that repose around us.'

'And I to your long life.'

He again took my arm and we proceeded.

'These vaults', he said, 'are extensive.'

'The Montresors', I replied, 'were a great and numerous family.'

'I forget your arms.'

'A huge human foot d'or, in a field azure; the foot crushes a serpent rampant whose fangs are embedded in the heel.'

'And the motto?'

'*Nemo me impune lacessit.*'

'Good!' he said.

The wine sparkled in his eyes and the bells jingled. My own fancy grew warm with the Medoc. We had passed through walls of piled bones, with casks and puncheons intermingling, into the inmost recesses of the catacombs. I paused again, and this time I made bold to seize Fortunato by an arm above the elbow.

'The nitre!' I said; 'see, it increases. It hangs like moss upon the vaults. We are below the river's bed. The drops of moisture trickle among the bones. Come, we will go back ere it is too late. Your cough——'

'It is nothing,' he said; 'let us go on. But first, another draught of the Medoc.'

I broke and reached him a flagon of De Grâve. He emptied it at a breath. His eyes flashed with a fierce light. He laughed and threw the bottle upward with a gesticulation I did not understand.

I looked at him in surprise. He repeated the movement—a grotesque one.

'You do not comprehend?' he said.

'Not I,' I replied.

'Then you are not of the brotherhood.'

'How?'

'You are not of the masons.'

'Yes, yes,' I said; 'yes, yes.'

'You? Impossible! A mason?'

'A mason,' I replied.

'A sign,' he said.

'It is this,' I answered, producing a trowel from beneath the folds of my *roquelaire.*

'You jest!' he exclaimed, recoiling a few paces. 'But let us proceed to the Amontillado.'

'Be it so,' I said, replacing the tool beneath the cloak, and again offering him my arm. He leaned upon it heavily. We continued our route in search of the Amontillado. We passed through a range of low arches, descended, passed on, and, descending again, arrived at a deep crypt, in which the foulness of the air caused our flambeaux rather to glow than flame.

At the most remote end of the crypt there appeared another less spacious. Its walls had been lined with human remains, piled to the vault overhead, in the fashion of the great catacombs of Paris. Three sides of this interior crypt were still ornamented in this manner. From the fourth the bones had been thrown down, and lay promiscuously upon the earth, forming at one point a mound of some size. Within the wall thus exposed by the displacing of the bones we perceived a still interior recess, in depth about four feet, in width three, in height six or seven. It seemed to have been constructed for no especial use within itself, but formed merely the interval between two of the colossal supports of the roof of the catacombs, and was backed by one of their circumscribing walls of solid granite.

It was in vain that Fortunato, uplifting his dull torch, endeavored to pry into the depth of the recess. Its termination the feeble light did not enable us to see.

'Proceed,' I said; 'herein is the Amontillado. As for Luchesi——'

'He is an ignoramus,' interrupted my friend, as he stepped unsteadily forward, while I followed immediately at his heels. In an instant he had reached the extremity of the niche, and, finding his progress arrested by the rock, stood stupidly bewildered. A moment more and I had fettered him to the granite. In its surface were two iron staples, distant from each other about two feet, horizontally. From one of these depended a short chain, from the other a padlock. Throwing the links about his waist, it was but the work of a few seconds to secure it. He was too much astounded to resist. Withdrawing the key I stepped back from the recess.

'Pass your hand', I said, 'over the wall; you cannot help feeling the nitre. Indeed it is very damp. Once more let me implore you to return.

No? Then I must positively leave you. But I must first render you all the little attentions in my power.'

'The Amontillado!' ejaculated my friend, not yet recovered from his astonishment.

'True,' I replied; 'the Amontillado.'

As I said these words I busied myself among the pile of bones of which I have before spoken. Throwing them aside, I soon uncovered a quantity of building stone and mortar. With these materials and with the aid of my trowel, I began vigorously to wall up the entrance of the niche.

I had scarcely laid the first tier of the masonry when I discovered that the intoxication of Fortunato had in a great measure worn off. The earliest indication I had of this was a low, moaning cry from the depth of the recess. It was not the cry of a drunken man. There was then a long and obstinate silence. I laid the second tier, and the third, and the fourth; and then I heard the furious vibrations of the chain. The noise lasted for several minutes, during which, that I might hearken to it with the more satisfaction, I ceased my labors and sat down upon the bones. When at last the clanking subsided, I resumed the trowel, and finished without interruption the fifth, the sixth, and seventh tier. The wall was now nearly upon a level with my breast. I again paused, and, holding the flambeaux over the masonwork, threw a few feeble rays upon the figure within.

A succession of loud and shrill screams, bursting suddenly from the throat of the chained form, seemed to thrust me violently back. For a brief moment I hesitated, I trembled. Unsheathing my rapier, I began to grope with it about the recess; but the thought of an instant reassured me. I placed my hand upon the solid fabric of the catacombs and felt satisfied. I reapproached the wall. I replied to the yells of him who clamored. I re-echoed, I aided, I surpassed them in volume and in strength. I did this, and the clamorer grew still.

It was now midnight, and my task was drawing to a close. I had completed the eighth, the ninth, and the tenth tier. I had finished a portion of the last and the eleventh; there remained but a single stone to be fitted and plastered in. I struggled with its weight; I placed it partially in its destined position. But now there came from out the niche a low laugh that erected the hairs upon my head. It was succeeded by a sad voice, which I had difficulty in recognizing as that of the noble Fortunato. The voice said:

'Ha! ha! ha!—he! he!—a very good joke indeed, an excellent jest. We will have many a rich laugh about it at the palazzo—he! he! he!—over our wine—he! he! he!'

'The Amontillado!' I said.

'He! he! he!—he! he! he!—yes, the Amontillado. But is it not getting late? Will not they be awaiting us at the palazzo—the Lady Fortunato and the rest? Let us be gone.'

'Yes,' I said, 'let us be gone.'

'For the love of God, Montresor!'

'Yes,' I said, 'for the love of God!'

But to these words I hearkened in vain for a reply. I grew impatient. I called aloud:

'Fortunato!'

No answer. I called again.

'Fortunato!'

No answer still. I thrust a torch through the remaining aperture and let it fall within. There came forth in return only a jingling of the bells. My heart grew sick—on account of the dampness of the catacombs. I hastened to make an end of my labor. I forced the last stone into its position; I plastered it up. Against the new masonry I re-erected the old rampart of bones. For the half of a century no mortal has disturbed them. *In pace requiescat!*

2

ELLIS PARKER BUTLER

The Silver Protector

When our new suburban house was completed, I took Sarah out to see it, and she liked it all but the stairs.

'Edgar,' she said, when she had ascended to the second floor, 'I don't know whether it is imagination or not, but it seems to me that these stairs are funny, some way. I can't understand it. They are not a long flight, and they are not unusually steep, but they seem to be unusually wearying. I never knew a short flight to tire me so, and I have climbed many flights in the six years we have lived in apartments.'

'Perhaps, Sarah,' I said, with mild dissimulation, 'you are unusually tired today.'

The fact was that I had planned those stairs myself, and for a particular reason I had made the rise of each step three inches more than the customary height, and in this way I had saved two steps. I had also made the tread of the steps unusually narrow; and the reason was that I had found, from long experience, that stair carpet wears first on the tread of the steps, where the foot falls. By making the steps tall enough to save two, and by making the tread narrow, I reduced the wear on the carpet to a minimum. I believe in economy where it is possible. For the same reason I had the stair banisters made wide, with a saddle-like top to the newel post, to tempt my son and daughter to slide downstairs. The less they used the stairs, the longer the carpet would last.

I need hardly say that Sarah has a fear of burglars; most women have. As for myself, I prefer not to meet a burglar. It is all very well to get up in the night and prowl about with a pistol in one hand, seeking to eliminate the life of a burglar, and some men may like it; but I am of a very excitable nature, and I am sure that if I did find a burglar and succeeded in shooting him, I should be in such an excited state that I could not sleep again that night—and no man can afford to lose his night's rest.

There are other objections to shooting a burglar in the house, and these objections apply with double force when the house and its furnishings are entirely new. Although some of the rugs in our house were red, not all of them were; and I had no guarantee that if I shot a burglar he would lie down on a red rug and bleed to death. A burglar does not consider one's feelings, and would be quite as apt to bleed on a green rug, and spoil it, as not. Until burglarizing is properly regulated and burglars are educated, as they should be, in technical burglary schools, we cannot hope that a shot burglar will staunch his wound until he can find a red rug to lie down on.

And there are still other objections to shooting a burglar. If all burglars were fat, one of these would be removed; but perhaps a thin burglar might get in front of my revolver, and in that case the bullet would be likely to go right through him and continue on its way, and perhaps break a mirror or a cut-glass dish. I am a thin man myself, and if a burglar shot at me he might damage some of our things in the same way.

I thought all these things over when we decided to build in the suburbs, for Sarah is very nervous about burglars, and makes me get up at the slightest noise and go poking about. Only the fact that no burglar had ever entered our apartment at night had prevented what might have been a serious accident to a burglar, for I made it a rule, when Sarah wakened me on such occasions, to waste no time, but to go through the rooms as hastily as possible and get back to bed; and at the speed I traveled I might have bumped into a burglar in the dark and knocked him over, and his head might have struck some hard object, causing concussion of the brain; and as a burglar has a small brain, a small amount of concussion might have ruined it entirely. But as I am a slight man it might have been my brain that got concussed. A father of a family has to think of these things.

The nervousness of Sarah regarding burglars had led me in this way to study the subject carefully, and my adoption of jet-black pajamas as nightwear was not due to cowardice on my part. I properly reasoned that if a burglar tried to shoot me while I was rushing around the house after him in the darkness, a suit of black pajamas would somewhat spoil his aim, and, not being able to see me, he would not shoot at all. In this way I should save Sarah the nerve shock that would follow the explosion of a pistol in the house. For Sarah was very much more afraid of pistols than of burglars. I am sure there were only two reasons why I had never killed a burglar with a pistol: one was that no burglar had ever entered our apartment, and the other was that I never had a pistol.

But I knew that one is much less protected in a suburb than in the city, and when I decided to build I studied the burglar protection matter most carefully. I said nothing to Sarah about it, for fear it would upset her nerves, but for months I considered every method that seemed to have any merit, and that would avoid getting a burglar's blood—or mine—spattered around on our new furnishings. I desired some method by which I could finish up a burglar properly without having to leave my bed, for although Sarah is brave enough in sending me out of bed to catch a burglar, I knew she must suffer severe nerve strain during the time I was wandering about in the dark. Her objection to explosives had also to be considered, and I really had to exercise my brain more than common before I hit upon what I may now consider the only perfect method of handling burglars.

Several things coincided to suggest my method. One of these was Sarah's foolish notion that our silver must, every night, be brought from the dining-room and deposited under our bed. This I considered a most foolhardy tempting of fate. It coaxed any burglar who ordinarily would have quietly taken the silver from the dining-room, and have then gone away peacefully, to enter our room. The knowledge that I lay in bed ready at any time to spring out upon him would make him prepare his revolver, and his nervousness might make him shoot me, which would quite upset Sarah's nerves. I told Sarah so, but she had a hereditary instinct for bringing the silver to the bedroom, and insisted. I saw that in the suburban house this would be continued as 'bringing the silver upstairs', and a trial of my carpet-saving stairs suggested to me my burglar-defeating plan. I had the apparatus built into the house, and I had the house planned to accommodate the apparatus.

For several months after we moved into the house I had no burglars, but I felt no fear of them in any event. I was prepared for them.

In order not to make Sarah nervous, I explained to her that my invention of a silver-elevator was merely a time-saving device. From the top of the dining-room sideboard I ran upright tracks through the ceiling to the back of the hall above, and in these I placed a glass case which could be run up and down the tracks like a dumb-waiter. All our servant had to do when she had washed the silver was to put it in the glass case, and I had attached to the top of the case a stout steel cable which ran to the ceiling of the hall above, over a pulley, and so to our bedroom, which was at the front of the hall upstairs. By this means I could, when I was in bed, pull the cable, and the glass case of silver would rise to the second floor. Our bedroom door opened upon the hall, and from the bed I could see the glass case; but in order that I might be sure that the silver was there I put a small electric light in the case and kept it burning all night.

Sarah was delighted with this arrangement, for in the morning all I had to do was to play out the steel cable and the silver would descend to the dining-room, and the maid could have the table all set by the time breakfast was ready. Not once did Sarah have a suspicion that all this was not merely a household economy, but my burglar trap.

On the sixth of August, at 2 o'clock in the morning, Sarah awakened me, and I immediately sat straight up in bed. There was an undoubtable noise of sawing, and I knew at once that a burglar was entering our home. Sarah was trembling, and I knew she was getting nervous.

'Sarah,' I said, in a whisper, 'be calm! There is not the least danger. I have been expecting this for some time, and I only hope the burglar has no dependent family or poor old mother to support. Whatever happens, be calm and keep perfectly quiet.'

With that I released the steel cable from the head of my bed and let the glass case full of silver slide noiselessly to the sideboard.

'Edgar!' whispered Sarah in agonized tones, 'are you *giving* him our silver?'

'Sarah!' I whispered sternly, 'remember what I have just said. Be calm and keep perfectly quiet.' And I would say no more.

In a very short time I heard the window below us open softly, and I knew the burglar was entering the parlor from the side porch. I counted twenty, which I had figured would be the time required for him to reach the dining-room, and then, when I was sure he must have seen the silver shining in the glass case, I slowly pulled on the steel cable and raised case and silver to the hall above. Sarah began to whisper to me, but I silenced her.

What I had expected happened. The burglar, seeing the silver rise through the ceiling, left the dining-room and went into the hall. There, from the foot of the stairs, he could see the case glowing in the hall above, and without hesitation he mounted the stairs. As he reached the top I had a good view of him, for he was silhouetted against the light that glowed from the silver case. He was a most brutal looking fellow of the prizefighting type, but I almost laughed aloud when I saw his build. He was short and chunky. As he stepped forward to grasp the silver case, I let the steel cable run through my fingers, and the case and its precious contents slid noiselessly down to the dining-room. For only one instant the burglar seemed disconcerted, then he turned and ran downstairs again.

This time I did not wait so long to draw up the silver. I hardly gave him time to reach the dining-room door before I jerked the cable, and the case was glowing in the upper hall. The burglar immediately stopped, turned, and mounted the stairs, but just as he reached the top I let the silver slide down again, and he had to turn and descend. Hardly had he reached the bottom step before I had the silver once more in the upper hall.

The burglar was a gritty fellow and was not to be so easily defeated. With some word which I could not catch, but which I have no doubt was profane, or at least vulgar, he dashed up the stairs, and just as his hand touched the case I let the silver drop to the dining-room. I smiled as I saw his next move. He carefully removed his coat and vest, rolled up his sleeves, and took off his collar. This evidently meant that he intended to get the silver if it took the whole night, and nothing could have pleased me more. I lay in my comfortable bed fairly shaking with suppressed laughter, and had to stuff a corner of a pillow in my mouth to smother the sound of my mirth. I did not allow the least pity for the fellow to weaken my nerve.

A low, long screech from the hall told me that I had a man of uncommon brain to contend with, for I knew the sound came from his hands drawing along the banister, and that to husband his strength and to save time, he was now sliding down. But this did not disconcert me. It pleased me. *The quicker he went down, the oftener he would have to walk up.*

For half an hour I played with him, giving him just time to get down to the foot of the stairs before I raised the silver, and just time to reach the top before I lowered it, and then I grew tired of the sport—for it was nothing else to me—and decided to finish him off. I was getting sleepy, but it was evident that the burglar was not, and I was a little afraid I might fall asleep and thus defeat myself. The burglar had that advantage because he was used to night work. So I quickened my movements a little. When the burglar slid down I gave him just time to see the silver rise through the ceiling, and when he climbed the stairs I only allowed him to see it descend through the floor. In this way I made him double his pace, and as I quickened my movements I soon had him dashing up the stairs and sliding down again as if for a wager. I did not give him a moment for rest, and he was soon panting terribly and beginning to stumble; but with almost superhuman nerve he kept up the chase. He was an unusually tough burglar.

But quick as he was I was always quicker, and a glimpse of the glowing case was all I let him have at either end of his climb or slide. No sooner was he down than it was up, and no sooner was the case up than he was after it. In this way I kept increasing his speed until it was something terrific, and the whole house shook. But still his speed increased. I saw then that I had brought him to the place I had prepared for, where he had but one object in life, and that was to beat the case up or downstairs; and as I was now so sleepy I could hardly keep my eyes open, I did what I had intended to do from the first. I lowered the case until it was exactly *halfway* between the ceiling of the dining-room and the floor of the hall above—and turned out the electric light. I then tied the steel cable securely to the head of my bed, turned over, and went to sleep, lulled by the shaking of the house as the burglar dashed up and down the stairs.

Just how long this continued I do not know, for my sleep was deep and dreamless, but I should judge that the burglar ran himself to death sometime between half-past 3 and a quarter after 4. So great had been his efforts that when I went to remove him I did not recognize him at all. When I had last seen him in the glow of the glass silver case he had been a stout, chunky fellow, and now his remains were those of an emaciated man. He must have run off one hundred and twenty pounds of flesh before he gave out.

Only one thing clouded my triumph. Our silver consisted of but half a dozen each of knives, forks, and spoons, a butter knife, and a sugar spoon, all plated, and worth probably ten dollars, and to save this I had made the burglar wear to rags a Wilton stair carpet worth fifty-nine dollars. But I have now corrected this. I have bought one hundred and fifty dollars' worth of silver.

3

SUSAN GLASPELL

A Jury of Her Peers

When Martha Hale opened the storm door and got a cut of the north wind, she ran back for her big woolen scarf. As she hurriedly wound that round her head her eye made a scandalized sweep of her kitchen. It was no ordinary thing that called her away—it was probably farther from ordinary than anything that had ever happened in Dickson County. But what her eye took in was that her kitchen was in no shape for leaving: her bread all ready for mixing, half the flour sifted and half unsifted.

She hated to see things half done; but she had been at that when the team from town stopped to get Mr Hale, and then the sheriff came running in to say his wife wished Mrs Hale would come too—adding, with a grin, that he guessed she was getting scarey and wanted another woman along. So she had dropped everything right where it was.

'Martha!' now came her husband's impatient voice. 'Don't keep folks waiting out here in the cold.'

She again opened the storm-door, and this time joined the three men and the one woman waiting for her in the big two-seated buggy.

After she had the robes tucked around her she took another look at the woman who sat beside her on the back seat. She had met Mrs Peters the year before at the county fair, and the thing she remembered about her was that she didn't seem like a sheriff's wife. She was small and thin and didn't have a strong voice. Mrs Gorman, sheriff's wife before Gorman went out and Peters came in, had a voice that somehow seemed to be backing up the law with every word. But if Mrs Peters didn't look like a sheriff's wife, Peters made it up in looking like a sheriff. He was to a dot the kind of man who could get

15

himself elected sheriff—a heavy man with a big voice, who was particularly genial with the law-abiding, as if to make it plain that he knew the difference between criminals and non-criminals. And right there it came into Mrs Hale's mind, with a stab, that this man who was so pleasant and lively with all of them was going to the Wrights' now as a sheriff.

'The country's not very pleasant this time of year,' Mrs Peters at last ventured, as if she felt they ought to be talking as well as the men.

Mrs Hale scarcely finished her reply, for they had gone up a little hill and could see the Wright place now, and seeing it did not make her feel like talking. It looked very lonesome this cold March morning. It had always been a lonesome-looking place. It was down in a hollow, and the poplar trees around it were lonesome-looking trees. The men were looking at it and talking about what had happened. The county attorney was bending to one side of the buggy, and kept looking steadily at the place as they drew up to it.

'I'm glad you came with me,' Mrs Peters said nervously, as the two women were about to follow the men in through the kitchen door.

Even after she had her foot on the door-step, her hand on the knob, Martha Hale had a moment of feeling she could not cross the threshold. And the reason it seemed she couldn't cross it now was simply because she hadn't crossed it before. Time and time again it had been in her mind, 'I ought to go over and see Minnie Foster'—she still thought of her as Minnie Foster, though for twenty years she had been Mrs Wright. And then there was always something to do and Minnie Foster would go from her mind. But *now* she could come.

The men went over to the stove. The women stood close together by the door. Young Henderson, the county attorney, turned around and said, 'Come up to the fire, ladies.'

Mrs Peters took a step forward, then stopped. 'I'm not—cold,' she said.

And so the two women stood by the door, at first not even so much as looking around the kitchen.

The men talked for a minute about what a good thing it was the sheriff had sent his deputy out that morning to make a fire for them, and then Sheriff Peters stepped back from the stove, unbuttoned his outer coat, and leaned his hands on the kitchen table in a way that seemed to mark the beginning of official business. 'Now, Mr Hale,' he said in a sort of semi-official voice, 'before we move things about, you tell Mr Henderson just what it was you saw when you came here yesterday morning.'

The county attorney was looking around the kitchen.

'By the way,' he said, 'has anything been moved?' He turned to the sheriff. 'Are things just as you left them yesterday?'

Peters looked from cupboard to sink; from that to a small worn rocker a little to one side of the kitchen table.

'It's just the same.'

'Somebody should have been left here yesterday,' said the county attorney.

'Oh—yesterday,' returned the sheriff, with a little gesture as of yesterday having been more than he could bear to think of. 'When I had to send Frank to Morris Center for that man who went crazy—let me tell you, I had my hands full *yesterday*. I knew you could get back from Omaha by today, George, and as long as I went over everything here myself—'

'Well, Mr Hale,' said the county attorney, in a way of letting what was past and gone go, 'tell just what happened when you came here yesterday morning.'

Mrs Hale, still leaning against the door, had that sinking feeling of the mother whose child is about to speak a piece. Lewis often wandered along and got things mixed up in a story. She hoped he would tell this straight and plain, and not say unnecessary things that would just make things harder for Minnie Foster. He didn't begin at once, and she noticed that he looked queer—as if standing in that kitchen and having to tell what he had seen there yesterday morning made him almost sick.

'Yes, Mr Hale?' the county attorney reminded.

'Harry and I had started to town with a load of potatoes,' Mrs Hale's husband began.

Harry was Mrs Hale's oldest boy. He wasn't with them now, for the very good reason that those potatoes never got to town yesterday and he was taking them this morning, so he hadn't been home when the sheriff stopped to say he wanted Mr Hale to come over to the Wright place and tell the county attorney his story there, where he could point it all out. With all Mrs Hale's other emotions came the fear that maybe Harry wasn't dressed warm enough—they hadn't any of them realized how that north wind did bite.

'We come along this road,' Hale was going on, with a motion of his hand to the road over which they had just come, 'and as we got in sight of the house I says to Harry, "I'm goin' to see if I can't get John Wright to take a telephone." You see,' he explained to Henderson, 'unless I can get somebody to go in with me they won't come out this branch road except for a price *I* can't pay. I'd spoke to Wright about it once before; but he put me off, saying folks talked too much anyway, and all he asked was peace and quiet—guess you know about how much he talked himself. But I thought maybe if I went to the house and talked about it before his wife, and said all the women-folks liked the telephones, and that in this lonesome stretch of road it would be a good thing—well, I said to Harry that that was what I was going to say— though I said at the same time that I didn't know as what his wife wanted made much difference to John—'

Now, there he was!—saying things he didn't need to say. Mrs Hale tried to catch her husband's eye, but fortunately the county attorney interrupted with:

'Let's talk about that a little later, Mr Hale. I do want to talk about that, but I'm anxious now to get along to just what happened when you got here.'

When he began this time, it was very deliberately and carefully:

'I didn't see or hear anything. I knocked at the door. And still it was all quiet inside. I knew they must be up—it was past eight o'clock. So I knocked again, louder, and I thought I heard somebody say "Come in". I wasn't sure—I'm not sure yet. But I opened the door—this door,' jerking a hand toward the door by which the two women stood, 'and there, in that rocker'—pointing to it—'sat Mrs Wright.'

Every one in the kitchen looked at the rocker. It came into Mrs Hale's mind that that rocker didn't look in the least like Minnie Foster—the Minnie Foster of twenty years before. It was a dingy red, with wooden rungs up the back, and the middle rung was gone, and the chair sagged to one side.

'How did she—look?' the county attorney was enquiring.

'Well,' said Hale, 'she looked—queer.'

'How do you mean—queer?'

As he asked it he took out a note-book and pencil. Mrs Hale did not like the sight of that pencil. She kept her eye fixed on her husband, as if to keep him from saying unnecessary things that would go into that note-book and make trouble.

Hale did speak guardedly, as if the pencil had affected him too.

'Well, as if she didn't know what she was going to do next. And kind of—done up.'

'How did she seem to feel about your coming?'

'Why, I don't think she minded—one way or other. She didn't pay much attention. I said, "Ho' do, Mrs Wright? It's cold, ain't it?" And she said, "Is it?"—and went on pleatin' at her apron.

'Well, I was surprised. She didn't ask me to come up to the stove, or to sit down, but just set there, not even lookin' at me. And so I said: "I want to see John."

'And then she—laughed. I guess you would call it a laugh.

'I thought of Harry and the team outside, so I said, a little sharp, "Can I see John?" "No," says she—kind of dull like. "Ain't he home?" says I. Then she looked at me. "Yes," says she, "he's home." "Then why can't I see him?" I asked her, out of patience with her now. "'Cause he's dead." says she, just as quiet and dull—and fell to pleatin' her apron. "Dead?" says I, like you do when you can't take in what you've heard.

'She just nodded her head, not getting a bit excited, but rockin' back and forth.

'"Why—where is he?" says I, not knowing *what* to say.

'She just pointed upstairs—like this'—pointing to the room above.

'I got up, with the idea of going up there myself. By this time I— didn't know what to do. I walked from there to here; then I says: "Why, what did he die of?"

'"He died of a rope around his neck," says she; and just went on pleatin' at her apron.'

Hale stopped speaking, and stood staring at the rocker, as if he were still seeing the woman who had sat there the morning before. Nobody spoke; it was as if every one were seeing the woman who had sat there the morning before.

'And what did you do then?' the county attorney at last broke the silence.

'I went out and called Harry. I thought I might—need help. I got Harry in, and we went upstairs.' His voice fell almost to a whisper. 'There he was—lying over the—'

'I think I'd rather have you go into that upstairs,' the county attorney interrupted, 'where you can point it all out. Just go on now with the rest of the story.'

'Well, my first thought was to get that rope off. It looked—'

He stopped, his face twitching.

'But Harry, he went up to him, and he said, "No, he's dead all right, and we'd better not touch anything." So we went downstairs.

'She was still sitting that same way. "Has anybody been notified?" I asked. "No," says she, unconcerned.

' "Who did this, Mrs Wright?" said Harry. He said it businesslike, and she stopped pleatin' at her apron. "I don't know," she says. "You don't *know?*" says Harry. "Weren't you sleepin' in the bed with him?" "Yes," says she, "but I was on the inside." "Somebody slipped a rope round his neck and strangled him, and you didn't wake up?" says Harry. "I didn't wake up," she said after him.

'We may have looked as if we didn't see how that could be, for after a minute she said, "I sleep sound."

'Harry was going to ask her more questions, but I said maybe that weren't our business; maybe we ought to let her tell her story first to the coroner or the sheriff. So Harry went fast as he could over to High Road—the Rivers' place, where there's a telephone.'

'And what did she do when she knew you had gone for the coroner?' The attorney got his pencil in his hand all ready for writing.

'She moved from that chair to this one over here'—Hale pointed to a small chair in the corner—'and just sat there with her hands held together and looking down. I got a feeling that I ought to make some conversation, so I said I had come in to see if John wanted to put in a telephone; and at that she started to laugh, and then she stopped and looked at me—scared.'

At the sound of a moving pencil the man who was telling the story looked up.

'I dunno—maybe it wasn't scared,' he hastened; 'I wouldn't like to say it was. Soon Harry got back, and then Dr Lloyd came, and you, Mr Peters, and so I guess that's all I know that you don't.'

He said that last with relief, and moved a little, as if relaxing. Every one moved a little. The county attorney walked toward the stair door.

'I guess we'll go upstairs first—then out to the barn and around there.'

He paused and looked around the kitchen.

'You're convinced there was nothing important here?' he asked the sheriff. 'Nothing that would—point to any motive?'

The sheriff too looked all around, as if to re-convince himself.

'Nothing here but kitchen things,' he said, with a little laugh for the insignificance of kitchen things.

The county attorney was looking at the cupboard—a peculiar, ungainly structure, half closet and half cupboard, the upper part of it being built in the wall, and the lower part just the old-fashioned kitchen cupboard. As if its queerness attracted him, he got a chair and opened the upper part and looked in. After a moment he drew his hand away sticky.

'Here's a nice mess,' he said resentfully.

The two women had drawn nearer, and now the sheriff's wife spoke.

'Oh—her fruit,' she said, looking to Mrs Hale for sympathetic understanding. She turned back to the county attorney and explained: 'She worried about that when it turned so cold last night. She said the fire would go out and her jars might burst.'

Mrs Peters's husband broke into a laugh.

'Well, can you beat the women! Held for murder, and worrying about her preserves!'

The young attorney set his lips.

'I guess before we're through with her she may have something more serious than preserves to worry about.'

'Oh, well,' said Mrs Hale's husband, with good-natured superiority, 'women are used to worrying over trifles.'

The two women moved a little closer together. Neither of them spoke. The county attorney seemed suddenly to remember his manners—and think of his future.

'And yet,' said he, with the gallantry of a young politician, 'for all their worries, what would we do without the ladies?'

The women did not speak, did not unbend. He went to the sink and began washing his hands. He turned to wipe them on the roller towel—whirled it for a cleaner place.

'Dirty towels! Not much of a housekeeper, would you say, ladies?'

He kicked his foot against some dirty pans under the sink.

'There's a great deal of work to be done on a farm,' said Mrs Hale stiffly.

'To be sure. And yet'—with a little bow to her—'I know there are some Dickson County farm-houses that do not have such roller towels.' He gave it a pull to expose its full length again.

'Those towels get dirty awful quick. Men's hands aren't always as clean as they might be.'

'Ah, loyal to your sex, I see,' he laughed. He stopped and gave her a keen look. 'But you and Mrs Wright were neighbors. I suppose you were friends, too.'

Martha Hale shook her head.

'I've seen little enough of her of late years. I've not been in this house—it's more than a year.'

'And why was that? You didn't like her?'

'I liked her well enough,' she replied with spirit. 'Farmers' wives have their hands full, Mr Henderson. And then'—She looked around the kitchen.

'Yes?' he encouraged.

'It never seemed a very cheerful place,' said she, more to herself than to him.

'No,' he agreed; 'I don't think any one would call it cheerful. I shouldn't say she had the home-making instinct.'

'Well, I don't know as Wright had, either,' she muttered.

'You mean they didn't get on very well?' he was quick to ask.

'No; I don't mean anything,' she answered, with decision. As she turned a little away from him, she added: 'But I don't think a place would be any the cheerfuler for John Wright's bein' in it.'

'I'd like to talk to you about that a little later, Mrs Hale,' he said. 'I'm anxious to get the lay of things upstairs now.'

He moved toward the stair door, followed by the two men.

'I suppose anything Mrs Peters does'll be all right?' the sheriff enquired. 'She was to take in some clothes for her, you know—and a few little things. We left in such a hurry yesterday.'

The county attorney looked at the two women whom they were leaving alone there among the kitchen things.

'Yes—Mrs Peters,' he said, his glance resting on the woman who was not Mrs Peters, the big farmer woman who stood behind the sheriff's wife. 'Of course Mrs Peters is one of us,' he said, in a manner of entrusting responsibility. 'And keep your eye out, Mrs Peters, for anything that might be of use. No telling; you women might come upon a clue to the motive—and that's the thing we need.'

Mr Hale rubbed his face after the fashion of a show man getting ready for a pleasantry.

'But would the women know a clue if they did come upon it?' he said; and, having delivered himself of this, he followed the others through the stair door.

The women stood motionless and silent, listening to the footsteps, first upon the stairs, then in the room above them.

Then, as if releasing herself from something strange, Mrs Hale began to arrange the dirty pans under the sink, which the county attorney's disdainful push of the foot had deranged.

'I'd hate to have men comin' into my kitchen,' she said testily— 'snoopin' round and criticizin'.'

'Of course it's no more than their duty,' said the sheriff's wife, in her manner of timid acquiescence.

'Duty's all right,' replied Mrs Hale bluffly; 'but I guess that deputy sheriff that come out to make the fire might have got a little of this on.' She gave the roller towel a pull. 'Wish I'd thought of that sooner! Seems mean to talk about her for not having things slicked up, when she had to come away in such a hurry.'

She looked around the kitchen. Certainly it was not 'slicked up'. Her eye was held by a bucket of sugar on a low shelf. The cover was off the wooden bucket, and beside it was a paper bag—half full.

Mrs Hale moved toward it.

'She was putting this in here,' she said to herself—slowly.

She thought of the flour in her kitchen at home—half sifted, half not sifted. She had been interrupted, and had left things half done. What had interrupted Minnie Foster? Why had that work been left half done? She made a move as if to finish it—unfinished things always bothered her—and then she glanced around and saw that Mrs Peters was watching her—and she didn't want Mrs Peters to get that feeling she had got of work begun and then—for some reason—not finished.

'It's a shame about her fruit,' she said, and walked toward the cupboard that the county attorney had opened, and got on the chair, murmuring: 'I wonder if it's all gone.'

It was a sorry enough looking sight, but 'Here's one that's all right,' she said at last. She held it toward the light. 'This is cherries, too.' She looked again. 'I declare I believe that's the only one.'

With a sigh, she got down from the chair, went to the sink, and wiped off the bottle.

'She'll feel awful bad, after all her hard work in the hot weather. I remember the afternoon I put up my cherries last summer.'

She set the bottle on the table, and, with another sigh, started to sit down in the rocker. But she did not sit down. Something kept her from sitting down in that chair. She straightened—stepped back, and, half turned away, stood looking at it, seeing the woman who sat there 'pleatin' at her apron'.

The thin voice of the sheriff's wife broke in upon her: 'I must be getting those things from the front room closet.' She opened the door into the other room, started in, stepped back. 'You coming with me, Mrs Hale?' she asked nervously. 'You—you could help me get them.'

They were soon back—the stark coldness of that shut-up room was not a thing to linger in.

'My!' said Mrs Peters, dropping the things on the table and hurrying to the stove.

Mrs Hale stood examining the clothes the woman who was being detained in town had said she wanted.

'Wright was close!' she exclaimed, holding up a shabby black skirt that bore the marks of much making over. 'I think maybe that's why she kept so much to herself. I s'pose she felt she couldn't do her part; and then, you don't enjoy things when you feel shabby. She used to wear pretty clothes and be lively—when she was Minnie Foster, one of the town girls, singing in the choir. But that—oh, that was twenty years ago.'

With a carefulness in which there was something tender, she folded the shabby clothes and piled them at one corner of the table. She looked at Mrs Peters, and there was something in the other woman's look that irritated her.

'She don't care,' she said to herself. 'Much difference it makes to her whether Minnie Foster had pretty clothes when she was a girl.'

Then she looked again, and she wasn't so sure; in fact, she hadn't at any time been perfectly sure about Mrs Peters. She had that shrinking manner, and yet her eyes looked as if they could see a long way into things.

'This all you was to take in?' asked Mrs Hale.

'No,' said the sheriff's wife; 'she said she wanted an apron. Funny thing to want,' she ventured in her nervous little way, 'for there's not much to get you dirty in jail, goodness knows. But I suppose just to make her feel more natural. If you're used to wearing an apron— She said they were in the bottom drawer of this cupboard. Yes—here they are. And then her little shawl that always hung on the stair door.'

She took the small gray shawl from behind the door leading upstairs, and stood a minute looking at it.

Suddenly Mrs Hale took a quick step toward the other woman.

'Mrs Peters!'

'Yes, Mrs Hale?'

'Do you think she—did it?'

A frightened look blurred the other things in Mrs Peters's eyes.

'Oh, I don't know,' she said, in a voice that seemed to shrink away from the subject.

'Well, I don't think she did,' affirmed Mrs Hale stoutly. 'Asking for an apron, and her little shawl. Worryin' about her fruit.'

'Mr Peters says—' Footsteps were heard in the room above; she stopped, looked up, then went on in a lowered voice: 'Mr Peters says—it looks bad for her. Mr Henderson is awful sarcastic in a speech, and he's going to make fun of her saying she didn't—wake up.'

For a moment Mrs Hale had no answer. Then, 'Well, I guess John Wright didn't wake up—when they was slippin' that rope under his neck,' she muttered.

'No, it's *strange*,' breathed Mrs Peters. 'They think it was such a—funny way to kill a man.'

She began to laugh; at the sound of the laugh, abruptly stopped.

'That's just what Mr Hale said,' said Mrs Hale, in a resolutely natural voice. 'There was a gun in the house. He says that's what he can't understand.'

'Mr Henderson said, coming out, that what was needed for the case was a motive. Something to show anger—or sudden feeling.'

'Well, I don't see any signs of anger around here,' said Mrs Hale. 'I don't—'

She stopped. It was as if her mind tripped on something. Her eye was caught by a dish-towel in the middle of the kitchen table. Slowly she moved toward the table. One half of it was wiped clean, the other half messy. Her eyes made a slow, almost unwilling turn to the bucket of sugar and the half empty bag beside it. Things begun—and not finished.

After a moment she stepped back, and said, in that manner of releasing herself:

'Wonder how they're finding things upstairs? I hope she had it a little more red up up there. You know,'—she paused, and feeling gathered—'it seems kind of *sneaking*; locking her up in town and coming out here to get her own house to turn against her!'

'But, Mrs Hale,' said the sheriff's wife, 'the law is the law.'

'I s'pose 'tis,' answered Mrs Hale shortly.

She turned to the stove, saying something about that fire not being much to brag of. She worked with it a minute, and when she straightened up she said aggressively:

'The law is the law—and a bad stove is a bad stove. How'd you like to cook on this?'—pointing with the poker to the broken lining. She opened the oven door and started to express her opinion of the oven; but she was swept into her own thoughts, thinking of what it would mean, year after year, to have that stove to wrestle with. The thought of Minnie Foster trying to bake in that oven—and the thought of her never going over to see Minnie Foster—

She was startled by hearing Mrs Peters say: 'A person gets discouraged—and loses heart.'

The sheriff's wife had looked from the stove to the sink—to the pail of water which had been carried in from outside. The two women stood there silent, above them the footsteps of the men who were looking for evidence against the woman who had worked in that kitchen. That look of seeing into things, of seeing through a thing to something else, was in the eyes of the sheriff's wife now. When Mrs Hale next spoke to her, it was gently:

'Better loosen up your things, Mrs Peters. We'll not feel them when we go out.'

Mrs Peters went to the back of the room to hang up the fur tippet she was wearing. A moment later she exclaimed, 'Why, she was piecing a quilt,' and held up a large sewing basket piled high with quilt pieces.

Mrs Hale spread some of the blocks on the table.

'It's log-cabin pattern,' she said, putting several of them together. 'Pretty, isn't it?'

They were so engaged with the quilt that they did not hear the footsteps on the stairs. Just as the stair door opened Mrs Hale was saying:

'Do you suppose she was going to quilt it or just knot it?'

The sheriff threw up his hands.

'They wonder whether she was going to quilt it or just knot it'

There was a laugh for the ways of women, a warming of hands over the stove, and then the county attorney said briskly:

'Well, let's go right out to the barn and get that cleared up.'

'I don't see as there's anything so strange,' Mrs Hale said resentfully, after the outside door had closed on the three men—'our taking up our time with little things while we're waiting for them to get the evidence. I don't see as it's anything to laugh about.'

'Of course they've got awful important things on their minds,' said the sheriff's wife apologetically.

They returned to an inspection of the blocks for the quilt. Mrs Hale was looking at the fine, even sewing, and preoccupied with thoughts of the woman who had done that sewing, when she heard the sheriff's wife say, in a queer tone:

'Why, look at this one.'

She turned to take the block held out to her.

'The sewing,' said Mrs Peters, in a troubled way. 'All the rest of them have been so nice and even—but—this one. Why, it looks as if she didn't know what she was about!'

Their eyes met—something flashed to life, passed between them; then, as if with an effort, they seemed to pull away from each other. A moment Mrs Hale sat there, her hands folded over that sewing which was so unlike all the rest of the sewing. Then she had pulled a knot and drawn the threads.

'Oh, what are you doing, Mrs Hale?' asked the sheriff's wife, startled.

'Just pulling out a stitch or two that's not sewed very good,' said Mrs Hale mildly.

'I don't think we ought to touch things,' Mrs Peters said, a little helplessly.

'I'll just finish up this end,' answered Mrs Hale, still in that mild, matter-of-fact fashion.

She threaded a needle and started to replace bad sewing with good. For a little while she sewed in silence. Then, in that thin, timid voice, she heard:

'Mrs Hale!'

'Yes, Mrs Peters?'

'What do you suppose she was so—nervous about?'

'Oh, *I* don't know,' said Mrs Hale, as if dismissing a thing not important enough to spend much time on. 'I don't know as she was—nervous. I sew awful queer sometimes when I'm just tired.'

She cut a thread, and out of the corner of her eye looked up at Mrs Peters. The small, lean face of the sheriff's wife seemed to have tightened up. Her eyes had that look of peering into something. But the next moment she moved, and said in her thin, indecisive way:

'Well, I must get those clothes wrapped. They may be through sooner than we think. I wonder where I could find a piece of paper—and string.'

'In that cupboard, maybe,' suggested Mrs Hale, after a glance around.

One piece of the crazy sewing remained unripped. Mrs Peters's back turned, Martha Hale now scrutinized that piece, compared it with the dainty, accurate sewing of the other blocks. The difference was startling. Holding this block made her feel queer, as if the distracted thoughts of the woman who had perhaps turned to it to try and quiet herself were communicating themselves to her.

Mrs Peters's voice roused her.

'Here's a birdcage,' she said. 'Did she have a bird, Mrs Hale?'

'Why, I don't know whether she did or not.' She turned to look at the cage Mrs Peters was holding up. 'I've not been here in so long.' She sighed. 'There was a man round last year selling canaries cheap—but I don't know as she took one. Maybe she did. She used to sing real pretty herself.'

Mrs Peters looked around the kitchen.

'Seems kind of funny to think of a bird here.' She half laughed—an attempt to put up a barrier. 'But she must have had one—or why would she have a cage? I wonder what happened to it.'

'I suppose maybe the cat got it,' suggested Mrs Hale, resuming her sewing.

'No, she didn't have a cat. She's got that feeling some people have about cats—being afraid of them. When they brought her to our house yesterday, my cat got in the room, and she was real upset and asked me to take it out.'

'My sister Bessie was like that,' laughed Mrs Hale.

The sheriff's wife did not reply. The silence made Mrs Hale turn around. Mrs Peters was examining the birdcage.

'Look at this door,' she said slowly. 'It's broke. One hinge has been pulled apart.'

Mrs Hale came nearer.

'Looks as if some one must have been—rough with it.'

Again their eyes met—startled, questioning, apprehensive. For a moment neither spoke nor stirred. Then Mrs Hale, turning away, said brusquely:

'If they're going to find any evidence, I wish they'd be about it. I don't like this place.'

'But I'm awful glad you came with me, Mrs Hale.' Mrs Peters put the birdcage on the table and sat down. 'It would be lonesome for me—sitting here alone.'

'Yes, it would, wouldn't it?' agreed Mrs Hale, a certain determined naturalness in her voice. She picked up the sewing, but now it dropped in her lap, and she murmured in a different voice: 'But I tell you what I *do* wish, Mrs Peters. I wish I had come over sometimes when she was here. I wish—I had.'

'But of course you were awful busy, Mrs Hale. Your house—and your children.'

'I could've come,' retorted Mrs Hale shortly. 'I stayed away because it weren't cheerful—and that's why I ought to have come. I'—she looked around—'I've never liked this place. Maybe because it's down in a hollow and you don't see the road. I don't know what it is, but it's a lonesome place, and always was. I wish I had come over to see Minnie Foster sometimes. I can see now—' She did not put it into words.

'Well, you mustn't reproach yourself,' counseled Mrs Peters. 'Somehow, we just don't see how it is with other folks till—something comes up.'

'Not having children makes less work,' mused Mrs Hale, after a silence, 'but it makes a quiet house—and Wright out to work all day—and no company when he did come in. Did you know John Wright, Mrs Peters?'

'Not to know him. I've seen him in town. They say he was a good man.'

'Yes—good,' conceded John Wright's neighbor grimly. 'He didn't drink, and kept his word as well as most, I guess, and paid his debts. But he was a hard man, Mrs Peters. Just to pass the time of day with him—' She stopped, shivered a little. 'Like a raw wind that gets to the bone.' Her eye fell upon the cage on the table before her, and she added, almost bitterly: 'I should think she would've wanted a bird!'

Suddenly she leaned forward, looking intently at the cage. 'But what do you s'pose went wrong with it?'

'I don't know,' returned Mrs Peters; 'unless it got sick and died.'

But after she said it she reached over and swung the broken door. Both women watched it as if somehow held by it.

'You didn't know—her?' Mrs Hale asked, a gentler note in her voice.

'Not till they brought her yesterday,' said the sheriff's wife.

'She—come to think of it, she was kind of like a bird herself. Real sweet and pretty, but kind of timid and—fluttery. How—she—did—change.'

That held her for a long time. Finally, as if struck with a happy thought and relieved to get back to everyday things, she exclaimed:

'Tell you what, Mrs Peters, why don't you take the quilt in with you? It might take up her mind.'

'Why, I think that's a real nice idea, Mrs Hale,' agreed the sheriff's wife, as if she too were glad to come into the atmosphere of a simple kindness. 'There couldn't possibly be any objection to that, could there? Now, just what will I take? I wonder if her patches are in here—and her things.'

They turned to the sewing basket.

'Here's some red,' said Mrs Hale, bringing out a roll of cloth. Underneath that was a box. 'Here, maybe her scissors are in here—and her things.' She held it up. 'What a pretty box! I'll warrant that was something she had a long time ago—when she was a girl.'

She held it in her hand a moment; then, with a little sigh, opened it. Instantly her hand went to her nose.

'Why—!'

Mrs Peters drew nearer—then turned away.

'There's something wrapped up in this piece of silk,' faltered Mrs Hale.

'This isn't her scissors,' said Mrs Peters in a shrinking voice.

Her hand not steady, Mrs Hale raised the piece of silk. 'Oh, Mrs Peters!' she cried. 'It's—'

Mrs Peters bent closer.

'It's the bird,' she whispered.

'But, Mrs Peters!' cried Mrs Hale. '*Look* at it! Its neck—look at its neck! It's all—other side *to*.'

She held the box away from her.

The sheriff's wife again bent closer.

'Somebody wrung its neck,' said she, in a voice that was slow and deep.

And then again the eyes of the two women met—this time clung together in a look of dawning comprehension, of growing horror. Mrs Peters looked from the dead bird to the broken door of the cage. Again their eyes met. And just then there was a sound at the outside door.

Mrs Hale slipped the box under the quilt pieces in the basket, and sank into the chair before it. Mrs Peters stood holding to the table. The county attorney and the sheriff came in from outside.

'Well, ladies,' said the county attorney, as one turning from serious things to little pleasantries, 'have you decided whether she was going to quilt it or knot it?'

'We think', began the sheriff's wife in a flurried voice, 'that she was going to—knot it.'

He was too preoccupied to notice the change that came in her voice on that last.

'Well, that's very interesting, I'm sure,' he said tolerantly. He caught sight of the birdcage. 'Has the bird flown?'

'We think the cat got it,' said Mrs Hale in a voice curiously even.

He was walking up and down, as if thinking something out.

'Is there a cat?' he asked absently.

Mrs Hale shot a look up at the sheriff's wife.

'Well, not *now*,' said Mrs Peters. 'They're superstitious, you know; they leave.'

She sank into her chair.

The county attorney did not heed her. 'No sign at all of any one having come in from the outside,' he said to Peters, in the manner of continuing an interrupted conversation. 'Their own rope. Now let's go upstairs again and go over it, piece by piece. It would have to have been some one who knew just the—'

The stair door closed behind them and their voices were lost.

The two women sat motionless, not looking at each other, but as if peering into something and at the same time holding back. When they spoke now it was as if they were afraid of what they were saying, but as if they could not help saying it.

'She liked the bird,' said Martha Hale, low and slowly. 'She was going to bury it in that pretty box.'

'When I was a girl,' said Mrs Peters, under her breath, 'my kitten—there was a boy took a hatchet, and before my eyes—before I could get there—' She covered her face an instant. 'If they hadn't held me back I would have'—she caught herself, looked upstairs where footsteps were heard, and finished weakly—'hurt him.'

Then they sat without speaking or moving.

'I wonder how it would seem,' Mrs Hale at last began, as if feeling her way over strange ground—'never to have had any children around?' Her eyes made a slow sweep of the kitchen, as if seeing what that kitchen had meant through all the years. 'No, Wright wouldn't like the bird,' she said after that—'a thing that sang. She used to sing. He killed that too.' Her voice tightened.

Mrs Peters moved uneasily.

'Of course we don't know who killed the bird.'

'I knew John Wright,' was Mrs Hale's answer.

'It was an awful thing was done in this house that night, Mrs Hale,' said the sheriff's wife. 'Killing a man while he slept—slipping a thing round his neck that choked the life out of him.'

Mrs Hale's hand went out to the birdcage.

'His neck. Choked the life out of him.'

'We don't *know* who killed him,' whispered Mrs Peters wildly. 'We don't *know*.'

Mrs Hale had not moved. 'If there had been years and years of—nothing, then a bird to sing to you, it would be awful—still—after the bird was still.'

It was as if something within her not herself had spoken, and it found in Mrs Peters something she did not know as herself.

'I know what stillness is,' she said, in a queer, monotonous voice. 'When we homesteaded in Dakota, and my first baby died—after he was two years old—and me with no other then—'

Mrs Hale stirred.

'How soon do you suppose they'll be through looking for evidence?'

'I know what stillness is,' repeated Mrs Peters, in just that same way. Then she too pulled back. 'The law has got to punish crime, Mrs Hale,' she said in her tight little way.

'I wish you'd seen Minnie Foster', was the answer, 'when she wore a white dress with blue ribbons, and stood up there in the choir and sang.'

The picture of that girl, the fact that she had lived neighbor to that girl for twenty years, and had let her die for lack of life, was suddenly more than she could bear.

'Oh, I *wish* I'd come over here once in a while!' she cried. 'That was a crime! That was a crime! Who's going to punish that?'

'We mustn't take on,' said Mrs Peters, with a frightened look toward the stairs.

'I might 'a' *known* she needed help! I tell you, it's *queer*, Mrs Peters. We live close together, and we live far apart. We all go through the same things—it's all just a different kind of the same thing! If it weren't—why do you and I *understand*? Why do we *know*—what we know this minute?'

She dashed her hand across her eyes. Then, seeing the jar of fruit on the table, she reached for it and choked out:

'If I was you I wouldn't *tell* her her fruit was gone! Tell her it *ain't*. Tell her it's all right—all of it. Here—take this in to prove it to her! She—she may never know whether it was broke or not.'

She turned away.

Mrs Peters reached out for the bottle of fruit as if she were glad to take it—as if touching a familiar thing, having something to do, could keep her from something else. She got up, looked about for something to wrap the fruit in, took a petticoat from the pile of clothes she had brought from the front room, and nervously started winding that round the bottle.

'My!' she began, in a high, false voice, 'it's a good thing the men couldn't hear us! Getting all stirred up over a little thing like a—dead canary.' She hurried over that. 'As if that could have anything to do with—with—My, wouldn't they *laugh*?'

Footsteps were heard on the stairs.

'Maybe they would,' muttered Mrs Hale—'maybe they wouldn't.'

'No, Peters,' said the county attorney incisively; 'it's all perfectly clear, except the reason for doing it. But you know juries when it comes to women. If there was some definite thing—something to show. Something to make a story about. A thing that would connect up with this clumsy way of doing it.'

In a covert way Mrs Hale looked at Mrs Peters. Mrs Peters was looking at her. Quickly they looked away from each other. The outer door opened and Mr Hale came in.

'I've got the team round now,' he said. 'Pretty cold out there.'

'I'm going to stay here awhile by myself,' the county attorney suddenly announced. 'You can send Frank out for me, can't you?' he asked the sheriff. 'I want to go over everything. I'm not satisfied we can't do better.'

Again, for one brief moment, the two women's eyes found one another.

The sheriff came up to the table.

'Did you want to see what Mrs Peters was going to take in?'

The county attorney picked up the apron. He laughed.

'Oh, I guess they're not very dangerous things the ladies have picked out.'

Mrs Hale's hand was on the sewing basket in which the box was concealed. She felt that she ought to take her hand off the basket. She did not seem able to. He picked up one of the quilt blocks which she had piled on to cover the box. Her eyes felt like fire. She had a feeling that if he took up the basket she would snatch it from him.

But he did not take it up. With another little laugh, he turned away, saying:

'No; Mrs Peters doesn't need supervising. For that matter, a sheriff's wife is married to the law. Ever think of it that way, Mrs Peters?'

Mrs Peters was standing beside the table. Mrs Hale shot a look up at her; but she could not see her face. Mrs Peters had turned away. When she spoke, her voice was muffled.

'Not—just that way,' she said.

'Married to the law!' chuckled Mrs Peters's husband. He moved toward the door into the front room, and said to the county attorney:

'I just want you to come in here a minute, George. We ought to take a look at these windows.'

'Oh—windows,' said the county attorney scoffingly.

'We'll be right out, Mr Hale,' said the sheriff to the farmer, who was still waiting by the door.

Hale went to look after the horses. The sheriff followed the county attorney into the other room. Again—for one moment—the two women were alone in that kitchen.

Martha Hale sprang up, her hands tight together, looking at that other woman, with whom it rested. At first she could not see her eyes, for the sheriff's wife had not turned back since she turned away at that suggestion of being married to the law. But now Mrs Hale made her turn back. Her eyes made her turn back. Slowly, unwillingly, Mrs Peters turned her head until her eyes met the eyes of the other woman. There was a moment when they held each other in a steady, burning look in which there was no evasion nor flinching. Then Martha Hale's eyes pointed the way to the basket in which was hidden the thing that would make certain the conviction of the other woman—that woman who was not there and yet who had been there with them all through the hour.

For a moment Mrs Peters did not move. And then she did it. With a rush forward, she threw back the quilt pieces, got the box, tried to put it in her handbag. It was too big. Desperately she opened it, started to take the bird out. But there she broke—she could not touch the bird. She stood helpless, foolish.

There was the sound of a knob turning in the inner door. Martha Hale snatched the box from the sheriff's wife, and got it in the pocket of her big coat just as the sheriff and the county attorney came back into the kitchen.

'Well, Henry,' said the county attorney facetiously, 'at least we found out that she was not going to quilt it. She was going to—what is it you call it, ladies?'

Mrs Hale's hand was against the pocket of her coat.

'We call it—knot it, Mr Henderson.'

4

CARTER DICKSON

The Other Hangman

'Why do they electrocute 'em instead of hanging 'em in Pennsylvania? What' (said my old friend, Judge Murchison, dexterously hooking the spittoon closer with his foot) 'do they teach you youngsters in these newfangled law schools, anyway? That, son, *was* a murder case. It turned the Supreme Court's whiskers grey to find a final ruling, and for thirty years it's been argued about by lawyers in the back room of every saloon from here to the Pacific coast. It happened right here in this county—when they hanged Fred Joliffe for the murder of Randall Fraser.

'It was in '92 or '93; anyway, it was the year they put the first telephone in the court-house, and you could talk as far as Pittsburg except when the wires blew down. Considering it was the county seat, we were mighty proud of our town (population 3,500). The hustlers were always bragging about how thriving and growing our town was, and we had just got to the point of enthusiasm where every ten years we were certain the census-taker must have forgotten half our population. Old Mark Sturgis, who owned the *Bugle Gazette* then, carried on something awful in an editorial when they printed in the almanac that we had a population of only 3,265. We were all pretty riled about it, naturally.

'We were proud of plenty of other things, too. We had good reason to brag about the McClellan House, which was the finest hotel in the county; and I mind when you could get room and board, with apple pie for breakfast every morning, for two dollars a week. We were proud of our old county families, that came over the mountains when Braddock's army was scalped by the Indians in seventeen fifty-five, and settled down in log huts to dry their wounds. But most of all we were proud of our legal batteries.

'Son, it was a grand assembly! Mind, I won't say that all of 'em were long on knowledge of the Statute Books; but they knew their *Blackstone* and their *Greenleaf on Evidence*, and they were powerful speakers. *And* there were some—the top-notchers—full of graces and book-knowledge and dignity, who were hell on the exact letter of the law. Scotch-Irish Presbyterians, all of us, who loved a good debate and a bottle o' whisky. There was Charley Connell, a Harvard graduate and the district attorney, who had fine white hands, and wore a fine high collar, and made such pathetic addresses to the jury that people flocked for miles around to hear him; though he generally lost his cases. There was Judge Hunt, who prided himself on his resemblance to Abe Lincoln, and in consequence always wore a frock coat and an elegant plug hat. Why, there was your own grandfather, who had over two hundred books in his library, and people used to go up nights to borrow volumes of the encyclopædia.

'You know the big stone court-house at the top of the street, with the flowers round it, and the jail adjoining? People went there as they'd go to a picture-show nowadays; it was a lot better, too. Well, from there it was only two minutes' walk across the meadow to Jim Riley's saloon. All the cronies gathered there—in the back room, of course, where Jim had an elegant brass spittoon and a picture of George Washington on the wall to make it dignified. You could see the footpath worn across the grass until they built over that meadow. Besides the usual crowd, there was Bob Moran, the sheriff, a fine, strapping big fellow, but very nervous about doing his duty strictly. And there was poor old Nabors, a big, quiet, reddish-eyed fellow, who'd been a doctor before he took to drink. He was always broke, and he had two daughters—one of 'em consumptive—and Jim Riley pitied him so much that he gave him all he wanted to drink for nothing. Those were fine, happy days, with a power of eloquence and theorizing and solving the problems of the nation in that back room, until our wives came to fetch us home.

'Then Randall Fraser was murdered, and there was hell to pay.

'Now if it had been anybody else but Fred Joliffe who killed him, naturally we wouldn't have convicted. You can't do it, son, not in a little community. It's all very well to talk about the power and grandeur of justice, and sounds fine in a speech. But here's somebody you've seen walking the streets about his business every day for years; and you know when his kids were born, and saw him crying when one of 'em died; and you remember how he loaned you ten dollars when you needed it. . . . Well, you can't take that person out in the cold light of day and string him up by the neck until he's dead. You'd always be seeing the look on his face afterwards. And you'd find excuses for him no matter what he did.

'But with Fred Joliffe it was different. Fred Joliffe was the worst and nastiest customer we ever had, with the possible exception of Randall Fraser himself. Ever seen a copperhead curled up on a flat stone? And a copperhead's worse than a rattlesnake—that won't strike unless you step on it, and gives warning before it does. Fred Joliffe had the same brownish colour and sliding movements. You always remembered his pale little eye and his nasty grin. When he drove his cart through town—he had some sort of rag-and-bone business, you understand— you'd see him sitting up there, a skinny little man in a brown coat, peeping round the side of his nose to find something for gossip. And grinning.

'It wasn't merely the things he said about people behind their backs. Or to their faces, for that matter, because he relied on the fact that he was too small to be thrashed. He was a slick customer. It was believed that he wrote those anonymous letters that caused . . . but never mind that. Anyhow, I can tell you his little smirk *did* drive Will Farmer crazy one time, and Will *did* beat him within an inch of his life. Will's livery stable was burnt down one night about a month later, with eleven horses inside, but nothing could ever be proved. He was too smart for us.

'That brings me to Fred Joliffe's only companion—I don't mean friend. Randall Fraser had a harness-and-saddle store in Market Street, a dusty place with a big dummy horse in the window. I reckon the only thing in the world Randall liked was that dummy horse, which was a dappled mare with vicious-looking glass eyes. He used to keep its mane combed. Randall was a big man with a fine moustache, a horseshoe pin in his tie, and sporty checked clothes. He was buttery polite, and mean as sin. He thought a dirty trick or a swindle was the funniest joke he ever heard. But the women liked him—a lot of them, it's no denying, sneaked in at the back door of that harness store. Randall itched to tell it at the barber shop, to show what fools they were and how virile he was; but he had to be careful. He and Fred Joliffe did a lot of drinking together.

'Then the news came. It was in October, I think, and I heard it in the morning, when I was putting on my hat to go down to the office. Old Withers was the town constable then. He got up early in the morning, although there was no need for it; and, when he was going down Market Street in the mist about five o'clock, he saw the gas still burning in the back room of Randall's store. The front door was wide open. Withers went in and found Randall lying on a pile of harness in his shirt-sleeves, and his forehead and face bashed in with a wedging-mallet. There wasn't much left of the face, but you could recognize him by his moustache and his horseshoe pin.

'I was in my office when somebody yelled up from the street that they had found Fred Joliffe drunk and asleep in the flour-mill, with blood on his hands and an empty bottle of Randall Fraser's whisky in his pocket. He was still in bad shape, and couldn't walk or understand what was going on, when the sheriff—that was Bob Moran I told you about—came to take him to the lock-up. Bob had to drive him in his own rag-and-bone cart. I saw them drive up Market Street in the rain, Fred lying in the back of the cart all white with flour, and rolling and cursing. People were very quiet. They were pleased, but they couldn't show it.

'That is, all except Will Farmer, who had owned the livery stable that was burnt down.

' "Now they'll hang him," says Will. "Now, by God they'll hang him."

'It's a funny thing, son: I didn't realize the force of that until I heard Judge Hunt pronounce sentence after the trial. They appointed me to defend him, because I was a young man without any particular practice, and somebody had to do it. The evidence was all over town before I got a chance to speak with Fred. You could see he was done for. A scissors-grinder who lived across the street (I forget his name now) had seen Fred go into Randall's place about eleven o'clock. An old couple who lived up over the store had heard 'em drinking and yelling downstairs; at near on midnight they'd heard a noise like a fight and a fall; but they knew better than to interfere. Finally, a couple of farmers driving home from town at midnight had seen Fred stumble out of the front door, slapping his clothes and wiping his hands on his coat like a man with delirium tremens.

'I went to see Fred at the jail. He was sober, although he jerked a good deal. Those pale watery eyes of his were as poisonous as ever. I can still see him sitting on the bunk in his cell, sucking a brown-paper cigarette, wriggling his neck, and jeering at me. He wouldn't tell me anything, because he said I would go and tell the judge if he did.

' "Hang *me?*" he says, and wrinkled his nose and jeered again. "Hang *me?* Don't you worry about that, mister. Them so-and-so's will never hang me. They're too much afraid of me, them so-and-so's are. Eh, mister?"

'And the fool couldn't get it through his head right up until the sentence. He strutted away in court; making smart remarks, and threatening to tell what he knew about people, and calling the judge by his first name. He wore a dew dickey shirtfront he bought to look spruce in.

'I was surprised how quietly everybody took it. The people who came to the trial didn't whisper or shove; they just sat still as death, and looked at him. All you could hear was a kind of breathing. It's funny about a courtroom, son: it has it's own particular smell, which won't bother you unless you get to thinking about what it means, but you notice worn places and cracks in the walls more than you would anywhere else. You would hear Charley Connell's voice for the prosecution, a little thin sound in a big room, and Charley's footsteps creaking. You would hear a cough in the audience, or a woman's dress rustle, or the gas-jets whistling. It was dark in the rainy season, so they lit the gas-jets by two o'clock in the afternoon.

'The only defence I could make was that Fred had been too drunk to be responsible, and remembered nothing of that night (which he admitted was true). But, in addition to being no defence in law, it was a terrible frost besides. My own voice sounded wrong. I remember that six of the jury had whiskers, and six hadn't; and Judge Hunt, up on the bench with the flag draped on the wall behind his head, looked more like Abe Lincoln than ever. Even Fred Joliffe began to notice. He kept twitching round to look at people, a little uneasy-like. Once he stuck out his neck at the jury and screeched: "*Say* something, can'tcha? Do something, can'tcha?"

'They did.

'When the foreman of the jury said: "Guilty of murder in the first degree," there was just a little noise from those people. Not a cheer, or anything like that. It hissed out all together, only once, like breath released, but it was terrible to hear. It didn't hit Fred until Judge Hunt was half-way through pronouncing sentence. Fred stood looking round with a wild, half-witted expression until he heard Judge Hunt say: "*And may God have mercy on your soul.*" Then he burst out, kind of pleading and kidding as though this was carrying the joke too far. He said: "Listen, now, you don't *mean* that, do you? You can't fool me. You're only Jerry Hunt; I know who you are. You can't do that to me." All of a sudden he began pounding the table and screaming: "You ain't really agoing to hang me, are you?"

'But we were.

'The date of execution was fixed for the twelfth of November. The order was all signed. " . . . within the precincts of the said county jail, between the hours of eight and nine a.m., the said Frederick Joliffe shall be hanged by the neck until he is dead; an executioner to be commissioned by the sheriff for this purpose, and the sentence to be carried out in the presence of a qualified medical practitioner; the body to be interred . . . " And the rest of it. Everybody was nervous. There hadn't been a hanging since any of that crowd had been in office, and nobody knew how to go about it exactly. Old Doc Macdonald, the coroner, was to be there; and of course they got hold of Reverend Phelps the preacher; and Bob Moran's wife was going to cook pancakes and sausage for the last breakfast. Maybe you think that's fool talk. But think for a minute of taking somebody you've known all your life, and binding his arms one cold morning, and walking him out in your own backyard to crack his neck on a rope—all religious and legal, with not a soul to interfere. Then you begin to get scared of the powers of life and death, and the thin partition between.

'Bob Moran was scared white for fear things wouldn't go off properly. He had appointed big, slow-moving, tipsy Ed Nabors as hangman. This was partly because Ed Nabors needed the fifty dollars that was the fee, and partly because Bob had a vague idea that an ex-medical man would be better able to manage an execution. Ed had sworn to keep sober; Bob Moran said he wouldn't get a dime unless he *was* sober; but you couldn't always tell.

'Nabors seemed in earnest. He had studied up the matter of scientific hanging in an old book he borrowed from your grandfather, and he and the carpenter had knocked together a big, shaky-looking contraption in the jail yard. It worked all right in practice, with sacks of meal; the trap went down with a boom that brought your heart up in your throat. But once they allowed for too much spring in the rope, and it tore a sack apart. Then old Doc Macdonald chipped in about that fellow John Lee, in England—and it nearly finished Bob Moran.

'That was late on the night before the execution. We were sitting round the lamp in Bob's office, trying to play stud poker. There were tops and skipping-ropes, all kinds of toys, all over that office. Bob let his kids play in there—which he shouldn't have done, because the door out of it led to a corridor of cells with Fred Joliffe in the last one. Of course the few other prisoners, disorderlies and chicken-thieves and the like, had been moved upstairs. Somebody had told Bob that the scent of an execution affects 'em like a cage of wild animals. Whoever it was, he was right. We could hear 'em shifting and stamping over our heads, and one old nigger singing hymns all night long.

'Well, it was raining hard on the tin roof; maybe that was what put Doc Macdonald in mind of it. Doc was a cynical old devil. When he saw that Bob couldn't sit still, and would throw in his hand without even looking at the buried card, Doc says:

' "Yes, I hope it'll go off all right. But you want to be careful about that rain. Did you read about that fellow they tried to hang in England?—and the rain had swelled the boards so's the trap wouldn't fall? They stuck him on it three times, but still it wouldn't work . . ."

'Ed Nabors slammed his hand down on the table. I reckon he felt bad enough as it was, because one of his daughters had run away and left him, and the other was dying of consumption. But he was twitchy and reddish about the eyes, he hadn't had a drink for two days, although there was a bottle on the table. He says:

' "You shut up or I'll kill you. Damn you, Macdonald," he says, and grabs the edge of the table. "I tell you nothing *can* go wrong. I'll go out and test the thing again, if you'll let me put the rope round your neck."

'And Bob Moran says: "What do you want to talk like that for, anyway, Doc? Ain't it bad enough as it is?" he says. "Now you've got me worrying about something else," he says. "I went down there a while ago to look at him, and he said the funniest thing I ever heard Fred Joliffe say. He's crazy. He giggled and said God wouldn't let them soand-so's hang him. It was terrible, hearing Fred Joliffe talk like that. What time is it, somebody?"

'I was cold that night. I dozed off in a chair, hearing the rain, and that animal-cage snuffling upstairs. The nigger was singing that part of the hymn about while the nearer waters roll, while the tempest still is high.

'They woke me about half-past eight to say that Judge Hunt and all the witnesses were out in the jail yard, and they were ready to start the march. Then I realized that they were really going to hang him after all. I had to join behind the procession as I was sworn, but I didn't see Fred Joliffe's face and I didn't want to see it. They had given him a good wash, and a clean flannel shirt that they tucked under at the neck. He stumbled coming out of the cell, and started to go in the wrong direction; but Bob Moran and the constable each had him by one arm. It was a cold, dark, windy morning. His hands were tied behind.

'The preacher was saying something I couldn't catch; everything went off smoothly enough until they got half-way across the jail yard. It's a pretty big yard. I didn't look at the contraption in the middle, but at the witnesses standing over against the wall with their hats off; and I smelled the clean air after the rain, and looked up at the mountains where the sky was getting pink. But Fred Joliffe did look at it, and went down flat on his knees. They hauled him up again. I heard them keep on walking, and go up the steps, which were creaky.

'I didn't look at the contraption until I heard a thumping sound, and we all knew something was wrong.

'Fred Joliffe was not standing on the trap, nor was the bag pulled over his head, although his legs were strapped. He stood with his eyes closed and his face towards the pink sky. Ed Nabors was clinging with both hands to the rope, twirling round a little and stamping on the trap. It didn't budge. Just as I heard Ed crying something about the rain having swelled the boards, Judge Hunt ran past me to the foot of the contraption.

'Bob Moran started cursing pretty obscenely. "Put him on and try it, anyway," he says, and grabs Fred's arm. "Stick that bag over his head and give the thing a chance."

' "In His name," says the preacher pretty steadily, "you'll not do it if I can help it."

'Bob ran over like a crazy man and jumped on the trap with both feet. It was stuck fast. Then Bob turned round and pulled an Ivor-Johnson .45 out of his hip-pocket. Judge Hunt got in front of Fred, whose lips were moving a little.

' "He'll have the law, and nothing but the law," says Judge Hunt. "Put that gun away, you lunatic, and take him back to the cell until you can make the thing work. Easy with him, now."

'To this day I don't think Fred Joliffe had realized what happened. I believe he only had his belief confirmed that they never meant to hang him after all. When he found himself going down the steps again, he opened his eyes. His face looked shrunken and dazed-like, but all of a sudden it came to him in a blaze.

' "I knew them so-and-so's would never hang me," says he. His throat was so dry he couldn't spit at Judge Hunt, as he tried to do; but he marched straight and giggling across the yard. "I knew them so-and-so's would never hang me," he says.

'We all had to sit down a minute, and we had to give Ed Nabors a drink. Bob made him hurry up, although we didn't say much, and he was leaving to fix the trap again when the court-house janitor came bustling into Bob's office.

' "Call," says he, "on the new machine over there. Telephone."

' "Lemme out of here!" yells Bob. "I can't listen to no telephone calls now. Come out and give us a hand."

' "But it's from Harrisburg," says the janitor. "It's from the Governor's office. You got to go."

' "Stay here, Bob," says Judge Hunt. He beckons to me. "Stay here, and I'll answer it," he says. We looked at each other in a queer way when we went across the Bridge of Sighs. The court-house clock was striking nine, and I could look down into the yard and see people hammering at the trap. After Judge Hunt had listened to that tele-phone call he had a hard time putting the receiver back on the hook.

' "I always believed in Providence, in a way," says he, "but I never thought it was so personal-like. Fred Joliffe is innocent. We're to call off this business," says he, "and wait for a messenger from the Gov-ernor. He's got the evidence of a woman. . . . Anyway, we'll hear it later."

'Now, I'm not much of a hand at describing mental states, so I can't tell you exactly what we felt then. Most of all was a fever and horror for fear they had already whisked Fred out and strung him up. But when we looked down into the yard from the Bridge of Sighs we saw Ed Nabors and the carpenter arguing over a cross-cut saw on the trap itself; and the blessed morning light coming up in a glory to show us we could knock the ugly contraption to pieces and burn it.

'The corridor downstairs was deserted. Judge Hunt had got his wind back, and, being one of those stern elocutionists who like to make complimentary remarks about God, he was going on some-thing powerful. He sobered up when he saw that the door to Fred Joliffe's cell was open.

' "Even Joliffe," says the judge, "deserves to get this news first."

'But Fred never did get that news, unless his ghost was listening. I told you he was very small and light. His heels were a good eighteen inches off the floor as he hung by the neck from an iron peg in the wall of the cell. He was hanging from a noose made in a child's skipping-rope; black-faced, dead already, with the whites of his eyes showing in slits, and his heels swinging over a kicked-away stool.

'No, son, we didn't think it was suicide for long. For a little while we were stunned, half crazy, naturally. It was like thinking about your troubles at three o'clock in the morning.

'But, you see, Fred's hands were still tied behind him. There was a bump on the back of his head, from a hammer that lay beside the stool. Somebody had walked in there with the hammer concealed behind his back, had stunned Fred when he wasn't looking, had run a slip-knot in that skipping-rope, and jerked him up a-flapping to stran-gle there. It was the creepiest part of the business, when we'd got that through our heads, and we began loudly to tell each other where we'd been during the confusion. Nobody had noticed much. I was scared green.

'When we gathered round the table in Bob's office, Judge Hunt took hold of his nerve with both hands. He looked at Bob Moran, at Ed Nabors, at Doc Macdonald, and at me. One of us was the other hangman.

' "This is a bad business, gentlemen," says he, clearing his throat a couple of times like a nervous orator before he starts. "What I want to know is, who under sanity would strangle a man when he thought we intended to do it, anyway, on a gallows?"

'Then Doc Macdonald turned nasty. "Well," says he, "if it comes to that, you might inquire where that skipping-rope came from, to begin with."

' "I don't get you," says Bob Moran, bewildered-like.

' "Oh, don't you?" says Doc, and sticks out his whiskers. "Well, then, who was so dead set on this execution going through as scheduled that he wanted to use a gun when the trap wouldn't drop?"

'Bob made a noise as though he'd been hit in the stomach. He stood looking at Doc for a minute, with his hands hanging down—and then he went for him. He had Doc back across the table, banging his head on the edge, when people began to crowd into the room at the yells. Funny, too; the first one in was the jail carpenter, who was pretty sore at not being told that the hanging had been called off.

' "What do you want to start fighting for?" he says, fretful-like. He was bigger than Bob, and had him off Doc with a couple of heaves. "Why didn't you tell me what was going on? They say there ain't going to be any hanging. Is that right?"

'Judge Hunt nodded, and the carpenter—Barney Hicks, that's who it was; I remember now—Barney Hicks looked pretty peevish, and says:

' "All right, all right, but you hadn't ought to fight all over the joint like that." Then he looks at Ed Nabors. "What I want is my hammer. Where's my hammer, Ed? I been looking all over the place for it. What did you do with it?"

'Ed Nabors sits up, pours himself four fingers of rye, and swallows it.

' "Beg pardon, Barney," says he in the coolest voice I ever heard. "I must have left it in the cell," he says, "when I killed Fred Joliffe."

'Talk about silences! It was like one of those silences when the magician at the Opera House fires a gun and six doves fly out of an empty box. I couldn't believe it. But I remember Ed Nabors sitting big in the corner by the barred window, in his shiny black coat and string tie. His hands were on his knees, and he was looking from one to the other of us, smiling a little. He looked as old as the prophets then; and he'd got enough liquor to keep the nerve from twitching beside his eye. So he just sat there, very quietly, shifting the plug of tobacco around in his cheek, and smiling.

' "Judge," he says in a reflective way, "you got a call from the Governor at Harrisburg, didn't you? Uh-huh. I knew what it would be. A woman had come forward, hadn't she, to confess Fred Joliffe was innocent and she had killed Randall Fraser? Uh-huh. The woman was my daughter. Jessie couldn't face telling it here, you see. That was why she ran away from me and went to the Governor. She'd have kept quiet if you hadn't convicted Fred."

' "But why . . ." shouts the judge. "*Why* . . ."

' "It was like this," Ed goes on in that slow way of his. 'She'd been on pretty intimate terms with Randall Fraser, Jessie had. And both Randall and Fred were having a whooping lot of fun threatening to tell the whole town about it. She was pretty near crazy, I think. And, you see, on the night of the murder Fred Joliffe was too drunk to remember anything that happened. He thought he *had* killed Randall, I suppose, when he woke up and found Randall dead and blood on his hands.

' "It's all got to come out now, I suppose," says he, nodding. "What did happen was that the three of 'em were in that back room, which Fred didn't remember. He and Randall had a fight while they were baiting Jessie; Fred whacked him hard enough with that mallet to lay him out, but all the blood he got was from a big splash over Randall's eye. Jessie. . . . Well, Jessie finished the job when Fred ran away, that's all."

' "But, you damned fool," cries Bob Moran, and begins to pound the table, "why did you have to go and kill Fred when Jessie had confessed?"

' "You fellows wouldn't have convicted Jessie, would you?" says Ed, blinking round at us. "No. But, if Fred had lived after her confession, you'd have *had* to, boys. That was how I figured it out. Once Fred learned what did happen, that he wasn't guilty and she was, he'd never have let up until he'd carried that case to the Superior Court out of your hands. He'd have screamed all over the State until they either had to hang her or send her up for life. I couldn't stand that. As I say, that was how I figured it out, although my brain's not so clear these days. So," says he, nodding and leaning over to take aim at the cuspidor, "when I heard about that telephone call, I went into Fred's cell and finished *my* job."

' "But don't you understand," says Judge Hunt, in the way you'd reason with a lunatic, "that Bob Moran will have to arrest you for murder, and——"

'It was the peacefulness of Ed's expression that scared us then. He got up from his chair, and dusted his shiny black coat, and smiled at us.

' "Oh, no," says he very clearly. "That's what you don't understand. You can't do a single damned thing to me. You can't even arrest me."

' "He's bughouse," says Bob Moran.

' "Am I?" says Ed affably. "Listen to me. I've committed what you might call a perfect murder, because I've done it legally . . . Judge, what time did you talk to the Governor's office, and get the order for the execution to be called off? Be careful now."

'And I said, with the whole idea of the business suddenly hitting me:

' "It was maybe five minutes past nine, wasn't it, Judge? I remember the court-house clock striking when we were going over the Bridge of Sighs."

' "I remember it too," says Ed Nabors. "And Doc Macdonald will tell you that Fred Joliffe was dead before ever that clock struck nine. I have in my pocket,' says he, unbuttoning his coat, 'a court order which authorizes me to kill Fred Joliffe, by means of hanging by the neck—which I did—between the hours of eight and nine in the morning—which I also did. And I did it in full legal style before the order was countermanded. Well?"

'Judge Hunt took off his stovepipe hat and wiped his face with a bandana. We all looked at him.

' "You can't get away with this," says the judge, and grabs the sheriff's orders off the table. "You can't trifle with the law in that way. And you can't execute sentence alone. Look here! 'In the presence of a qualified medical practitioner.' What do you say to that?"

' "Well, I can produce my medical diploma," says Ed, nodding again. "I may be a booze-hister, and mighty unreliable, but they haven't struck me off the register yet. . . . You lawyers are hell on the wording of the law," says he admiringly, "and it's the wording that's done for you this time. Until you get the law altered with some fancy words, there's nothing in that document to say that the doctor and the hangman can't be the same person."

'After a while Bob Moran turned round to the judge with a funny expression on his face. It might have been a grin.

' "This ain't according to morals," says he. "A fine citizen like Fred shouldn't get murdered like that. It's awful. Something's got to be done about it. As you said yourself this morning, Judge, he ought to have the law and nothing but the law. Is Ed right, Judge?"

' "Frankly, I don't know," says Judge Hunt, wiping his face again. "But, so far as I know, he is. What are you doing, Robert?"

' "I'm writing him out a cheque for fifty dollars," says Bob Moran, surprised-like. "We got to have it all nice and legal, haven't we?" '

5

CORNELL WOOLRICH

Murder at the Automat

Nelson pushed through the revolving-door at twenty to one in the morning, his squadmate, Sarecky, in the compartment behind him. They stepped clear and looked around. The place looked funny. Almost all the little white tables had helpings of food on them, but no one was at them eating. There was a big black crowd ganged up over in one corner, thick as bees and sending up a buzz. One or two were standing up on chairs, trying to see over the heads of the ones in front, rubbering like a flock of cranes.

The crowd burst apart, and a cop came through. 'Now, stand back. Get away from this table, all of you,' he was saying. 'There's nothing to see. The man's dead—that's all.'

He met the two dicks halfway between the crowd and the door. 'Over there in the corner,' he said unnecessarily. 'Indigestion, I guess.' He went back with them.

They split the crowd wide open again, this time from the outside. In the middle of it was one of the little white tables, a dead man in a chair, an ambulance doctor, a pair of stretcher-bearers, and the automat manager.

'He gone?' Nelson asked the interne.

'Yep. We got here too late.' He came closer so the mob wouldn't overhear. 'Better send him down to the morgue and have him looked at. I think he did the Dutch. There's a white streak on his chin, and a half-eaten sandwich under his face spiked with some more of it, whatever it is. That's why I got in touch with you fellows. Good night,' he wound up pleasantly and elbowed his way out of the crowd, the two stretcher-bearers tagging after him. The ambulance clanged

51

dolorously outside, swept its fiery headlights around the corner, and whined off.

Nelson said to the cop: 'Go over to the door and keep everyone in here, until we get the three others that were sitting at this table with him.'

The manager said: 'There's a little balcony upstairs. Couldn't he be taken up there, instead of being left down here in full sight like this?'

'Yeah, pretty soon,' Nelson agreed, 'but not just yet.'

He looked down at the table. There were four servings of food on it, one on each side. Two had barely been touched. One had been finished and only the soiled plates remained. One was hidden by the prone figure sprawled across it, one arm out, the other hanging limply down toward the floor.

'Who was sitting here?' said Nelson, pointing to one of the unconsumed portions. 'Kindly step forward and identify yourself.' No one made a move. 'No one', said Nelson, raising his voice, 'gets out of here until we have a chance to question the three people that were at this table with him when it happened.'

Someone started to back out of the crowd from behind. The woman who had wanted to go home so badly a minute ago, pointed accusingly. '*He* was—that man there! I remember him distinctly. He bumped into me with his tray just before he sat down.'

Sarecky went over, took him by the arm, and brought him forward again. 'No one's going to hurt you,' Nelson said, at sight of his pale face. 'Only don't make it any tougher for yourself than you have to.'

'I never even saw the guy before,' wailed the man, as if he had already been accused of murder, 'I just happened to park my stuff at the first vacant chair I—' Misery liking company, he broke off short and pointed in turn. '*He* was at the table, too. Why doncha hold him, if you're gonna hold me?'

'That's just what we're going to do,' said Nelson dryly. 'Over here, you,' he ordered the new witness. 'Now, who was eating spaghetti on the right here? As soon as we find that out, the rest of you can go home.'

The crowd looked around indignantly in search of the recalcitrant witness that was the cause of detaining them all. But this time no one was definitely able to single him out. A white-uniformed busman finally edged forward and said to Nelson: 'I think he musta got out of the place right after it happened. I looked over at this table a minute before it happened, and he was already through eating, picking his teeth and just holding down the chair.'

'Well, he's not as smart as he thinks he is,' said Nelson. 'We'll catch up with him, whether he got out or didn't. The rest of you clear out of here now. And don't give fake names and addresses to the cop at the door, or you'll be making trouble for yourselves.'

The place emptied itself like magic, self-preservation being stronger than curiosity in most people. The two table-mates of the dead man, the manager, the staff, and the two dicks remained inside.

An assistant medical examiner arrived, followed by two men with the usual basket, and made a brief preliminary investigation. While this was going on, Nelson was questioning the two witnesses, the busman, and the manager. He got an illuminating composite picture.

The man was well known to the staff by sight, and was considered an eccentric. He always came in at the same time each night, just before closing time, and always helped himself to the same snack— coffee and a bologna sandwich. It hadn't varied for six months now. The remnants that the busman removed from where the man sat each time were always the same. The manager was able to corroborate this. He, the dead man, had raised a kick one night about a week ago, because the bologna-sandwich slots had all been emptied before he came in. The manager had had to remind him that it's first come first served at an automat, and you can't reserve your food ahead of time. The man at the change-booth, questioned by Nelson, added to the old fellow's reputation for eccentricity. Other, well-dressed people came in and changed a half-dollar, or at the most a dollar bill. He, in his battered hat and derelict's overcoat, never failed to produce a ten and sometimes even a twenty.

'One of these misers, eh?' said Nelson. 'They always end up behind the eight-ball, one way or another.'

The old fellow was removed, also the partly consumed sandwich. The assistant examiner let Nelson know: 'I think you've got something here, brother. I may be wrong, but that sandwich was loaded with cyanide.'

Sarecky, who had gone through the man's clothes, said: 'The name was Leo Avram, and here's the address. Incidentally, he had seven hundred dollars, in C's, in his right shoe and three hundred in his left. Want me to go over there and nose around?'

'Suppose I go,' Nelson said. 'You stay here and clean up.'

'My pal,' murmured the other dick dryly.

The waxed paper from the sandwich had been left lying under the chair. Nelson picked it up, wrapped it in a paper-napkin, and put it in his pocket. It was only a short walk from the automat to where Avram lived, an outmoded, walk-up building, falling to pieces with neglect.

Nelson went into the hall and there was no such name listed. He thought at first Sarecky had made a mistake, or at least been misled by whatever memorandum it was he had found that purported to give the old fellow's address. He rang the bell marked *Superintendent*, and went down to the basement-entrance to make sure. A stout blonde woman in an old sweater and carpet-slippers came out.

'Is there anyone named Avram living in this building?'

'That's my husband—he's the superintendent. He's out right now, I expect him back any minute.'

Nelson couldn't understand, himself, why he didn't break it to her then and there. He wanted to get a line, perhaps, on the old man's surroundings while they still remained normal. 'Can I come in and wait a minute?' he said.

'Why not?' she said indifferently.

She led him down a barren, unlit basement-way, stacked with empty ashcans, into a room green-yellow with a tiny bud of gaslight. Old as the building upstairs was, it had been wired for electricity, Nelson had noted. For that matter, so was this basement down here. There was a cord hanging from the ceiling ending in an empty socket. It had been looped up out of reach. 'The old bird sure was a miser,' thought Nelson. 'Walking around on one grand and living like this!' He couldn't help feeling a little sorry for the woman.

He noted to his further surprise that a pot of coffee was boiling on a one-burner gas stove over in the corner. He wondered if she knew that he treated himself away from home each night. 'Any idea where he went?' he asked, sitting down in a creaking rocker.

'He goes two blocks down to the automat for a bite to eat every night at this time,' she said.

'How is it,' he asked curiously, 'he'll go out and spend money like that, when he could have coffee right here where he lives with you?'

A spark of resentment showed in her face, but a defeated resentment that had long turned to resignation. She shrugged. 'For himself, nothing's too good. He goes there because the light's better, he says. But for me and the kids, he begrudges every penny.'

'You've got kids, have you?'

'They're mine, not his,' she said dully.

Nelson had already caught sight of a half-grown girl and a little boy peeping shyly out at him from another room. 'Well,' he said, getting up, 'I'm sorry to have to tell you this, but your husband had an accident a little while ago at the automat, Mrs Avram. He's gone.'

The weary stolidity on her face changed very slowly. But it did change—to fright. 'Cyanide—what's that?' she breathed, when he'd told her.

'Did he have any enemies?'

She said with utter simplicity. 'Nobody loved him. Nobody hated him that much, either.'

'Do you know of any reason he'd have to take his own life?'

'Him? Never! He held on tight to life, just like he did to his money.'

There was some truth in that, the dick had to admit. Misers seldom commit suicide.

The little girl edged into the room fearfully, holding her hands behind her. 'Is—is he dead, Mom?'

The woman just nodded, dry-eyed.

'Then, can we use this now?' She was a holding a flyblown electric bulb in her hands.

Nelson felt touched, hard-boiled dick though he was. 'Come down to headquarters tomorrow, Mrs Avram. There's some money there you can claim. G'night.' He went outside and clanged the basement-gate shut after him. The windows alongside him suddenly bloomed feebly with electricity, and the silhouette of a woman standing up on a chair was outlined against them.

'It's a funny world,' thought the dick with a shake of his head, as he trudged up to sidewalk-level.

It was now two in the morning. The automat was dark when Nelson returned there, so he went down to headquarters. They were questioning the branch-manager and the unseen counterman who prepared the sandwiches and filled the slots from the inside.

Nelson's captain said: 'They've already telephoned from the chem lab that the sandwich is loaded with cyanide crystals. On the other hand, they give the remainder of the loaf that was used, the leftover bologna from which the sandwich was prepared, the breadknife, the cutting-board, and the scraps in the garbage-receptacle—all of which we sent over there—a clean bill of health. There was clearly no slip-up or carelessness in the automat pantry. Which means that cyanide got into that sandwich on the consumer's side of the apparatus. He committed suicide or was deliberately murdered by one of the other customers.'

'I was just up there,' Nelson said. 'It wasn't suicide. People don't worry about keeping their light bills down when they're going to take their own lives.'

'Good psychology,' the captain nodded. 'My experience is that miserliness is simply a perverted form of self-preservation, an exaggerated clinging to life. The choice of method wouldn't be in character, either. Cyanide's expensive, and it wouldn't be sold to a man of Avram's type, just for the asking. It's murder, then. I think it's highly important you men bring in whoever the fourth man at that table was tonight. Do it with the least possible loss of time.'

A composite description of him, pieced together from the few scraps that could be obtained from the busman and the other two at the table, was available. He was a heavy-set dark-complected man, wearing a light-tan suit. He had been the first of the four at the table, and already through eating, but had lingered on. Mannerisms—had kept looking back over his shoulder, from time to time, and picking his teeth. He had had a small black satchel, or sample-case, parked at his feet under the table. Both survivors were positive on this point. Both had stubbed their toes against it in sitting down, and both had glanced to the floor to see what it was.

Had he reached down toward it at any time, after their arrival, as if to open it or take anything out of it?

To the best of their united recollections—no.

Had Avram, *after* bringing the sandwich to the table, gotten up again and left it unguarded for a moment?

Again, no. In fact the whole thing had been over with in a flash. He had noisily unwrapped it, taken a huge bite, swallowed without chewing, heaved convulsively once or twice, and fallen prone across the tabletop.

'Then it must have happened right outside the slot—I mean the inserting of the stuff—and not at the table, at all,' Sarecky told Nelson privately. 'Guess he laid it down for a minute while he was drawing his coffee.'

'Absolutely not!' Nelson contradicted. 'You're forgetting it was all wrapped up in wax-paper. How could anyone have opened, then closed it again, without attracting his attention? And if we're going to suspect the guy with the satchel—and the cap seems to want us to—he was already *at* the table and all through eating when Avram came over. How could he know ahead of time which table the old guy was going to select?'

'Then how did the stuff get on it? Where did it come from?' the other dick asked helplessly.

'It's little things like that we're paid to find out,' Nelson reminded him dryly.

'Pretty large order, isn't it?'

'You talk like a layman. You've been on the squad long enough by now to know how damnably unescapable little habits are, how impossible it is to shake them off, once formed. The public at large thinks detective work is something miraculous like pulling rabbits out of a silk-hat. They don't realize that no adult is a free agent—that they're tied hand and foot by tiny, harmless little habits, and held helpless. This man has a habit of taking a snack to eat at midnight in a public place. He has a habit of picking his teeth after he's through, of lingering on at the table, of looking back over his shoulder aimlessly from time to time. Combine that with a stocky build, a dark complexion, and you have him! What more d'ya want—a spotlight trained on him?'

It was Sarecky himself, in spite of his misgivings, who picked him up forty-eight hours later in another automat, sample-case and all, at nearly the same hour as the first time, and brought him in for questioning! The busman from the former place, and the two customers, called in, identified him unhesitatingly, even if he was now wearing a gray suit.

His name, he said, was Alexander Hill, and he lived at 215 Such-and-such a street.

'What business are you in?' rapped out the captain.

The man's face got livid. His Adam's apple went up and down like an elevator. He could barely articulate the words. 'I'm—I'm a salesman for a wholesale drug concern,' he gasped terrifiedly.

'Ah!' said two of his three questioners expressively. The sample-case, opened, was found to contain only tooth-powders, aspirins, and headache remedies.

But Nelson, rummaging through it, thought: 'Oh, nuts, it's too pat. And he's too scared, too defenseless, to have really done it. Came in here just now without a bit of mental build-up prepared ahead of time. The real culprit would have been all primed, all rehearsed, for just this. Watch him go all to pieces. The innocent ones always do.'

The captain's voice rose to a roar. 'How is it everyone else stayed in the place that night, but you got out in such a hurry?'

'I—I don't know. It happened so close to me, I guess I—I got nervous.'

That wasn't necessarily a sign of guilt; Nelson was thinking. It was his duty to take part in the questioning, so he shot out at him: 'You got nervous, eh? What reason d'you have for getting nervous? How'd *you* know it wasn't just a heart attack or malnutrition—unless you were the cause of it?'

He stumbled badly over that one. 'No! No! I don't handle that stuff! I don't carry anything like that—'

'So you know what it was? How'd you know? We didn't tell you,' Sarecky jumped on him.

'I—I read it in the papers next morning,' he wailed.

Well, it had been in all of them, Nelson had to admit.

'You didn't reach out in front of you—toward him—for anything that night? You kept your hands to yourself?' Then, before he could get a word out, '*What about sugar?*'

The suspect went from bad to worse: 'I don't use any!' he whimpered.

Sarecky had been just waiting for that. 'Don't lie to us!' he yelled, and swung at him. 'I watched you for ten full minutes tonight before I went over and tapped your shoulder. You emptied half the container into your cup!' His fist hit him a glancing blow on the side of the jaw, knocked him and the chair he was sitting on both off-balance. Fright was making the guy sew himself up twice as badly as before.

'Aw, we're just barking up the wrong tree,' Nelson kept saying to himself. 'It's just one of those fluke coincidences. A drug salesman happens to be sitting at the same table where a guy drops from cyanide poisoning!' Still, he knew that more than one guy had been strapped into the chair just on the strength of such a coincidence and nothing more. You couldn't expect a jury not to pounce on it for all it was worth.

The captain took Nelson out of it at this point, somewhat to his relief, took him aside and murmured: 'Go over there and give his place a good cleaning while we're holding him here. If you can turn up any of that stuff hidden around there, that's all we need. He'll break down like a stack of cards.' He glanced over at the cowering figure in the chair. 'We'll have him before morning,' he promised.

'That's what I'm afraid of,' thought Nelson, easing out. 'And then what'll we have? Exactly nothing.' He wasn't the kind of a dick that would have rather had a wrong guy than no guy at all, like some of them. He wanted the right guy—or none at all. The last he saw of the captain, he was stripping off his coat for action, more as a moral threat than a physical one, and the unfortunate victim of circumstances was wailing, 'I didn't do it, I didn't do it,' like a record with a flaw in it.

Hill was a bachelor and lived in a small one-room flat on the upper West Side. Nelson let himself in with the man's own key, put on the lights, and went to work. In half an hour, he had investigated the place upside-down. There was not a grain of cyanide to be found, nor anything beyond what had already been revealed in the sample-case. This did not mean, of course, that he couldn't have obtained some either through the firm he worked for, or some of the retail druggists whom he canvassed. Nelson found a list of the latter and took it with him to check over the following day.

Instead of returning directly to headquarters, he detoured on an impulse past the Avram house, and, seeing a light shining in the basement windows, went over and rang the bell.

The little girl came out, her brother behind her. 'Mom's not in,' she announced.

'She's out with Uncle Nick,' the boy supplied.

His sister whirled on him. 'She told us not to tell anybody that, didn't she!'

Nelson could hear the instructions as clearly as if he'd been in the room at the time, "If that man comes around again, don't you tell him I've gone out with Uncle Nick, now!"

Children are after all very transparent. They told him most of what he wanted to know without realizing they were doing it. 'He's not really your uncle, is he?'

A gasp of surprise. 'How'd you know that?'

'Your ma gonna marry him?'

They both nodded approvingly. 'He's gonna be our new Pop.'

'What was the name of your real Pop—the one before the last?'

'Edwards,' they chorused proudly.

'What happened to him?'

'He died.'

'In Dee-troit,' added the little boy.

He only asked them one more question. 'Can you tell me his full name?'

'Albert J. Edwards,' they recited.

He gave them a friendly push. 'All right, kids, go back to bed.'

He went back to headquarters, sent a wire to the Bureau of Vital Statistics in Detroit, on his own hook. They were still questioning Hill down to the bone, meanwhile, but he hadn't caved in yet. 'Nothing,' Nelson reported. 'Only this account-sheet of where he places his orders.'

'I'm going to try framing him with a handful of bicarb of soda, or something—pretend we got the goods on him. I'll see if that'll open him up,' the captain promised wrathfully. 'He's not the pushover I expected. You start in at seven this morning and work your way through this list of retail druggists. Find out if he ever tried to contract them for any of that stuff.'

Meanwhile, he had Hill smuggled out the back way to an outlying precinct, to evade the statute governing the length of time a prisoner can be held before arraignment. They didn't have enough of a case against him to arraign him, but they weren't going to let him go.

Nelson was even more surprised than the prisoner at what he caught himself doing. As they stood Hill up next to him in the corridor, for a minute, waiting for the Black Maria, he breathed over his shoulder, 'Hang on tight, or you're sunk!'

The man acted too far gone even to understand what he was driving at.

Nelson was present the next morning when Mrs Avram showed up to claim the money, and watched her expression curiously. She had the same air of weary resignation as the night he had broken the news to her. She accepted the money from the captain, signed for it, turned apathetically away, holding it in her hand. The captain, by pre-arrangement, had pulled another of his little tricks—purposely withheld one of the hundred-dollar bills to see what her reaction would be.

Halfway to the door, she turned in alarm, came hurrying back. 'Gentlemen, there must be a mistake! There's—there's a hundred-dollar bill here on top!' She shuffled through the roll hastily. 'They're all hundred-dollar bills!' she cried out aghast. 'I knew he had a little money in his shoes—he slept with them under his pillow at nights—but I thought maybe, fifty, seventy dollars—'

'There was a thousand in his shoes,' said the captain, 'and another thousand stitched all along the seams of his overcoat.'

She let the money go, caught the edge of the desk he was sitting behind with both hands, and slumped draggingly down it to the floor in a dead faint. They had to hustle in with a pitcher of water to revive her.

Nelson impatiently wondered what the heck was the matter with him, what more he needed to be convinced she hadn't known what she was coming into? And yet, he said to himself, how are you going to tell a real faint from a fake one? They close their eyes and they flop, and which is it?

He slept three hours, and then he went down and checked at the wholesale drug concern Hill worked for. The firm did not handle cyanide or any other poisonous substance, and the man had a very good record there. He spent the morning working his way down the list of retail druggists who had placed their orders through Hill, and again got nowhere. At noon he quit and went back to the automat where it had happened—not to eat but to talk to the manager. He was really working on two cases simultaneously—an official one for his captain and a private one of his own. The captain would have had a fit if he'd known it.

'Will you lemme have that busman of yours, the one we had down at headquarters the other night? I want to take him out of here with me for about half an hour.'

'You're the Police Department,' the manager smiled acquiescently.

Nelson took him with him in his streetclothes. 'You did a pretty good job of identifying Hill, the fourth man at that table,' he told him. 'Naturally, I don't expect you to remember every face that was in there that night. Especially with the quick turnover there is in an automat. However, here's what you do. Go down this street here to Number One-twenty-one—you can see it from here. Ring the super-intendent's bell. You're looking for an apartment, see? But while you're at it, you take a good look at the woman you'll see, and then come back and tell me if you remember seeing her face in the automat that night or any other night. Don't stare now—just size her up.'

It took him a little longer than Nelson had counted on. When he finally rejoined the dick around the corner, where the latter was wait-ing, he said: 'Nope, I've never seen her in our place, that night or any other, to my knowledge. But don't forget—I'm not on the floor every minute of the time. She could have been in and out often without my spotting her.'

'But not', thought Nelson, 'without Avram seeing her, if she went anywhere near him at all.' She hadn't been there, then. That was prac-tically certain. 'What took you so long?' he asked him.

'Funny thing. There was a guy there in the place with her that used to work for us. He remembered me right away.'

'Oh, yeah?' The dick drew up short. 'Was *he* in there that night?'

'Naw, he quit six months ago. I haven't seen him since.'

'What was he, sandwich-maker?'

'No, busman like me. He cleaned up the tables.'

Just another coincidence, then. But, Nelson reminded himself, if one coincidence was strong enough to put Hill in jeopardy, why should the other be passed over as harmless? Both cases—his and the captain's—now had their coincidences. It remained to be seen which was just that—a coincidence and nothing more—and which was the McCoy.

He went back to headquarters. No wire had yet come from Detroit in answer to his, but he hadn't expected any this soon—it took time. The captain, bulldog-like, wouldn't let Hill go. They had spirited him away to still a third place, were holding him on some technicality or other that had nothing to do with the Avram case. The bicarbonate of soda trick hadn't worked, the captain told Nelson ruefully.

'Why?' the dick wanted to know. 'Because he caught on just by looking at it that it wasn't cyanide—is that it? I think that's an important point, right there.'

'No, he thought it was the stuff all right. But he hollered blue murder it hadn't come out of his room.'

'Then if he doesn't know the difference between cyanide and bicarb of soda at sight, doesn't that prove he didn't put any on that sandwich?'

The captain gave him a look. 'Are you for us or against us?' he wanted to know acidly. 'You go ahead checking that list of retail druggists until you find out where he got it. And if we can't dig up any other motive, unhealthy scientific curiosity will satisfy me. He wanted to study the effects at first hand, and picked the first stranger who came along.'

'Sure, in an automat—the most conspicuous, crowded public eating-place there is. The one place where human handling of the food is reduced to a minimum.'

He deliberately disobeyed orders, a thing he had never done before—or rather, postponed carrying them out. He went back and commenced a one-man watch over the basement entrance of the Avram house.

In about an hour, a squat, foreign-looking man came up the steps and walked down the street. This was undoubtedly 'Uncle Nick',

Mrs Avram's husband-to-be, and former employee of the automat. Nelson tailed him effortlessly on the opposite side, boarded the same bus he did a block below, and got off at the same stop. 'Uncle Nick' went into a bank, and Nelson into a cigar-store across the way that had transparent telephone booths commanding the street through the glass front.

When he came out again, Nelson didn't bother following him any more. Instead, he went into the bank himself. 'What'd that guy do—open an account just now? Lemme see the deposit-slip.'

He had deposited a thousand dollars cash under the name of Nicholas Krassin, half of the sum Mrs Avram had claimed at headquarters only the day before. Nelson didn't have to be told that this by no means indicated Krassin and she had had anything to do with the old man's death. The money was rightfully hers as his widow, and, if she wanted to divide it with her groom-to-be, that was no criminal offence. Still, wasn't there a stronger motive here than the 'unhealthy scientific curiosity' the captain had pinned on Hill? The fact remained that she wouldn't have had possession of the money had Avram still been alive. It would have still been in his shoes and coat-seams where she couldn't get at it.

Nelson checked Krassin at the address he had given at the bank, and, somewhat to his surprise, found it to be on the level, not fictitious. Either the two of them weren't very bright, or they were innocent. He went back to headquarters at six, and the answer to his telegram to Detroit had finally come. 'Exhumation order obtained as per request stop Albert J. Edwards deceased January 1936 stop death certificate gives cause fall from steel girder while at work building under construction stop—autopsy—'

Nelson read it to the end, folded it, put it in his pocket without changing his expression.

'Well, did you find out anything?' the captain wanted to know.

'No, but I'm on the way to,' Nelson assured him, but he may have been thinking of that other case of his own, and not the one they were all steamed up over. He went out again without saying where.

He got to Mrs Avram's at quarter to seven, and rang the bell. The little girl came out to the basement-entrance. At sight of him, she called out shrilly, but without humorous intent, 'Ma, that man's here again.'

Nelson smiled a little and walked back to the living-quarters. A sudden hush had fallen thick enough to cut with a knife. Krassin was there again, in his shirt-sleeves, having supper with Mrs Avram and the two kids. They not only had electricity now but a midget radio as well, he noticed. You can't arrest people for buying a midget radio. It was silent as a tomb, but he let the back of his hand brush it, surreptitiously, and the front of the dial was still warm from recent use.

'I'm not butting in, am I?' he greeted them cheerfully.

'N-no, sit down,' said Mrs Avram nervously. 'This is Mr Krassin, a friend of the family. I don't know your name—'

'Nelson.'

Krassin just looked at him watchfully.

The dick said: 'Sorry to trouble you. I just wanted to ask you a couple questions about your husband. About what time was it he had the accident?'

'You know better than I,' she objected. 'You were the one came here and told me.'

'I don't mean Avram, I mean Edwards, in Detroit—the riveter that fell off the girder.'

Her face went a little gray, as if the memory were painful. Krassin's face didn't change color, but only showed considerable surprise.

'About what time of day?' he repeated.

'Noon,' she said almost inaudibly.

'Lunchtime,' said the dick softly, as if to himself. 'Most workmen carry their lunch from home in a pail—' He looked at her thoughtfully. Then he changed the subject, wrinkled up his nose appreciatively. 'That coffee smells good,' he remarked.

She gave him a peculiar, strained smile. 'Have a cup, Mr Detective,' she offered. He saw her eyes meet Krassin's briefly.

'Thanks, don't mind if I do,' drawled Nelson.

She got up. Then, on her way to the stove, she suddenly flared out at the two kids for no apparent reason: 'What are you hanging around here for? Go to bed. Get out of here now, I say!' She banged the door shut on them, stood before it with her back to the room for a minute. Nelson's sharp ears caught the faint but unmistakable click of a key.

She turned back again, purred to Krassin: 'Nick, go outside and take a look at the furnace, will you, while I'm pouring Mr Nelson's coffee? If the heat dies down, they'll all start complaining from upstairs right away. Give it a good shaking up.'

The hairs at the back of Nelson's neck stood up a little as he watched the man get up and sidle out. But he'd asked for the cup of coffee, himself.

He couldn't see her pouring it—her back was turned toward him again as she stood over the stove. But he could hear the splash of the hot liquid, see her elbow-motions, hear the clink of the pot as she replaced it. She stayed that way a moment longer, after it had been poured, with her back to him—less than a moment, barely thirty seconds. One elbow moved slightly. Nelson's eyes were narrow slits. It was thirty seconds too long, one elbow-motion too many.

She turned, came back, set the cup down before him. 'I'll let you put your own sugar in, yes?' she said almost playfully. 'Some like a lot, some like a little.' There was a disappearing ring of froth in the middle of the black steaming liquid.

Outside somewhere, he could hear Krassin raking up the furnace.

'Drink it while it's still hot,' she urged.

He lifted it slowly to his lips. As the cup went up, her eyelids went down. Not all the way, not enough to completely shut out sight, though.

He blew the steam away. 'Too hot—burn my mouth. Gotta give it a minute to cool,' he said. 'How about you—ain't you having any? I couldn't drink alone. Ain't polite.'

'I had mine,' she breathed heavily, opening her eyes again. 'I don't think there's any left.'

'Then I'll give you half of this.'

Her hospitable alarm was almost overdone. She all but jumped back in protest. 'No, no! Wait, I'll look. Yes, there's more, there's plenty!'

He could have had an accident with it while her back was turned a second time, upset it over the floor. Instead, he took a kitchen-match out of his pocket, broke the head off short with his thumbnail. He threw the head, not the stick, over on top of the warm stove in front of which she was standing. It fell to one side of her, without making any noise, and she didn't notice it. If he'd thrown stick and all, it would have clicked as it dropped and attracted her attention.

She came back and sat down opposite him. Krassin's footsteps could be heard shuffling back toward them along the cement corridor outside.

'Go ahead. Don't be bashful—drink up,' she encouraged. There was something ghastly about her smile, like a death's-head grinning across the table from him.

The match-head on the stove, heated to the point of combustion, suddenly flared up with a little spitting sound and a momentary gleam. She jumped a little, and her head turned nervously to see what it was. When she looked back again, he already had his cup to his lips. She raised hers, too, watching him over the rim of it. Krassin's footfalls had stopped somewhere just outside the room door, and there wasn't another sound from him, as if he were standing there, waiting.

At the table, the cat-and-mouse play went on a moment longer. Nelson started swallowing with a dry constriction of the throat. The woman's eyes, watching him above her cup, were greedy half-moons of delight. Suddenly, her head and shoulders went down across the table with a bang, like her husband's had at the automat that other night, and the crash of the crushed cup sounded from underneath her.

Nelson jumped up watchfully, throwing his chair over. The door shot open, and Krassin came in, with an axe in one hand and an empty burlap-bag in the other.

'I'm not quite ready for cremation yet,' the dick gritted, and threw himself at him.

Krassin dropped the superfluous burlap-bag, the axe flashed up overhead. Nelson dipped his knees, down in under it before it could fall. He caught the shaft with one hand, midway between the blade and Krassin's grip, and held the weapon teetering in mid-air. With his other fist he started imitating a hydraulic drill against his assailant's teeth. Then he lowered his barrage suddenly to solar-plexus level, sent in two body-blows that caved his opponent in—and that about finished it.

Out in the wilds of Corona, an hour later, in a sub-basement locker-room, Alexander Hill—or at least what was left of him—was saying: 'And you'll lemme sleep if I do? And you'll get it over real quick, send me up and put me out of my misery?'

'Yeah, yeah!' said the haggard captain, flicking ink out of a fountain pen and jabbing it at him. 'Why dincha do this days ago, make it easier for us all?'

'Never saw such a guy,' complained Sarecky, rinsing his mouth with water over in a corner.

'What's that man signing?' exploded Nelson's voice from the stairs.

'Whaddye think he's signing?' snarled the captain. 'And where you been all night, incidentally?'

'Getting poisoned by the same party that croaked Avram!' He came the rest of the way down, and Krassin walked down alongside at the end of a short steel link.

'Who's this guy?' they both wanted to know.

Nelson looked at the first prisoner, in the chair. 'Take him out of here a few minutes, can't you?' he requested. 'He don't have to know all our business.'

'Just like in the story-books,' muttered Sarecky jealously. 'One-Man Nelson walks in at the last minute and cops all the glory.'

A cop led Hill upstairs. Another cop brought down a small brown-paper parcel at Nelson's request. Opened, it revealed a small tin that had once contained cocoa. Nelson turned it upside down and a few threads of whitish substance spilled lethargically out, filling the close air of the room with a faint odor of bitter almonds.

'There's your cyanide,' he said. 'It came off the shelf above Mrs Avram's kitchen-stove. Her kids, who are being taken care of at headquarters until I can get back there, will tell you it's roach-powder and they were warned never to go near it. She probably got it in Detroit, way back last year.'

'She did it?' said the captain. 'How could she? It was on the automat-sandwich, not anything he ate at home. *She* wasn't at the automat that night, she was home, you told us that yourself.'

'Yeah, she was at home, but she poisoned him at the automat just the same. Look, it goes like this.' He unlocked his manacle, refastened his prisoner temporarily to a plumbing-pipe in the corner. He took a paper napkin out of his pocket, and, from within that, the carefully preserved waxpaper wrapper the death-sandwich had been done in.

Nelson said: 'This has been folded over twice, once on one side, once on the other. You can see that, yourself. Every crease in it is double-barreled. Meaning what? The sandwich was taken out, doctored, and rewrapped. Only, in her hurry, Mrs Avram slipped up and put the paper back the other way around.

'As I told Sarecky already, there's death in little habits. Avram was a miser. Bologna is the cheapest sandwich that automat sells. For six months straight, he never bought any other kind. This guy here used to work there. He knew at what time the slots were refilled for the last time. He knew that that was just when Avram always showed up. And, incidentally, the old man was no fool. He didn't go there because the light was better—he went there to keep from getting poisoned at home. Ate all his meals out.

'All right, so what did they do? They got him, anyway—like this. Krassin, here, went in, bought a bologna sandwich, and took it home to her. She spiked it, rewrapped it, and, at eleven-thirty, he took it back there in his pocket. The sandwich-slots had just been refilled for the last time. They wouldn't put any more in till next morning. There are three bologna-slots. He emptied all three, to make sure the victim wouldn't get any but the lethal sandwich. After they're taken out, the glass slides remain ajar. You can lift them and reach in without inserting a coin. He put his death-sandwich in, stayed by it so no one else would get it. The old man came in. Maybe he's near-sighted and didn't recognize Krassin. Maybe he didn't know him at all—I haven't cleared that point up yet. Krassin eased out of the place. The old man is a miser. He sees he can get a sandwich for nothing, thinks something went wrong with the mechanism, maybe. He grabs it up twice as quick as anyone else would have. There you are.

'What was in his shoes is the guy's motive. As for her, that was only partly her motive. She was a congenital killer, anyway, outside of that. He would have married her, and it would have happened to him in his turn some day. She got rid of her first husband, Edwards, in Detroit that way. She got a wonderful break. He ate the poisoned lunch she'd given him way up on the cross-beams of a building under construction, and it looked like he'd lost his balance and toppled to his death. They exhumed the body and performed an autopsy at my request. This telegram says they found traces of cyanide poisoning even after all this time.

'I paid out rope to her tonight, let her know I was onto her. I told her her coffee smelled good. Then I switched cups on her. She's up there now, dead. I can't say that I wanted it that way, but it was me or her. You never would have gotten her to the chair, anyway. She was unbalanced of course, but not the kind that's easily recognizable. She'd have spent a year in an institution, been released, and gone out and done it all over again. It grows on 'em, gives 'em a feeling of power over their fellow human beings.

'This louse, however, is *not* insane. He did it for exactly one thousand dollars and no cents—and he knew what he was doing from first to last. So I think he's entitled to a chicken-and-ice-cream dinner in the death-house, at the state's expense.'

'The Sphinx,' growled Sarecky under his breath, shrugging into his coat. 'Sees all, knows all, keeps all to himself.'

'Who stinks?' corrected the captain, misunderstanding. 'If anyone does, it's you and me. He brought home the bacon!'

6

RAYMOND CHANDLER

Red Wind

There was a desert wind blowing that night. It was one of those hot dry Santa Anas that come down through the mountain passes and curl your hair and make your nerves jump and your skin itch. On nights like that every booze party ends in a fight. Meek little wives feel the edge of the carving knife and study their husbands' necks. Anything can happen. You can even get a full glass of beer at a cocktail lounge.

I was getting one in a flossy new place across the street from the apartment house where I lived. It had been open about a week and it wasn't doing any business. The kid behind the bar was in his early twenties and looked as if he had never had a drink in his life.

There was only one other customer, a souse on a bar stool with his back to the door. He had a pile of dimes stacked neatly in front of him, about two dollars' worth. He was drinking straight rye in small glasses and he was all by himself in a world of his own.

I sat farther along the bar and got my glass of beer and said: 'You sure cut the clouds off them, buddy. I will say that for you.'

'We just opened up,' the kid said. 'We got to build up trade. Been in before, haven't you, mister?'

'Uh-huh.'

'Live around here?'

'In the Berglund Apartments across the street,' I said. 'And the name is Philip Marlowe.'

'Thanks, mister. Mine's Lew Petrolle.' He leaned close to me across the polished dark bar. 'Know that guy?'

'No.'

'He ought to go home, kind of. I ought to call a taxi and send him home. He's doing his next week's drinking too soon.'

'A night like this,' I said. 'Let him alone.'

'It's not good for him,' the kid said, scowling at me.

'Rye!' the drunk croaked, without looking up. He snapped his fingers so as not to disturb his piles of dimes by banging on the bar.

The kid looked at me and shrugged. 'Should I?'

'Whose stomach is it? Not mine.'

The kid poured him another straight rye and I think he doctored it with water down behind the bar because when he came up with it he looked as guilty as if he'd kicked his grandmother. The drunk paid no attention. He lifted coins off his pile with the exact care of a crack surgeon operating on a brain tumor.

The kid came back and put more beer in my glass. Outside the wind howled. Every once in a while it blew the stained-glass door open a few inches. It was a heavy door.

The kid said: 'I don't like drunks in the first place and in the second place I don't like them getting drunk in here, and in the third place I don't like them in the first place.'

'Warner Brothers could use that,' I said.

'They did.'

Just then we had another customer. A car squeaked to a stop outside and the swinging door came open. A fellow came in who looked a little in a hurry. He held the door and ranged the place quickly with flat, shiny, dark eyes. He was well set up, dark, good-looking in a narrow-faced, tight-lipped way. His clothes were dark and a white handkerchief peeped coyly from his pocket and he looked cool as well as under a tension of some sort. I guessed it was the hot wind. I felt a bit the same myself only not cool.

He looked at the drunk's back. The drunk was playing checkers with his empty glasses. The new customer looked at me, then he looked along the line of half-booths at the other side of the place. They were all empty. He came on in—down past where the drunk sat swaying and muttering to himself—and spoke to the bar kid.

'Seen a lady in here, buddy? Tall, pretty, brown hair, in a print bolero jacket over a blue crêpe silk dress. Wearing a wide-brimmed straw hat with a velvet band.' He had a tight voice I didn't like.

'No, sir. Nobody like that's been in,' the bar kid said.

'Thanks. Straight Scotch. Make it fast, will you?'

The kid gave it to him and the fellow paid and put the drink down in a gulp and started to go out. He took three or four steps and stopped, facing the drunk. The drunk was grinning. He swept a gun from somewhere so fast that it was just a blur coming out. He held it steady and he didn't look any drunker than I was. The tall dark guy stood quite still and then his head jerked back a little and then he was still again.

A car tore by outside. The drunk's gun was a .22 target automatic, with a large front sight. It made a couple of hard snaps and a little smoke curled—very little.

'So long, Waldo,' the drunk said.

Then he put the gun on the barman and me.

The dark guy took a week to fall down. He stumbled, caught himself, waved one arm, stumbled again. His hat fell off, and then he hit the floor with his face. After he hit it he might have been poured concrete for all the fuss he made.

The drunk slid down off the stool and scooped his dimes into a pocket and slid towards the door. He turned sideways, holding the gun across his body. I didn't have a gun. I hadn't thought I needed one to buy a glass of beer. The kid behind the bar didn't move or make the slightest sound.

The drunk felt the door lightly with his shoulder, keeping his eyes on us, then pushed through it backwards. When it was wide a hard gust of air slammed in and lifted the hair of the man on the floor. The drunk said: 'Poor Waldo. I bet I made his nose bleed.'

The door swung shut. I started to rush it—from long practice in doing the wrong thing. In this case it didn't matter. The car outside let out a roar and when I got onto the sidewalk it was flicking a red smear of tail-light around the nearby corner. I got its license number the way I got my first million.

There were people and cars up and down the block as usual. Nobody acted as if a gun had gone off. The wind was making enough noise to make the hard quick rap of .22 ammunition sound like a slammed door, even if anyone heard it. I went back into the cocktail bar.

The kid hadn't moved, even yet. He just stood with his hands flat on the bar, leaning over a little and looking down at the dark guy's back.

The dark guy hadn't moved either. I bent down and felt his neck artery. He wouldn't move—ever.

The kid's face had as much expression as a cut of round steak and was about the same color. His eyes were more angry than shocked.

I lit a cigarette and blew smoke at the ceiling and said shortly: 'Get on the phone.'

'Maybe he's not dead,' the kid said.

'When they use a twenty-two that means they don't make mistakes. Where's the phone?'

'I don't have one. I got enough expenses without that. Boy, can I kick eight hundred bucks in the face!'

'You own this place?'

'I did till this happened.'

He pulled his white coat off and his apron and came around the inner end of the bar. 'I'm locking this door,' he said, taking keys out.

He went out, swung the door to and jiggled the lock from the outside until the bolt clicked into place. I bent down and rolled Waldo over. At first I couldn't even see where the shots went in. Then I could. A couple of tiny holes in his coat, over his heart. There was a little blood on his shirt.

The drunk was everything you could ask—as a killer.

The prowl-car boys came in about eight minutes. The kid, Lew Petrolle, was back behind the bar by then. He had his white coat on again and he was counting his money in the register and putting it in his pocket and making notes in a little book.

I sat at the edge of one of the half-booths and smoked cigarettes and watched Waldo's face get deader and deader. I wondered who the girl in the print coat was, why Waldo had left the engine of his car running outside, why he was in a hurry, whether the drunk had been waiting for him or just happened to be there.

The prowl-car boys came in perspiring. They were the usual large size and one of them had a flower stuck under his cap and his cap on a bit crooked. When he saw the dead man he got rid of the flower and leaned down to feel Waldo's pulse.

'Seems to be dead,' he said, and rolled him around a little more. 'Oh yeah, I see where they went in. Nice clean work. You two see him get it?'

I said yes. The kid behind the bar said nothing. I told them about it, that the killer seemed to have left in Waldo's car.

The cop yanked Waldo's wallet out, went through it rapidly and whistled. 'Plenty jack and no driver's license.' He put the wallet away. 'OK, we didn't touch him, see? Just a chance we could find did he have a car and put it on the air.'

'The hell you didn't touch him,' Lew Patrolle said.

The cop gave him one of those looks. 'OK, pal,' he said softly. 'We touched him.'

The kid picked up a clean highball glass and began to polish it. He polished it all the rest of the time we were there.

In another minute a homicide fast-wagon sirened up and screeched to a stop outside the door and four men came in, two dicks, a photographer and a laboratory man. I didn't know either of the dicks. You can be in the detecting business a long time and not know all the men on a big city force.

One of them was a short, smooth, dark, quiet, smiling man, with curly black hair and soft intelligent eyes. The other was big, rawboned, long-jawed, with a veined nose and glassy eyes. He looked like a heavy drinker. He looked tough, but he looked as if he thought he was a little tougher than he was. He shooed me into the last booth against the wall and his partner got the kid up front and the bluecoats went out. The fingerprint man and photographer set about their work.

A medical examiner came, stayed just long enough to get sore because there was no phone for him to call the morgue wagon.

The short dick emptied Waldo's pockets and then emptied his wallet and dumped everything into a large handkerchief on a booth table. I saw a lot of currency, keys, cigarettes, another handkerchief, very little else.

The big dick pushed me back into the end of the half-booth. 'Give,' he said. 'I'm Copernik, Detective Lieutenant.'

I put my wallet in front of him. He looked at it, went through it, tossed it back, made a note in a book.

'Philip Marlowe, huh? A shamus. You here on business?'

'Drinking business,' I said. 'I live just across the street in the Berglund.'

'Know this kid up front?'

'I've been in here once since he opened up.'

'See anything funny about him now?'

'No.'

'Takes it too light for a young fellow, don't he? Never mind answering. Just tell the story.'

I told it—three times. Once for him to get the outline, once for him to get the details and once for him to see if I had it too pat. At the end he said: 'This dame interests me. And the killer called the guy Waldo, yet didn't seem to be anyways sure he would be in. I mean, if Waldo wasn't sure the dame would be here, nobody could be sure Waldo would be here.'

'That's pretty deep,' I said.

He studied me. I wasn't smiling. 'Sounds like a grudge job, don't it? Don't sound planned. No getaway except by accident. A guy don't leave his car unlocked much in this town. And the killer works in front of two good witnesses. I don't like that.'

'I don't like being a witness,' I said. 'The pay's too low.'

He grinned. His teeth had a freckled look. 'Was the killer drunk really?'

'With that shooting? No.'

'Me too. Well, it's a simple job. The guy will have a record and he's left plenty prints. Even if we don't have his mug here we'll make him in hours. He had something on Waldo, but he wasn't meeting Waldo tonight. Waldo just dropped in to ask about a dame he had a date with and had missed connections on. It's a hot night and this wind would kill a girl's face. She'd be apt to drop in somewhere to wait. So the killer feeds Waldo two in the right place and scrams and don't worry about you boys at all. It's that simple.'

'Yeah,' I said.

'It's so simple it stinks,' Copernik said.

He took his felt hat off and tousled up his ratty blond hair and leaned his head on his hands. He had a long mean horse face. He got a handkerchief out and mopped it, and the back of his neck and the back of his hands. He got a comb out and combed his hair—he looked worse with it combed—and put his hat back on.

'I was just thinking,' I said.

'Yeah? What?'

'This Waldo knew just how the girl was dressed. So he must already have been with her tonight.'

'So, what? Maybe he had to go to the can. And when he came back she's gone. Maybe she changed her mind about him.'

'That's right,' I said.

But that wasn't what I was thinking at all. I was thinking that Waldo had described the girl's clothes in a way the ordinary man wouldn't know how to describe them. Printed bolero jacket over blue crêpe silk dress. I didn't even know what a bolero jacket was. And I might have said blue dress or even blue silk dress, but never blue crêpe silk dress.

After a while two men came with a basket. Lew Petrolle was still polishing his glass and talking to the short dark dick.

We all went down to Headquarters.

Lew Petrolle was all right when they checked on him. His father had a grape ranch near Antioch in Contra Costa County. He had given Lew a thousand dollars to go into business and Lew had opened the cocktail bar, neon sign and all, on eight hundred flat.

They let him go and told him to keep the bar closed until they were sure they didn't want to do any more printing. He shook hands all around and grinned and said he guessed the killing would be good for business after all, because nobody believed a newspaper account of anything and people would come to him for the story and buy drinks while he was telling it.

'There's a guy won't ever do any worrying,' Copernik said, when he was gone. 'Over anybody else.'

'Poor Waldo,' I said. 'The prints any good?'

'Kind of smudged,' Copernik said sourly. 'But we'll get a classification and teletype it to Washington some time tonight. If it don't click, you'll be in for a day on the steel picture racks downstairs.'

I shook hands with him and his partner, whose name was Ybarra, and left. They didn't know who Waldo was yet either. Nothing in his pockets told.

I got back to my street about 9 p.m. I looked up and down the block before I went into the Berglund. The cocktail bar was farther down on the other side, dark, with a nose or two against the glass, but no real crowd. People had seen the law and the morgue wagon, but they didn't know what had happened. Except the boys playing pinball games in the drugstore on the corner. They know everything, except how to hold a job.

The wind was still blowing, oven-hot, swirling dust and torn paper up against the walls.

I went into the lobby of the apartment house and rode the automatic elevator up to the fourth floor. I unwound the doors and stepped out and there was a tall girl standing there waiting for the car.

She had brown wavy hair under a wide-brimmed straw hat with a velvet band and loose bow. She had wide blue eyes and eyelashes that didn't quite reach her chin. She wore a blue dress that might have been crêpe silk, simple in lines but not missing any curves. Over it she wore what might have been a print bolero jacket.

I said: 'Is that a bolero jacket?'

She gave me a distant glance and made a motion as if to brush a cobweb out of the way.

'Yes. Would you mind—I'm rather in a hurry. I'd like—'

I didn't move. I blocked her off from the elevator. We stared at each other and she flushed very slowly.

'Better not go out on the street in those clothes,' I said.

'Why, how dare you—'

The elevator clanked and started down again. I didn't know what she was going to say. Her voice lacked the edgy twang of a beer-parlor frill. It had a soft light sound, like spring rain.

'It's not a make,' I said. 'You're in trouble. If they come to this floor in the elevator, you have just that much time to get off the hall. First take off the hat and jacket—and snap it up!'

She didn't move. Her face seemed to whiten a little behind the not-too-heavy make-up.

'Cops', I said, 'are looking for you. In those clothes. Give me the chance and I'll tell you why.'

She turned her head swiftly and looked back along the corridor. With her looks I didn't blame her for trying one more bluff.

'You're impertinent, whoever you are. I'm Mrs Leroy in Apartment Thirty-one. I can assure—'

'That you're on the wrong floor,' I said. 'This is the fourth.' The elevator had stopped down below. The sound of doors being wrenched open came up the shaft.

'Off!' I rapped. 'Now!'

She switched her hat off and slipped out of the bolero jacket, fast. I grabbed them and wadded them into a mess under my arm. I took her elbow and turned her and we were going down the hall.

'I live in Forty-two. The front one across from yours, just a floor up. Take your choice. Once again—I'm not on the make.'

She smoothed her hair with that quick gesture, like a bird preening itself. Ten thousand years of practice behind it.

'Mine,' she said, and tucked her bag under her arm and strode down the hall fast. The elevator stopped at the floor below. She stopped when it stopped. She turned and faced me.

'The stairs are back by the elevator shaft,' I said gently.

'I don't have an apartment,' she said.

'I didn't think you had.'

'Are they searching for me?'

'Yes, but they won't start gouging the block stone by stone before tomorrow. And then only if they don't make Waldo.'

She stared at me. 'Waldo?'

'Oh, you don't know Waldo,' I said.

She shook her head slowly. The elevator started down in the shaft again. Panic flicked in her blue eyes like a ripple on water.

'No,' she said breathlessly, 'but take me out of this hall.'

We were almost at my door. I jammed the key in and shook the lock around and heaved the door inward. I reached in far enough to switch lights on. She went in past me like a wave. Sandalwood floated on the air, very faint.

I shut the door, threw my hat into a chair and watched her stroll over to a card table on which I had a chess problem set out that I couldn't solve. Once inside, with the door locked, her panic had left her.

'So you're a chess player,' she said, in that guarded tone, as if she had come to look at my etchings. I wished she had.

We both stood still then and listened to the distant clang of elevator doors and then steps—going the other way.

I grinned, but with strain, not pleasure, went out into the kitchenette and started to fumble with a couple of glasses and then realized I still had her hat and bolero jacket under my arm. I went into the dressing room behind the wall bed and stuffed them into a drawer, went back out to the kitchenette, dug out some extra-fine Scotch and made a couple of highballs.

When I went in with the drinks she had a gun in her hand. It was a small automatic with a pearl grip. It jumped up at me and her eyes were full of horror.

I stopped, with a glass in each hand, and said: 'Maybe this hot wind has got you crazy too. I'm a private detective. I'll prove it if you let me.'

She nodded slightly and her face was white. I went over slowly and put a glass down beside her, and went back and set mine down and got a card out that had no bent corners. She was sitting down, smoothing one blue knee with her left hand, and holding the gun on the other. I put the card down beside her drink and sat with mine.

'Never let a guy get that close to you,' I said. 'Not if you mean business. And your safety catch is on.'

She flashed her eyes down, shivered, and put the gun back in her bag. She drank half the drink without stopping, put the glass down hard and picked the card up.

'I don't give many people that liquor,' I said. 'I can't afford to.'

Her lips curled. 'I supposed you would want money.'

'Huh?'

She didn't say anything. Her hand was close to her bag again.

'Don't forget the safety catch,' I said. Her hand stopped. I went on: 'This fellow I called Waldo is quite tall, say five-eleven, slim, dark, brown eyes with a lot of glitter. Nose and mouth too thin. Dark suit, white handkerchief showing, and in a hurry to find you. Am I getting anywhere?'

She took her glass again. 'So that's Waldo,' she said. 'Well, what about him?' Her voice seemed to have a slight liquor edge now.

'Well, a funny thing. There's a cocktail bar across the street ... Say, where have you been all evening?'

'Sitting in my car,' she said coldly, 'most of the time.'

'Didn't you see a fuss across the street up the block?'

Her eyes tried to say no and missed. Her lips said: 'I knew there was some kind of disturbance. I saw policemen and red searchlights. I supposed someone had been hurt.'

'Someone was. And this Waldo was looking for you before that. In the cocktail bar. He described you and your clothes.'

Her eyes were set like rivets now and had the same amount of expression. Her mouth began to tremble and kept on trembling.

'I was in there,' I said, 'talking to the kid that runs it. There was nobody in there but a drunk on a stool and the kid and myself. The drunk wasn't paying any attention to anything. Then Waldo came in and asked about you and we said no, we hadn't seen you and he started to leave.'

I sipped my drink. I like an effect as well as the next fellow. Her eyes ate me.

'Just started to leave. Then this drunk that wasn't paying any attention to anyone called him Waldo and took a gun out. He shot him twice'—I snapped my fingers twice—'like that. Dead.'

She fooled me. She laughed in my face. 'So my husband hired you to spy on me,' she said. 'I might have known the whole thing was an act. You and your Waldo.'

I gawked at her.

'I never thought of him as jealous,' she snapped. 'Not of a man who had been our chauffeur anyhow. A little about Stan, of course—that's natural. But Joseph Coates—'

I made motions in the air. 'Lady, one of us has this book open at the wrong page,' I grunted. 'I don't know anybody named Stan or Joseph Coates. So help me, I didn't even know you had a chauffeur. People around here don't run to them. As for husbands—yeah, we do have a husband once in a while. Not often enough.'

She shook her head slowly and her hand stayed near her bag and her blue eyes had glitters in them.

'Not good enough, Mr Marlowe. No, not nearly good enough. I know you private detectives. You're all rotten. You tricked me into your apartment, if it is your apartment. More likely it's the apartment of some horrible man who will swear anything for a few dollars. Now you're trying to scare me. So you can blackmail me—as well as get money from my husband. All right,' she said breathlessly, 'how much do I have to pay?'

I put my empty glass aside and leaned back. 'Pardon me if I light a cigarette,' I said. 'My nerves are frayed.'

I lit it while she watched me without enough fear for any real guilt to be under it. 'So Joseph Coates is his name,' I said. 'The guy that killed him in the cocktail bar called him Waldo.'

She smiled a bit disgustedly, but almost tolerantly. 'Don't stall. How much?'

'Why were you trying to meet this Joseph Coates?'

'I was going to buy something he stole from me, of course. Something that's valuable in the ordinary way too. Almost fifteen thousand dollars. The man I loved gave it to me. He's dead. There! He's dead! He died in a burning plane. Now, go back and tell my husband that, you slimy little rat!'

'I'm not little and I'm not a rat,' I said.

'You're still slimy. And don't bother about telling my husband. I'll tell him myself. He probably knows anyway.'

I grinned. 'That's smart. Just what was I supposed to find out?'

She grabbed her glass and finished what was left of her drink. 'So he thinks I'm meeting Joseph. Well, perhaps I was. But not to make love. Not with a chauffeur. Not with a bum I picked off the front step and gave a job to. I don't have to dig down that far, if I want to play around.'

'Lady,' I said, 'you don't indeed.'

'Now, I'm going,' she said. 'You just try and stop me.' She snatched the pearl-handled gun out of her bag. I didn't move.

'Why, you nasty little string of nothing,' she stormed. 'How do I know you're a private detective at all? You might be a crook. This card you gave me doesn't mean anything. Anybody can have cards printed.'

'Sure,' I said. 'And I suppose I'm smart enough to live here two years because you were going to move in today so I could blackmail you for not meeting a man named Joseph Coates who was bumped off across the street under the name of Waldo. Have you got the money to buy this something that cost fifteen grand?'

'Oh! You think you'll hold me up, I suppose!'

'Oh!' I mimicked her, 'I'm a stick-up artist now, am I? Lady, will you please either put that gun away or take the safety catch off? It hurts my professional feelings to see a nice gun made a monkey of that way.'

'You're a full portion of what I don't like,' she said. 'Get out of my way.'

I didn't move. She didn't move. We were both sitting down—and not even close to each other.

'Let me in on one secret before you go,' I pleaded. 'What in hell did you take the apartment down on the floor below for? Just to meet a guy down on the street?'

'Stop being silly,' she snapped. 'I didn't. I lied. It's his apartment.'

'Joseph Coates'?'

She nodded sharply.

'Does my description of Waldo sound like Joseph Coates?'

She nodded sharply again.

'All right. That's one fact learned at last. Don't you realize Waldo described your clothes before he was shot—when he was looking for you—that the description was passed on to the police—that the police don't know who Waldo is—and are looking for somebody in those clothes to help tell them? Don't you get that much?'

The gun suddenly started to shake in her hand. She looked down at it, sort of vacantly, and slowly put it back in her bag.

'I'm a fool,' she whispered, 'to be even talking to you.' She stared at me for a long time, then pulled in a deep breath. 'He told me where he was staying. He didn't seem afraid. I guess blackmailers are like that. He was to meet me on the street, but I was late. It was full of police when I got here. So I went back and sat in my car for a while. Then I came up to Joseph's apartment and knocked. Then I went back to my car and waited again. I came up here three times in all. The last time I walked up a flight to take the elevator. I had already been seen twice on the third floor. I met you. That's all.'

'You said something about a husband,' I grunted. 'Where is he?'

' He's at a meeting.'

'Oh, a meeting,' I said, nastily.

'My husband's a very important man. He has lots of meetings. He's a hydroelectric engineer. He's been all over the world. I'd have you know—'

'Skip it,' I said. 'I'll take him to lunch some day and have him tell me himself. Whatever Joseph had on you is dead stock now. Like Joseph.'

'He's really dead?' she whispered. 'Really?'

'He's dead,' I said. 'Dead, dead, dead. Lady, he's dead.'

She believed it at last. I hadn't thought she ever would somehow. In the silence, the elevator stopped at my floor.

I heard steps coming down the hall. We all have hunches. I put my finger to my lips. She didn't move now. Her face had a frozen look. Her big blue eyes were as black as the shadows below them. The hot wind boomed against the shut windows. Windows have to be shut when a Santa Ana blows, heat or no heat.

The steps that came down the hall were the casual ordinary steps of one man. But they stopped outside my door, and somebody knocked.

I pointed to the dressing room behind the wall bed. She stood up without a sound, her bag clenched against her side. I pointed again, to her glass. She lifted it swiftly, slid across the carpet, through the door, drew the door quietly shut after her.

I didn't know just what I was going to all this trouble for.

The knocking sounded again. The backs of my hands were wet. I creaked my chair and stood up and made a loud yawning sound. Then I went over and opened the door—without a gun. That was a mistake.

I didn't know him at first. Perhaps for the opposite reason Waldo hadn't seemed to know him. He'd had a hat on all the time over at the cocktail bar and he didn't have one on now. His hair ended completely and exactly where his hat would start. Above that line was hard white sweatless skin almost as glaring as scar tissue. He wasn't just twenty years older. He was a different man.

But I knew the gun he was holding, the .22 target automatic with the big front sight. And I knew his eyes. Bright, brittle, shallow eyes like the eyes of a lizard.

He was alone. He put the gun against my face very lightly and said between his teeth: 'Yeah, me. Let's go on in.'

I backed in just far enough and stopped. Just the way he would want me to, so he could shut the door without moving much. I knew from his eyes that he would want me to do just that.

I wasn't scared. I was paralyzed.

When he had the door shut he backed me some more, slowly, until there was something against the back of my legs. His eyes looked into mine.

'That's a card table,' he said. 'Some goon here plays chess. You?'

I swallowed. 'I don't exactly play it. I just fool around.'

'That means two,' he said with a kind of hoarse softness, as if some cop had hit him across the windpipe with a blackjack once, in a third-degree session.

'It's a problem,' I said. 'Not a game. Look at the pieces.'

'I wouldn't know.'

'Well, I'm alone,' I said, and my voice shook just enough.

'It don't make any difference,' he said. 'I'm washed up anyway. Some nose puts the bulls on me tomorrow, next week, what the hell? I just didn't like your map, pal. And that smug-faced pansy in the bar coat that played left tackle for Fordham or something. To hell with guys like you guys.'

I didn't speak or move. The big front sight raked my cheek lightly almost caressingly. The man smiled.

'It's kind of good business too,' he said. 'Just in case. An old con like me don't make good prints, all I got against me is two witnesses. The hell with it.'

'What did Waldo do to you?' I tried to make it sound as if I wanted to know, instead of just not wanting to shake too hard.

'Stooled on a bank job in Michigan and got me four years. Got himself a nolle prosse. Four years in Michigan ain't no summer cruise. They make you be good in them lifer states.'

'How'd you know he'd come in there?' I croaked.

'I didn't. Oh yeah, I was lookin' for him. I was wanting to see him all right. I got a flash of him on the street night before last but I lost him. Up to then I wasn't lookin' for him. Then I was. A cute guy, Waldo. How is he?'

'Dead,' I said.

'I'm still good,' he chuckled. 'Drunk or sober. Well, that don't make no doughnuts for me now. They make me downtown yet?'

I didn't answer him quick enough. He jabbed the gun into my throat and I choked and almost grabbed for it by instinct.

'Naw,' he cautioned me softly. 'Naw. You ain't that dumb.'

I put my hands back, down at my sides, open, the palms towards him. He would want them that way. He hadn't touched me, except with the gun. He didn't seem to care whether I might have one too. He wouldn't—if he just meant the one thing.

He didn't seem to care very much about anything, coming back on that block. Perhaps the hot wind did something to him. It was booming against my shut windows like the surf under a pier.

'They got prints,' I said. 'I don't know how good.'

'They'll be good enough—but not for teletype work. Take 'em airmail time to Washington and back to check 'em right. Tell me why I came here, pal.'

'You heard the kid and me talking in the bar. I told him my name, where I lived.'

'That's how, pal. I said why.' He smiled at me. It was a lousy smile to be the last one you might see.

'Skip it,' I said. 'The hangman won't ask you to guess why he's there.'

'Say, you're tough at that. After you, I visit that kid. I tailed him home from Headquarters, but I figure you're the guy to put the bee on first. I tail him home from the city hall, in the rent car Waldo had. From Headquarters, pal. Them funny dicks. You can sit in their laps and they don't know you. Start runnin' for a streetcar and they open up with machine guns and bump two pedestrians, a hacker asleep in his cab, and an old scrubwoman on the second floor workin' a mop. And they miss the guy they're after. Them funny lousy dicks.'

He twisted the gun muzzle in my neck. His eyes looked madder than before.

'I got time,' he said. 'Waldo's rent car don't get a report right away. And they don't make Waldo very soon. I know Waldo. Smart he was. A smooth boy, Waldo.'

'I'm going to vomit,' I said, 'if you don't take that gun out of my throat.'

He smiled and moved the gun down to my heart. 'This about right? Say when.'

I must have spoken louder than I meant to. The door of the dressing-room by the wall bed showed a crack of darkness. Then an inch. Then four inches. I saw eyes, but didn't look at them. I stared hard into the bald-headed man's eyes. Very hard. I didn't want him to take his eyes off mine.

'Scared?' he asked softly.

I leaned against his gun and began to shake. I thought he would enjoy seeing me shake. The girl came out through the door. She had her gun in her hand again. I was sorry as hell for her. She'd try to make the door—or scream. Either way it would be curtains—for both of us.

'Well, don't take all night about it,' I bleated. My voice sounded far away, like a voice on a radio on the other side of a street.

'I like this, pal,' he smiled. 'I'm like that.'

The girl floated in the air, somewhere behind him. Nothing was ever more soundless than the way she moved. It wouldn't do any good though. He wouldn't fool around with her at all. I had known him all my life but I had been looking into his eyes for only five minutes.

'Suppose I yell,' I said.

'Yeah, suppose you yell. Go ahead and yell,' he said with his killer's smile.

She didn't go near the door. She was right behind him.

'Well—here's where I yell,' I said.

As if that was the cue, she jabbed the little gun hard into his short ribs, without a single sound.

He had to react. It was like a knee reflex. His mouth snapped open and both his arms jumped out from his sides and he arched his back just a little. The gun was pointing at my right eye.

I sank and kneed him with all my strength, in the groin.

His chin came down and I hit it. I hit it as if I was driving the last spike on the first transcontinental railroad. I can still feel it when I flex my knuckles.

His gun raked the side of my face but it didn't go off. He was already limp. He writhed down gasping, his left side against the floor. I kicked his right shoulder—hard. The gun jumped away from him, skidded on the carpet, under a chair. I heard the chessmen tinkling on the floor behind me somewhere.

The girl stood over him, looking down. Then her wide dark horrified eyes came up and fastened on mine.

'That buys me,' I said. 'Anything I have is yours—now and forever.'

She didn't hear me. Her eyes were strained open so hard that the whites showed under the vivid blue iris. She backed quickly to the door with her little gun up, felt behind her for the knob and twisted it. She pulled the door open and slipped out.

The door shut.

She was bareheaded and without her bolero jacket.

She had only the gun, and the safety catch on that was still set so that she couldn't fire it.

It was silent in the room then, in spite of the wind. Then I heard him gasping on the floor. His face had a greenish pallor. I moved behind him and pawed him for more guns, and didn't find any. I got a pair of store cuffs out of my desk and pulled his arms in front of him and snapped them on his wrists. They would hold if he didn't shake them too hard.

His eyes measured me for a coffin, in spite of their suffering. He lay in the middle of the floor, still on his left side, a twisted, wizened, bald-headed little guy with drawn-back lips and teeth spotted with cheap silver fillings. His mouth looked like a black pit and his breath came in little waves, choked, stopped, came on again, limping.

I went into the dressing room and opened the drawer of the chest. Her hat and jacket lay there on my shirts. I put them underneath, at the back, and smoothed the shirts over them. Then I went out to the kitchenette and poured a stiff jolt of whiskey and put it down and stood a moment listening to the hot wind howl against the window glass. A garage door banged, and a power-line wire with too much play between the insulators thumped the side of the building with a sound like somebody beating a carpet.

The drink worked on me. I went back into the living room and opened a window. The guy on the floor hadn't smelled her sandal-wood, but somebody else might.

I shut the window again, wiped the palms of my hands and used the phone to dial Headquarters.

Copernik was still there. His smart-aleck voice said: 'Yeah? Marlowe? Don't tell me. I bet you got an idea.'

'Make that killer yet?'

'We're not saying, Marlowe. Sorry as all hell and so on. You know how it is.'

'OK, I don't care who he is. Just come and get him off the floor of my apartment.'

'Holy Christ!' Then his voice hushed and went down low. 'Wait a minute, now. Wait a minute.' A long way off I seemed to hear a door shut. Then his voice again. 'Shoot,' he said softly.

'Handcuffed,' I said. 'All yours. I had to knee him, but he'll be all right. He came here to eliminate a witness.'

Another pause. The voice was full of honey. 'Now listen, boy, who else is in this with you?'

'Who else? Nobody. Just me.'

'Keep it that way, boy. All quiet. OK?'

'Think I want all the bums in the neighborhood in here sightseeing?'

'Take it easy, boy. Easy. Just sit tight and sit still. I'm practically there. No touch nothing. Get me?'

'Yeah.' I gave him the address and apartment number again to save him time.

I could see his big bony face glisten. I got the .22 target gun from under the chair and sat holding it until feet hit the hallway outside my door and knuckles did a quiet tattoo on the door panel.

Copernik was alone. He filled the doorway quickly, pushed me back into the room with a tight grin and shut the door. He stood with his back to it, his hand under the left side of his coat. A big hard bony man with flat cruel eyes.

He lowered them slowly and looked at the man on the floor. The man's neck was twitching a little. His eyes moved in short stabs — sick eyes.

'Sure it's the guy?' Copernik's voice was hoarse.

'Positive. Where's Ybarra?'

'Oh, he was busy.' He didn't look at me when he said that. 'Those your cuffs?'

'Yeah.'

'Key.'

I tossed it to him. He went down swiftly on one knee beside the killer and took my cuffs off his wrists, tossed them to one side. He got his own off his hip, twisted the bald man's hands behind him and snapped the cuffs on.

'All right, you bastard,' the killer said tonelessly.

Copernik grinned and balled his fist and hit the handcuffed man in the mouth a terrific blow. His head snapped back almost enough to break his neck. Blood dribbled from the lower corner of his mouth.

'Get a towel,' Copernik ordered.

I got a hand towel and gave it to him. He stuffed it between the handcuffed man's teeth, viciously, stood up and rubbed his bony fingers through his ratty blond hair.

'All right. Tell it.'

I told it—leaving the girl out completely. It sounded a little funny. Copernik watched me, said nothing. He rubbed the side of his veined nose. Then he got his comb out and worked on his hair just as he had done earlier in the evening, in the cocktail bar.

I went over and gave him the gun. He looked at it casually, dropped it into his side pocket. His eyes had something in them and his face moved in a hard bright grin.

I bent down and began picking up my chessmen and dropping them into the box. I put the box on the mantel, straightened out a leg of the card table, played around for a while. All the time Copernik watched me. I wanted him to think something out.

At last he came out with it. 'This guy uses a twenty-two,' he said. 'He uses it because he's good enough to get by with that much gun. That means he's good. He knocks at your door, pokes that gat in your belly, walks you back into the room, says he's here to close your mouth for keeps—and yet you take him. You not having any gun. You take him alone. You're kind of good yourself, pal.'

'Listen,' I said, and looked at the floor. I picked up another chessman and twisted it between my fingers. 'I was doing a chess problem,' I said 'Trying to forget things.'

'You got something on your mind, pal,' Copernik said softly. 'You wouldn't try to fool an old copper, would you, boy?'

'It's a swell pinch and I'm giving it to you,' I said. 'What the hell more do you want?'

The man on the floor made a vague sound behind the towel. His bald head glistened with sweat.

'What's the matter, pal? You been up to something?' Copernik almost whispered.

I looked at him quickly, looked away again. 'All right,' I said. 'You know damn well I couldn't take him alone. He had the gun on me and he shoots where he looks.'

Copernik closed one eye and squinted at me amiably with the other. 'Go on, pal. I kind of thought of that too.'

I shuffled around a little more, to make it look good. I said, slowly: 'There was a kid here who pulled a job over in Boyle Heights, a heist job. It didn't take. A two-bit service station stick-up. I know his family. He's not really bad. He was here trying to beg train money off me. When the knock came he sneaked in—there.'

I pointed at the wall bed and the door beside. Copernik's head swiveled slowly, swiveled back. His eyes winked again. 'And this kid had a gun,' he said.

I nodded. 'And he got behind him. That takes guts, Copernik. You've got to give the kid a break. You've got to let him stay out of it.'

'Tag out for this kid?' Copernik asked softly.

'Not yet, he says. He's scared there will be.'

Copernik smiled. 'I'm a homicide man,' he said. 'I wouldn't know—or care.'

I pointed down at the gagged and handcuffed man on the floor. 'You took him, didn't you?' I said gently.

Copernik kept on smiling. A big whitish tongue came out and massaged his thick lower lip. 'How'd I do it?' he whispered.

'Get the slugs out of Waldo?'

'Sure. Long twenty-two's. One smashed a rib, one good.'

'You're a careful guy. You don't miss any angles. You know anything about me? You dropped in on me to see what guns I had.'

Copernik got up and went down on one knee again beside the killer. 'Can you hear me, guy?' he asked with his face close to the face of the man on the floor.

The man made some vague sound. Copernik stood up and yawned. 'Who the hell cares what he says? Go on, pal.'

'You wouldn't expect to find I had anything, but you wanted to look around my place. And while you were mousing around in there'—I pointed to the dressing room—'and me not saying anything, being a little sore, maybe, a knock came on the door. So he came in. So after a while you sneaked out and took him.'

'Ah,' Copernik grinned widely, with as many teeth as a horse.

'You're on, pal. I socked him and I kneed him and I took him. You didn't have no gun and the guy swiveled on me pretty sharp and I left-hooked him down the backstairs. OK?'

'OK,' I said.

'You'll tell it like that downtown?'

'Yeah,' I said.

'I'll protect you, pal. Treat me right and I'll always play ball. Forget about that kid. Let me know if he needs a break.'

He came over and held out his hand. I shook it. It was as clammy as a dead fish. Clammy hands and the people who own them make me sick.

'There's just one thing,' I said. 'This partner of yours—Ybarra. Won't he be a bit sore you didn't bring him along on this?'

Copernik tousled his hair and wiped his hatband with a large yellowish silk handkerchief.

'That guinea?' he sneered. 'To hell with him!' He came close to me and breathed in my face. 'No mistakes, pal—about that story of ours.'

His breath was bad. It would be.

There were just five of us in the chief-of-detectives' office when Copernik laid it before them. A stenographer, the chief, Copernik, myself, Ybarra. Ybarra sat on a chair tilted against the side wall. His hat was down over his eyes but their softness loomed underneath, and the small still smile hung at the corners of the clean-cut Latin lips. He didn't look directly at Copernik. Copernik didn't look at him at all.

Outside in the corridor there had been photos of Copernik shaking hands with me, Copernik with his hat on straight and his gun in his hand and a stern, purposeful look on his face.

They said they knew who Waldo was, but they wouldn't tell me. I didn't believe they knew, because the chief-of-detectives had a morgue photo of Waldo on his desk. A beautiful job, his hair combed, his tie straight, the light hitting his eyes just right to make them glisten. Nobody would have known it was a photo of a dead man with two bullet holes in his heart. He looked like a dance-hall sheikh making up his mind whether to take the blonde or the redhead.

It was about midnight when I got home. The apartment door was locked and while I was fumbling for my keys a low voice spoke to me out of the darkness.

All it said was: 'Please!' but I knew it. I turned and looked at a dark Cadillac coupe parked just off the loading zone. It had no lights. Light from the street touched the brightness of a woman's eyes.

I went over there. 'You're a darn fool,' I said.

She said: 'Get in.'

I climbed in and she started the car and drove it a block and a half along Franklin and turned down Kingsley Drive. The hot wind still burned and blustered. A radio lilted from an open, sheltered side window of an apartment house. There were a lot of parked cars but she found a vacant space behind a small brand-new Packard cabriolet that had the dealer's sticker on the windshield glass. After she'd jockeyed us up to the curb she leaned back in the corner with her gloved hands on the wheel.

She was all in black now, or dark brown, with a small foolish hat. I smelled the sandalwood in her perfume.

'I wasn't very nice to you, was I?' she said.

'All you did was save my life.'

'What happened?'

'I called the law and fed a few lies to a cop I don't like and gave him all the credit for the pinch and that was that. That guy you took away from me was the man who killed Waldo.'

'You mean—you didn't tell them about me?'

'Lady,' I said again, 'all you did was save my life. What else do you want done? I'm ready, willing, and I'll try to be able.'

She didn't say anything, or move.

'Nobody learned who you are from me,' I said. 'Incidentally, I don't know myself.'

'I'm Mrs Frank C. Barsaly, Two-twelve Fremont Place, Olympia Two-four-five-nine-six. Is that what you wanted?'

'Thanks,' I mumbled, and rolled a dry unlit cigarette around in my fingers. 'Why did you come back?' Then I snapped the fingers of my left hand. 'The hat and jacket,' I said. 'I'll go up and get them.'

'It's more than that,' she said. 'I want my pearls.' I might have jumped a little. It seemed as if there had been enough without pearls.

A car tore by down the street going twice as fast as it should. A thin bitter cloud of dust lifted in the street lights and whirled and vanished. The girl ran the window up quickly against it.

'All right,' I said. 'Tell me about the pearls. We have had a murder and a mystery woman and a mad killer and a heroic rescue and a police detective framed into making a false report. Now we will have pearls. All right—feed it to me.'

'I was to buy them for five thousand dollars. From the man you call Waldo and I call Joseph Coates. He should have had them.'

'No pearls,' I said. 'I saw what came out of his pockets. A lot of money, but no pearls.'

'Could they be hidden in his apartment?'

'Yes,' I said. 'So far as I know he could have had them hidden anywhere in California except in his pockets. How's Mr Barsaly this hot night?'

'He's still downtown at his meeting. Otherwise I couldn't have come.'

'Well, you could have brought him,' I said. 'He could have sat in the rumble seat.'

'Oh, I don't know,' she said. 'Frank weighs two hundred pounds and he's pretty solid. I don't think he would like to sit in the rumble seat, Mr Marlowe.'

'What the hell are we talking about anyway?'

She didn't answer. Her gloved hands tapped lightly, provokingly on the rim of the slender wheel. I threw the unlit cigarette out the window, turned a little and took hold of her.

When I let go of her, she pulled as far away from me as she could against the side of the car and rubbed the back of her glove against her mouth. I sat quite still.

We didn't speak for some time. Then she said very slowly: 'I meant you to do that. But I wasn't always that way. It's only been since Stan Phillips was killed in his plane. If it hadn't been for that, I'd be Mrs Phillips now. Stan gave me the pearls. They cost fifteen thousand dollars, he said once. White pearls, forty-one of them, the largest about a third of an inch across. I don't know how many grains. I never had them appraised or showed them to a jeweler, so I don't know those things. But I loved them on Stan's account. I loved Stan. The way you do just the one time. Can you understand?'

'What's your first name?' I asked.

'Lola.'

'Go on talking, Lola.' I got another dry cigarette out of my pocket and fumbled it between my fingers just to give them something to do.

'They had a simple silver clasp in the shape of a two-bladed propeller. There was one small diamond where the boss would be. I told Frank they were store pearls I had bought myself. He didn't know the difference. It's not so easy to tell, I dare say. You see—Frank is pretty jealous.'

In the darkness she came closer to me and her side touched my side. But I didn't move this time. The wind howled and the trees shook. I kept on rolling the cigarette around in my fingers.

'I suppose you've read that story,' she said. 'About the wife and the real pearls and her telling her husband they were false?'

'I've read it,' I said, 'Maugham.'

'I hired Joseph. My husband was in Argentina at the time. I was pretty lonely.'

'*You* should be lonely,' I said.

'Joseph and I went driving a good deal. Sometimes we had a drink or two together. But that's all. I don't go around—'

'You told him about the pearls,' I said. 'And when your two hundred pounds of beef came back from Argentina and kicked him out—he took the pearls, because he knew they were real. And then offered them back to you for five grand.'

'Yes,' she said simply. 'Of course I didn't want to go to the police. And of course in the circumstance Joseph wasn't afraid of my knowing where he lived.'

'Poor Waldo,' I said. 'I feel kind of sorry for him. It was a hell of a time to run into an old friend that had a down on you.'

I struck a match on my shoe sole and lit the cigarette. The tobacco was so dry from the hot wind that it burned like grass. The girl sat quietly beside me, her hands on the wheel again.

'Hell with women—these fliers,' I said. 'And you're still in love with him, or think you are. Where did you keep the pearls?'

'In a Russian malachite jewelry box on my dressing table. With some other costume jewelry. I had to, if I ever wanted to wear them.'

'And they were worth fifteen grand. And you think Joseph might have hidden them in his apartment. Thirty-one, wasn't it?'

'Yes,' she said. 'I guess it's a lot to ask.'

I opened the door and got out of the car. 'I've been paid,' I said. 'I'll go look. The doors in my apartment are not very obstinate. The cops will find out where Waldo lived when they publish his photo, but not tonight, I guess.'

'It's awfully sweet of you,' she said. 'Shall I wait here?'

I stood with a foot on the running board, leaning in, looking at her. I didn't answer her question. I just stood there looking in at the shine of her eyes. Then I shut the car door and walked up the street towards Franklin.

Even with the wind shriveling my face I could still smell the sandalwood in her hair. And feel her lips.

I unlocked the Berglund door, walked through the silent lobby to the elevator, and rode up to Three. Then I soft-footed along the silent corridor and peered down at the sill of Apartment 31. No light. I rapped—the old light, confidential tattoo of the bootlegger with the big smile and the extra-deep hip pockets. No answer. I took the piece of thick hard celluloid that pretended to be a window over the driver's license in my wallet, and eased it between the lock and the jamb, leaning hard on the knob, pushing it toward the hinges. The edge of the celluloid caught the slope of the spring lock and snapped it back with a small brittle sound, like an icicle breaking. The door yielded and I went into near darkness. Street light filtered in and touched a high spot here and there.

I shut the door and snapped the light on and just stood. There was a queer smell in the air. I made it in a moment—the smell of dark-cured tobacco. I prowled over to a smoking stand by the window and looked down at four brown butts—Mexican or South American cigarettes.

Upstairs, on my floor, feet hit the carpet and somebody went into a bathroom. I heard the toilet flush. I went into the bathroom of Apartment 31. A little rubbish, nothing, no place to hide anything. The kitchenette was a longer job, but I only half searched. I knew there were no pearls in that apartment. I knew Waldo had been on his way out and that he was in a hurry and that something was riding him when he turned and took two bullets from an old friend.

I went back to the living room and swung the wall bed and looked past its mirror side into the dressing room for signs of still current occupancy. Swinging the bed farther I was no longer looking for pearls. I was looking at a man.

He was small, middle-aged, iron-gray at the temples, with a very dark skin, dressed in a fawn-colored suit with a wine-colored tie. His neat little brown hands hung limply by his sides. His small feet, in pointed polished shoes, pointed almost at the floor.

He was hanging by a belt around his neck from the metal top of the bed. His tongue stuck out farther than I thought it possible for a tongue to stick out.

He swung a little and I didn't like that, so I pulled the bed shut and he nestled quietly between the two clamped pillows. I didn't touch him yet. I didn't have to touch him to know that he would be cold as ice.

I went around him into the dressing room and used my handkerchief on drawer knobs. The place was stripped clean except for the light litter of a man living alone.

I came out of there and began on the man. No wallet. Waldo would have taken that and ditched it. A flat box of cigarettes, half full, stamped in gold: 'Louis Tapia y Cia, Calle de Paysandú, 19, Montevideo.' Matches from the Spezia Club. An under-arm holster of dark-grained leather and in it a 9-millimeter Mauser.

The Mauser made him a professional, so I didn't feel so badly. But not a very good professional, or bare hands would not have finished him, with the Mauser—a gun you can blast through a wall with—undrawn in his shoulder holster.

I made a little sense of it, not much. Four of the brown cigarettes had been smoked, so there had been either waiting or discussion. Somewhere along the line Waldo had got the little man by the throat and held him in just the right way to make him pass out in a matter of seconds. The Mauser had been less useful to him than a toothpick. Then Waldo had hung him up by the strap, probably dead already. That would account for haste, cleaning out the apartment, for Waldo's anxiety about the girl. It would account for the car left unlocked outside the cocktail bar.

That is, it would account for these things if Waldo had killed him, if this was really Waldo's apartment—if I wasn't just being kidded.

I examined some more pockets. In the left trouser one I found a gold penknife, some silver. In the left hip pocket a handkerchief, folded, scented. On the right hip another, unfolded but clean. In the right leg pocket four or five tissue handkerchiefs. A clean little guy. He didn't like to blow his nose on his handkerchief. Under these there was a small new keytainer holding four new keys—car keys. Stamped in gold on the keytainer was: Compliments of R. K. Vogelsang, Inc. 'The Packard House.'

I put everything as I had found it, swung the bed back, used my handkerchief on knobs and other projections, and flat surfaces, killed the light and poked my nose out the door. The hall was empty. I went down to the street and around the corner to Kingsley Drive. The Cadillac hadn't moved.

I opened the car door and leaned on it. She didn't seem to have moved, either. It was hard to see any expression on her face. Hard to see anything but her eyes and chin, but not hard to smell the sandalwood.

'That perfume,' I said, 'would drive a deacon nuts ... no pearls.'

'Well, thanks for trying,' she said in a low, soft vibrant voice. 'I guess I can stand it. Shall I ... Do we ... Or ... ?'

'You go on home now,' I said. 'And whatever happens you never saw me before. Whatever happens. Just as you may never see me again.'

'I'd hate that.'

'Good luck, Lola.' I shut the car door and stepped back.

The lights blazed on, the motor turned over. Against the wind at the corner the big coupe made a slow contemptuous turn and was gone. I stood there by the vacant space at the curb where it had been.

It was quite dark there now. Windows, had become blanks in the apartment where the radio sounded. I stood looking at the back of a Packard cabriolet which seemed to be brand new. I had seen it before—before I went upstairs, in the same place, in front of Lola's car. Parked, dark, silent, with a blue sticker pasted to the right-hand corner of the shiny windshield.

And in my mind I was looking at something else, a set of brand-new car keys in a keytainer stamped: 'The Packard House', upstairs, in a dead man's pocket.

I went up to the front of the cabriolet and put a small pocket flash on the blue slip. It was the same dealer all right. Written in ink below his name and slogan was a name and address—Eugénie Kolchenko, 5315 Arvieda Street, West Los Angeles.

It was crazy. I went back up to Apartment 31, jimmied the door as I had done before, stepped in behind the wall bed and took the keytainer from the trousers pocket of the neat brown dangling corpse. I was back down on the street beside the cabriolet in five minutes. The keys fitted.

It was a small house, near a canyon rim out beyond Sawtelle, with a circle of writhing eucalyptus trees in front of it. Beyond that, on the other side of the street, one of those parties was going on where they come out and smash bottles on the sidewalk with a whoop like Yale making a touchdown against Princeton.

There was a wire fence at my number and some rose trees, and a flagged walk and a garage that was wide open and had no car in it. There was no car in front of the house either. I rang the bell. There was a long wait, then the door opened rather suddenly.

I wasn't the man she had been expecting. I could see it in her glittering kohl-rimmed eyes. Then I couldn't see anything in them. She just stood and looked at me, a long, lean, hungry brunette, with rouged cheekbones, thick black hair parted in the middle, a mouth made for three-decker sandwiches, coral-and-gold pajamas, sandals— and gilded toenails. Under her ear lobes a couple of miniature temple bells gonged lightly in the breeze. She made a slow disdainful motion with a cigarette in a holder as long as a baseball bat.

'We-el, what ees it, little man? You want sometheeng? You are lost from the bee-ootiful party across the street, hein?'

'Ha-ha,' I said. 'Quite a party, isn't it? No, I just brought your car home. Lost it, didn't you?'

Across the street somebody had delirium tremens in the front yard and a mixed quartet tore what was left of the night into small strips and did what they could to make the strips miserable. While this was going on the exotic brunette didn't move more than one eyelash.

She wasn't beautiful, she wasn't even pretty, but she looked as if things would happen where she was.

'You have said what?' she got out, at last, in a voice as silky as a burnt crust of toast.

'Your car.' I pointed over my shoulder and kept my eyes on her. She was the type that uses a knife.

The long cigarette holder dropped very slowly to her side and the cigarette fell out of it. I stamped it out, and that put me in the hall. She backed away from me and I shut the door.

The hall was like the long hall of a railroad flat. Lamps glowed pinkly in iron brackets. There was a bead curtain at the end, a tiger skin on the floor. The place went with her.

'You're Miss Kolchenko?' I asked, not getting any more action.

'Ye-es. I am Mees Kolchenko. What the 'ell you want?'

She was looking at me now as if I had come to wash the windows, but at an inconvenient time.

I got a card out with my left hand, held it out to her. She read it in my hand, moving her head just enough. 'A detective?' she breathed.

'Yeah.'

She said something in a spitting language. Then in English: 'Come in! Thees damn wind dry up my skeen like so much teesue paper.'

'We're in,' I said. 'I just shut the door. Snap out of it, Nazimova. Who was he? The little guy?'

Beyond the bead curtain a man coughed. She jumped as if she had been stuck with an oyster fork. Then she tried to smile. It wasn't very successful.

'A reward,' she said softly. 'You weel wait 'ere? Ten dollars it is fair to pay, no?'

'No,' I said.

I reached a finger towards her slowly and added: 'He's dead.'

She jumped about three feet and let out a yell.

A chair creaked harshly. Feet pounded beyond the bead curtain, a large hand plunged into view and snatched it aside, and a big hard-looking blond man was with us. He had a purple robe over his pajamas, his right hand held something in his robe pocket. He stood quite still as soon as he was through the curtain, his feet planted solidly, his jaw out, his colorless eyes like gray ice. He looked like a man who would be hard to take out on an off-tackle play.

'What's the matter, honey?' He had a solid, burring voice, with just the right sappy tone to belong to a guy who would go for a woman with gilded toenails.

'I came about Miss Kolchenko's car,' I said.

'Well, you could take your hat off,' he said. 'Just for a light work-out.'

I took it off and apologized.

'OK,' he said, and kept his right hand shoved down hard in the purple pocket. 'So you came about Miss Kolchenko's car. Take it from there.'

I pushed past the woman and went closer to him. She shrank back against the wall and flattened her palms against it. Camille in a high-school play. The long holder lay empty at her toes.

When I was six feet from the big man he said easily: 'I can hear you from there. Just take it easy. I've got a gun in this pocket and I've had to learn to use one. Now about the car?'

'The man who borrowed it couldn't bring it,' I said, and pushed the card I was still holding towards his face. He barely glanced at it. He looked back at me.

'So what?' he said.

'Are you always this tough?' I asked. 'Or only when you have your pajamas on?'

'So why couldn't he bring it himself?' he asked. 'And skip the mushy talk.'

The dark woman made a stuffed sound at my elbow.

'It's all right, honeybunch,' the man said. 'I'll handle this. Go on.'

She slid past both of us and flicked through the bead curtain.

I waited a little while. The big man didn't move a muscle. He didn't look any more bothered than a toad in the sun.

'He couldn't bring it because somebody bumped him off,' I said. 'Let's see you handle that.'

'Yeah?' he said. 'Did you bring him with you to prove it?'

'No,' I said. 'But if you put your tie and crush hat on, I'll take you down and show you.'

'Who the hell did you say you were, now?'

'I didn't say. I thought maybe you could read.' I held the card at him some more.

'Oh, that's right,' he said. 'Philip Marlowe, Private Investigator. Well, well. So I should go with you to look at who, why?'

'Maybe he stole the car,' I said.

The big man nodded. 'That's a thought. Maybe he did. Who?'

'The little brown guy who had the keys to it in his pocket, and had it parked around the corner from the Berglund Apartments.'

He thought that over, without any apparent embarrassment. 'You've got something there,' he said. 'Not much. But a little. I guess this must be the night of the Police Smoker. So you're doing all their work for them.'

'Huh?'

'The card says private detective to me,' he said. 'Have you got some cops outside that were too shy to come in?'

'No, I'm alone.'

He grinned. The grin showed white ridges in his tanned skin. 'So you find somebody dead and take some keys and find a car and come riding out here—all alone. No cops. Am I right?'

'Correct.'

He sighed. 'Let's go inside,' he said. He yanked the bead curtain aside and made an opening for me to go through. 'It might be you have an idea I ought to hear.'

I went past him and he turned, keeping his heavy pocket towards me. I hadn't noticed until I got quite close that there were beads of sweat on his face. It might have been the hot wind but I didn't think so.

We were in the living room of the house.

We sat down and looked at each other across a dark floor, on which a few Navajo rugs and a few dark Turkish rugs made a decorating combination with some well-used overstuffed furniture. There was a fireplace, a small baby grand, a Chinese screen, a tall Chinese lantern on a teakwood pedestal, and gold net curtains against lattice windows. The windows to the south were open. A fruit tree with a white-washed trunk whipped about outside the screen, adding its bit to the noise from across the street.

The big man eased back into a brocaded chair and put his slippered feet on a footstool. He kept his right hand where it had been since I met him—on his gun.

The brunette hung around in the shadows and a bottle gurgled and her temple bells gonged in her ears.

'It's all right, honeybunch,' the man said. 'It's all under control. Somebody bumped somebody off and this lad thinks we're interested. Just sit down and relax.'

The girl tilted her head and poured half a tumbler of whiskey down her throat. She sighed, said, 'Goddam,' in a casual voice, and curled up on a davenport. It took all of the davenport. She had plenty of legs. Her gilded toenails winked at me from the shadowy corner where she kept herself quiet from then on.

I got a cigarette out without being shot at, lit it and went into my story. It wasn't all true, but some of it was. I told them about the Berglund Apartments and that I had lived there and that Waldo was living there in Apartment 31 on the floor below mine and that I had been keeping an eye on him for business reasons.

'Waldo what?' the blond man put in. 'And what business reasons?'

'Mister,' I said, 'have you no secrets?' He reddened slightly.

I told him about the cocktail lounge across the street from the Berglund and what had happened there. I didn't tell him about the printed bolero jacket or the girl who had worn it. I left her out of the story altogether.

'It was an undercover job—from my angle,' I said. 'If you know what I mean.' He reddened again, bit his teeth. I went on: 'I got back from the city hall without telling anybody I knew Waldo. In due time, when I decided they couldn't find out where he lived that night, I took the liberty of examining his apartment.'

'Looking for what?' the big man said thickly.

'For some letters. I might mention in passing there was nothing there at all—except a dead man. Strangled and hanging by a belt to the top of the wall bed—well out of sight. A small man, about forty-five, Mexican or South American, well-dressed in a fawn-colored——'

'That's enough,' the big man said. 'I'll bite, Marlowe. Was it a black-mail job you were on?'

'Yeah. The funny part was this little brown man had plenty of gun under his arm.'

'He wouldn't have five hundred bucks in twenties in his pocket, of course? Or are you saying?'

'He wouldn't. But Waldo had over seven hundred in currency when he was killed in the cocktail bar.'

'Looks like I underrated this Waldo,' the big man said calmly. 'He took my guy and his pay-off money, gun and all. Waldo have a gun?'

'Not on him.'

'Get us a drink, honeybunch,' the big man said. 'Yes, I certainly did sell this Waldo person shorter than a bargain-counter shirt.'

The brunette unwound her legs and made two drinks with soda and ice. She took herself another gill without trimmings, wound herself back on the davenport. Her big glittering black eyes watched me solemnly.

'Well, here's how,' the big man said, lifting his glass in salute. 'I haven't murdered anybody, but I've got a divorce suit on my hands from now on. You haven't murdered anybody, the way you tell it, but you laid an egg down at police Headquarters. What the hell! Life's a lot of trouble, anyway you look at it. I've still got honeybunch here. She's a white Russian I met in Shanghai. She's safe as a vault and she looks as if she could cut your throat for a nickel. That's what I like about her. You get the glamor without the risk.'

'You talk damn foolish,' the girl spat him.

'You look OK to me,' the big man went on ignoring her. 'That is, for a keyhole peeper. Is there an out?'

'Yeah. But it will cost a little money.'

'I expected that. How much?'

'Say another five hundred.'

'Goddam, thees hot wind make me dry like the ashes of love,' the Russian girl said bitterly.

'Five hundred might do,' the blond man said. 'What do I get for it?'

'If I swing it—you get left out of the story. If I don't—you don't pay.'

He thought it over. His face looked lined and tired now. The small beads of sweat twinkled in his short blond hair.

'This murder will make you talk,' he grumbled. 'The second one, I mean. And I don't have what I was going to buy. And if it's a hush, I'd rather buy it direct.'

'Who was the little brown man?' I asked.

'Name's Leon Valesanos, a Uruguayan. Another of my importations. I'm in a business that takes me a lot of places. He was working in the Spezzia Club in Chiseltown—you know, the strip of Sunset next to Beverly Hills. Working on roulette, I think. I gave him the five hundred to go down to this—this Waldo—and buy back some bills for stuff Miss Kolchenko had charged to my account and delivered here.

That wasn't bright, was it? I had them in my briefcase and this Waldo got a chance to steal them. What's your hunch about what happened?'

I sipped my drink and looked at him down my nose. 'Your Uruguayan pal probably talked curt and Waldo didn't listen good. Then the little guy thought maybe that Mauser might help his argument—and Waldo was too quick for him. I wouldn't say Waldo was a killer—not by intention. A blackmailer seldom is. Maybe he lost his temper and maybe he just held on to the little guy's neck too long. Then he had to take it on the lam. But he had another date, with more money coming up. And he worked the neighborhood looking for the party. And accidentally he ran into a pal who was hostile enough and drunk enough to blow him down.'

'There's a hell of a lot of coincidence in all this business,' the big man said.

'It's the hot wind,' I grinned. 'Everybody's screwy tonight.'

'For the five hundred you guarantee nothing? If I don't get my cover-up, you don't get your dough. Is that it?'

'That's it,' I said, smiling at him.

'Screwy is right,' he said, and drained his highball. 'I'm taking you up on it.'

'There are just two things,' I said softly, leaning forward in my chair. 'Waldo had a getaway car parked outside the cocktail bar where he was killed, unlocked with the motor running. The killer took it. There's always the chance of a kickback from that direction. You see, all Waldo's stuff must have been in that car.'

'Including my bills, and your letters.'

'Yeah. But the police are reasonable about things like that—unless you're good for a lot of publicity. If you're not, I think I can eat some stale dog downtown and get by. If you are—that's the second thing. What did you say your name was?'

The answer was a long time coming. When it came I didn't get as much kick out of it as I thought I would. All at once it was too logical.

'Frank C. Barsaly,' he said.

After a while the Russian girl called me a taxi. When I left, the party across the street was doing all that a party could do. I noticed the walls of the house were still standing. That seemed a pity.

When I unlocked the glass entrance door of the Berglund I smelled policeman. I looked at my wrist watch. It was nearly 3 a.m. In the dark corner of the lobby a man dozed in a chair with a newspaper over his face. Large feet stretched out before him. A corner of the paper lifted an inch, dropped again. The man made no other movement.

I went on along the hall to the elevator and rode up to my floor. I soft-footed along the hallway, unlocked my door, pushed it wide and reached in for the light switch.

A chain switch tinkled and light glared from a standing lamp by the easy chair, beyond the card table on which my chessmen were still scattered.

Copernik sat there with a stiff unpleasant grin on his face. The short dark man, Ybarra, sat across the room from him, on my left, silent, half smiling as usual.

Copernik showed more of his big yellow horse teeth and said: 'Hi. Long time no see. Been out with the girls?'

I shut the door and took my hat off and wiped the back of my neck slowly, over and over again. Copernik went on grinning. Ybarra looked at nothing with his soft dark eyes.

'Take a seat, pal,' Copernik drawled. 'Make yourself to home. We got pow-wow to make. Boy, do I hate this night sleuthing. Did you know you were low on hooch?'

'I could have guessed it,' I said. I leaned against the wall.

Copernik kept on grinning. 'I always did hate private dicks,' he said, 'but I never had a chance to twist one like I got tonight.'

He reached down lazily beside his chair and picked up a printed bolero jacket, tossed it on the card table. He reached down again and put a wide-brimmed hat beside it.

'I bet you look cuter than all hell with these on,' he said.

I took hold of a straight chair, twisted it around and straddled it, leaned my folded arms on the chair and looked at Copernik.

He got up very slowly—with an elaborate slowness, walked across the room and stood in front of me smoothing his coat down. Then he lifted his open right hand and hit me across the face with it—hard. It stung but I didn't move.

Ybarra looked at the wall, looked at the floor, looked at nothing.

'Shame on you, pal,' Copernik said lazily. 'The way you was taking care of this nice exclusive merchandise. Wadded down behind your old shirts. You punk peepers always did make me sick.'

He stood there over me for a moment. I didn't move or speak. I looked into his glazed drinker's eyes. He doubled a fist at his side, then shrugged and turned and went back to the chair.

'OK,' he said. 'The rest will keep. Where did you get these things?'

'They belong to a lady.'

'Do tell. They belong to a lady. Ain't you the lighthearted bastard! I'll tell you what lady they belong to. They belong to the lady a guy named Waldo asked about in a bar across the street—about two minutes before he got shot kind of dead. Or would that have slipped your mind?'

I didn't say anything.

'You was curious about her yourself,' Copernik sneered on. 'But you were smart, pal. You fooled me.'

'That wouldn't make me smart,' I said.

His face twisted suddenly and he started to get up. Ybarra laughed, suddenly and softly, almost under his breath. Copernik's eyes swung on him, hung there. Then he faced me again, bland-eyed.

'The guinea likes you,' he said. 'He thinks you're good.'

The smile left Ybarra's face, but no expression took its place. No expression at all.

Copernik said: 'You knew who the dame was all the time. You knew who Waldo was and where he lived. Right across the hall a floor below you. You knew this Waldo person had bumped a guy off and started to lam, only this broad came into his plans somewhere and he was anxious to meet up with her before he went away. Only he never got the chance. A heist guy from back East named Al Tessilore took care of that by taking care of Waldo. So you met the gal and hid her clothes and sent her on her way and kept your trap glued. That's the way guys like you make your beans. Am I right?'

'Yeah,' I said. 'Except that I only knew these things very recently. Who was Waldo?'

Copernik bared his teeth at me. Red spots burned high on his sallow cheeks. Ybarra, looking down at the floor, said very softly: 'Waldo Ratigan. We got him from Washington by Teletype. He was a two-bit porch climber with a few small terms on him. He drove a car in a bank

107

stick-up job in Detroit. He turned the gang in later and got a nolle prosse. One of the gang was this Al Tessilore. He hasn't talked a word, but we think the meeting across the street was purely accidental.'

Ybarra spoke in the soft quiet modulated voice of a man for whom sounds have a meaning. I said: 'Thanks, Ybarra. Can I smoke—or would Copernik kick it out of my mouth?'

Ybarra smiled suddenly. 'You may smoke, sure,' he said.

'The guinea likes you all right,' Copernik jeered. 'You never know what a guinea will like, do you?'

I lit a cigarette. Ybarra looked at Copernik and said very softly: 'The word guinea—you overwork it. I don't like it so well applied to me.'

'The hell with what you like, guinea.'

Ybarra smiled a little more. 'You are making a mistake,' he said. He took a pocket nail file out and began to use it, looking down.

Copernik blared: 'I smelled something rotten on you from the start, Marlowe. So when we make these two mugs, Ybarra and me think we'll drift over and dabble a few more words with you. I bring one of Waldo's morgue photos—nice work, the light just right in his eyes, his tie all straight and a white handkerchief showing just right in his pocket. Nice work. So on the way up, just as a matter of routine, we rout out the manager here and let him lamp it. And he knows the guy. He's here as A. B. Hummel, Apartment Thirty-one. So we go in there and find a stiff. Then we go round and round with that. Nobody knows him yet, but he's got some swell finger bruises under that strap and I hear they fit Waldo's fingers very nicely.'

'That's something,' I said. 'I thought maybe I murdered him.'

Copernik stared at me a long time. His face had stopped grinning and was just a hard brutal face now. 'Yeah. We got something else even,' he said. 'We got Waldo's getaway car—and what Waldo had in it to take with him.'

I blew cigarette smoke jerkily. The wind pounded the shut windows. The air in the room was foul.

'Oh, we're bright boys,' Copernik sneered. 'We never figured you with that much guts. Take a look at this.'

He plunged his bony hand into his coat pocket and drew something up slowly over the edge of the card table, drew it along the green top and left it there stretched out, gleaming. A string of white pearls with a clasp like a two-bladed propeller. They shimmered softly in the thick smoky air.

Lola Barsaly's pearls. The pearls the flier had given her. The guy who was dead, the guy she still loved.

I stared at them, but I didn't move. After a long moment Copernik said almost gravely: 'Nice, ain't they? Would you feel like telling us a story about now, Mis-ter Marlowe?'

I stood up and pushed the chair from under me, walked slowly across the room and stood looking down at the pearls. The largest was perhaps a third of an inch across. They were pure white, iridescent, with a mellow softness. I lifted them slowly off the card table from beside her clothes. They felt heavy, smooth, fine.

'Nice,' I said. 'A lot of the trouble was about these. Yeah, I'll talk now. They must be worth a lot of money.'

Ybarra laughed behind me. It was a very gentle laugh. 'About a hundred dollars,' he said. 'They're good phonies—but they're phony.'

I lifted the pearls again. Copernik's glassy eyes gloated at me. 'How do you tell?' I asked.

'I know pearls,' Ybarra said. 'These are good stuff, the kind women very often have made on purpose, as a kind of insurance. But they are slick like glass. Real pearls are gritty between the edges of the teeth. Try.'

I put two or three of them between my teeth and moved my teeth back and forth, then sideways. Not quite biting them. The beads were hard and slick.

'Yes. They are very good,' Ybarra said. 'Several even have little waves and flat spots, as real pearls might have.'

'Would they cost fifteen grand—if they were real?' I asked.

'Sí. Probably. That's hard to say. It depends on a lot of things.'

'This Waldo wasn't so bad,' I said.

Copernik stood up quickly, but I didn't see him swing. I was still looking down at the pearls. His fist caught me on the side of the face, against the molars. I tasted blood at once. I staggered back and made it look like a worse blow than it was.

'Sit down and talk, you bastard!' Copernik almost whispered.

I sat down and used a handkerchief to pat my cheek. I licked at the cut inside my mouth. Then I got up again and went over and picked up the cigarette he had knocked out of my mouth. I crushed it out in a tray and sat down again.

Ybarra filed at his nails and held one up against the lamp. There were beads of sweat on Copernik's eyebrows, at the inner ends.

'You found the beads in Waldo's car,' I said, looking at Ybarra. 'Find any papers?'

He shook his head without looking up.

'I'd believe you,' I said. 'Here it is. I never saw Waldo until he stepped into the cocktail bar tonight and asked about the girl. I knew nothing I didn't tell. When I got home and stepped out of the elevator this girl, in the printed bolero jacket and the wide hat and the blue silk crêpe dress—all as he had described them—was waiting for the elevator, here on my floor. And she looked like a nice girl.'

Copernik laughed jeeringly. It didn't make any difference to me. I had him cold. All he had to do was know that. He was going to know it now, very soon.

'I knew what she was up against as a police witness,' I said. 'And I suspected there was something else to it. But I didn't suspect for a minute that there was anything wrong with her. She was just a nice girl in a jam—and she didn't even know she was in a jam. I got her in here. She pulled a gun on me. But she didn't mean to use it.'

Copernik sat up very suddenly and he began to lick his lips. His face had a stony look now. A look like wet gray stone. He didn't make a sound.

'Waldo had been her chauffeur,' I went on. 'His name was then Joseph Coates. Her name is Mrs Frank C. Barsaly. Her husband is a big hydroelectric engineer. Some guy gave her the pearls once and she told her husband they were just store pearls. Waldo got wise somehow there was a romance behind them and when Barsaly came home from South America and fired him, because he was too good-looking, he lifted the pearls.'

Ybarra lifted his head suddenly and his teeth flashed. 'You mean he didn't know they were phony?'

'I thought he fenced the real ones and had imitations fixed up,' I said.

Ybarra nodded. 'It's possible.'

'He lifted something else,' I said. 'Some stuff from Barsaly's briefcase that showed he was keeping a woman—out in Brentwood. He was blackmailing wife and husband both, without either knowing about the other. Get it so far?'

'I get it,' Copernik said harshly, between his tight lips. His face was still wet gray stone. 'Get the hell on with it.'

'Waldo wasn't afraid of them,' I said. 'He didn't conceal where he lived. That was foolish, but it saved a lot of finagling, if he was willing to risk it. The girl came down here tonight with five grand to buy back her pearls. She didn't find Waldo. She came here to look for him and walked up a floor before she went back down. A woman's idea of being cagey. So I met her. So I brought her in here. So she was in that dressing room when Al Tessilore visited me to rub out a witness.' I pointed to the dressing-room door. 'So she came out with her little gun and stuck it in his back and saved my life,' I said.

Copernik didn't move. There was something horrible in his face now. Ybarra slipped his nail file into a small leather case and slowly tucked it into his pocket.

'Is that all?' he said gently.

I nodded. 'Except that she told me where Waldo's apartment was and I went in there and looked for the pearls. I found the dead man. In his pocket I found new car keys in a case from a Packard agency. And down on the street I found the Packard and took it to where it came from. Barsaly's kept woman. Barsaly had sent a friend from the Spezzia Club down to buy something and he had tried to buy it with his gun instead of the money Barsaly gave him. And Waldo beat him to the punch.'

'Is that all?' Ybarra said softly.

'That's all,' I said licking the torn place on the inside of my cheek.

Ybarra said slowly: 'What do you want?'

Copernik's face convulsed and he slapped his long hard thigh. 'This guy's good,' he jeered. 'He falls for a stray broad and breaks every law in the book and you ask him what does he want? I'll give him what he wants, guinea!'

Ybarra turned his head slowly and looked at him. 'I don't think you will,' he said. 'I think you'll give him a clean bill of health and anything else he wants. He's giving you a lesson in police work.'

Copernik didn't move or make a sound for a long minute. None of us moved. Then Copernik leaned forward and his coat fell open. The butt of his service gun looked out of his underarm holster.

'So what do you want?' he asked me.

'What's on the card table there. The jacket and hat and the phony pearls. And some names kept away from the papers. Is that too much?'

'Yeah—it's too much,' Copernik said almost gently. He swayed sideways and his gun jumped neatly into his hand. He rested his forearm on his thigh and pointed the gun at my stomach.

'I like better that you get a slug in the guts resisting arrest,' he said. 'I like that better, because of a report I made out on Al Tessilore's arrest and how I made the pinch. Because of some photos of me that are in the morning sheets going out about now. I like it better that you don't live long enough to laugh about that baby.'

My mouth felt suddenly hot and dry. Far off I heard the wind booming. It seemed like the sound of guns.

Ybarra moved his feet on the floor and said coldly: 'You've got a couple of cases all solved, policeman. All you do for it is leave some junk here and keep some names from the papers. Which means from the DA. If he gets them anyway, too bad for you.'

Copernik said: 'I like the other way.' The blue gun in his hand was like a rock. 'And God help you, if you don't back me up on it.'

Ybarra said: 'If the woman is brought out into the open, you'll be a liar on a police report and a chisler on your own partner. In a week they won't even speak your name at Headquarters. The taste of it would make them sick.'

The hammer clicked back on Copernik's gun and I watched his big finger slide in farther around the trigger.

Ybarra stood up. The gun jumped at him. He said: 'We'll see how yellow a guinea is. I'm telling you to put that gun up, Sam.'

He started to move. He moved four even steps. Copernik was a man without a breath of movement, a stone man.

Ybarra took one more step and quite suddenly the gun began to shake.

Ybarra spoke evenly: 'Put it up, Sam. If you keep your head everything lies the way it is. If you don't—you're gone.'

He took one more step. Copernik's mouth opened wide and made a gasping sound and then he sagged in the chair as if he had been hit on the head. His eyelids dropped.

Ybarra jerked the gun out of his hand with a movement so quick it was no movement at all. He stepped back quickly, held the gun low at his side.

'It's the hot wind, Sam. Let's forget it,' he said in the same even, almost dainty voice.

Copernik's shoulders sagged lower and he put his face in his hands. 'OK,' he said between his fingers.

Ybarra went softly across the room and opened the door. He looked at me with lazy, half-closed eyes. 'I'd do a lot for a woman who saved my life, too,' he said. 'I'm eating this dish, but as a cop you can't expect me to like it.'

I said: 'The little man in the bed is called Leon Valesanos. He was a croupier at the Spezzia Club.'

'Thanks,' Ybarra said. 'Let's go, Sam.'

Copernik got up heavily and walked across the room and out of the open door and out of my sight. Ybarra stepped through the door after him and started to close it.

I said: 'Wait a minute.'

He turned his head slowly, his left hand on the door, the blue gun hanging down close to his right side.

'I'm not in this for money,' I said. 'The Barsalys live at Two-twelve Fremont Place. You can take the pearls to her. If Barsaly's name stays out of the paper, I get five C's. It goes to the Police Fund. I'm not so damn smart as you think. It just happened that way—and you had a heel for a partner.'

Ybarra looked across the room at the pearls on the card table. His eyes glistened. 'You take them,' he said. 'The five hundred's OK. I think the fund has it coming.'

He shut the door quietly and in a moment I heard the elevator doors clang.

I opened a window and stuck my head out into the wind and watched the squad car tool off down the block. The wind blew in hard and I let it blow. A picture fell off the wall and two chessmen rolled off the card table. The material of Lola Barsaly's bolero jacket lifted and shook.

I went out to the kitchenette and drank some Scotch and went back into the living room and called her—late as it was.

She answered the phone herself, very quickly, with no sleep in her voice.

'Marlowe,' I said. 'OK your end?'

'Yes ... yes,' she said. 'I'm alone.'

'I found something,' I said. 'Or rather the police did. But your dark boy gypped you. I have a string of pearls. They're not real. He sold the real ones, I guess, and made you up a string of ringers, with your clasp.'

She was silent for a long time. Then, a little faintly: 'The police found them?'

'In Waldo's car. But they're not telling. We have a deal. Look at the papers in the morning and you'll be able to figure out why.'

'There doesn't seem to be anything more to say,' she said. 'Can I have the clasp?'

'Yes. Can you meet me tomorrow at four in the Club Esquire bar?'

'You're really rather sweet,' she said in a dragged out voice. 'I can. Frank is still at his meeting.'

'Those meetings—they take it out of a guy,' I said. We said good-bye.

I called a West Los Angeles number. He was still there, with the Russian girl.

'You can send me a check for five hundred in the morning,' I told him. 'Made out to the Police Relief Fund, if you want to. Because that's where it's going.'

Copernik made the third page of the morning papers with two photos and a nice half-column. The little brown man in Apartment 31 didn't make the paper at all. The Apartment House Association has a good lobby too.

I went out after breakfast and the wind was all gone. It was soft, cool, a little foggy. The sky was close and comfortable and gray. I rode down to the boulevard and picked out the best jewelry store on it and laid a string of pearls on a black velvet mat under a daylight-blue lamp. A man in a wing collar and striped trousers looked down at them languidly.

'How good?' I asked.

'I'm sorry, sir. We don't make appraisals. I can give you the name of an appraiser.'

'Don't kid me,' I said. 'They're Dutch.'

He focused the light a little and leaned down and toyed with a few inches of the string.

'I want a string just like them, fitted to that clasp, and in a hurry,' I added.

'How, like them?' He didn't look up. 'And they're not Dutch. They're Bohemian.'

'OK, can you duplicate them?'

He shook his head and pushed the velvet pad away as if it soiled him. 'In three months, perhaps. We don't blow glass like that in this country. If you wanted them matched—three months at least. And this house would not do that sort of thing at all.'

'It must be swell to be that snooty,' I said. I put a card under his black sleeve. 'Give me a name that will—and not in three months—and maybe not exactly like them.'

He shrugged, went away with the card, came back in five minutes and handed it back to me. There was something written on the back.

The old Levantine had a shop on Melrose, a junk shop with everything in the window from a folding baby carriage to a French horn, from a mother-of-pearl lorgnette in a faded plush case to one of those .44 Special Single Action six-shooters they still make for Western peace officers whose grandfathers were tough.

The old Levantine wore a skull cap and two pairs of glasses and a full beard. He studied my pearls, shook his head sadly, and said: 'For twenty dollars, almost so good. Not so good, you understand. Not so good glass.'

'How alike will they look?'

He spread his firm strong hands. 'I am telling you the truth,' he said. 'They would not fool a baby.'

'Make them up,' I said. 'With this clasp. And I want the others back, too, of course.'

'Yah. Two o'clock,' he said.

Leon Valesanos, the little brown man from Uruguay, made the afternoon papers. He had been found hanging in an unnamed apartment. The police were investigating.

At four o'clock I walked into the long cool bar of the Club Esquire and prowled along the row of booths until I found one where a woman sat alone. She wore a hat like a shallow soup plate with a very wide edge, a brown tailor-made suit with a severe mannish shirt and tie.

I sat down beside her and slipped a parcel along the seat. 'You don't open that,' I said. 'In fact you can slip it into the incinerator as is, if you want to.'

She looked at me with dark tired eyes. Her fingers twisted a thin glass that smelled of peppermint. 'Thanks.' Her face was very pale.

I ordered a highball and the waiter went away. 'Read the papers?'

'Yes.'

'You understand now about this fellow Copernik who stole your act? That's why they won't change the story or bring you into it.'

'It doesn't matter now,' she said. 'Thank you, all the same. Please—please show them to me.'

I pulled the string of pearls out of the loosely wrapped tissue paper in my pocket and slid them across to her. The silver propeller clasp winked in the light of the wall bracket. The little diamond winked. The pearls were as dull as white soap. They didn't even match in size.

'You were right,' she said tonelessly. 'They are not my pearls.'

The waiter came with my drink and she put her bag on them deftly. When he was gone she fingered them slowly once more, dropped them into the bag and gave me a dry mirthless smile.

I stood there a moment with a hand hard on the table.

'As you said—I'll keep the clasp.'

I said slowly: 'You don't know anything about me. You saved my life last night and we had a moment, but it was just a moment. You still don't know anything about me. There's a detective downtown named Ybarra, a Mexican of the nice sort, who was on the job when the pearls were found in Waldo's suitcase. That is in case you would like to make sure—'

She said: 'Don't be silly. It's all finished. It was a memory. I'm too young to nurse memories. It may be for the best. I loved Stan Phillips—but he's gone—long gone.'

I stared at her, didn't say anything.

She added quietly: 'This morning my husband told me something

I hadn't known. We are to separate. So I have very little to laugh about today.'

'I'm sorry,' I said lamely. 'There's nothing to say. I may see you sometime. Maybe not. I don't move much in your circle. Good luck.'

I stood up. We looked at each other for a moment. 'You haven't touched your drink,' she said.

'You drink it. That peppermint stuff will just make you sick.'

I stood there a moment with a hand on the table.

'If anybody ever bothers you,' I said, 'let me know.'

I went out of the bar without looking back at her, got into my car and drove west on Sunset and down all the way to the Coast Highway. Everywhere along the way gardens were full of withered and blackened leaves and flowers which the hot wind had burned.

But the ocean looked cool and languid and just the same as ever. I drove on almost to Malibu and then parked and went and sat on a big rock that was inside somebody's wire fence. It was about half-tide and coming in. The air smelled of kelp. I watched the water for a while and then I pulled a string of Bohemian glass imitation pearls out of my pocket and cut the knot at one end and slipped the pearls off one by one.

When I had them all loose in my left hand I held them like that for a while and thought. There wasn't really anything to think about. I was sure.

'To the memory of Mr Stan Phillips,' I said aloud. 'Just another four-flusher.'

I flipped her pearls out into the water one by one at the floating seagulls.

They made little splashes and the seagulls rose off the water and swooped at the splashes.

MARGARET MILLAR

The Couple Next Door

It was by accident that they lived next door to each other, but by design that they became neighbors—Mr Sands, who had retired to California after a life of crime investigation, and the Rackhams, Charles and Alma. Rackham was a big, innocent-looking man in his fifties. Except for the accumulation of a great deal of money, nothing much had ever happened to Rackham, and he liked to listen to Sands talk, while Alma sat with her knitting, plump and contented, unimpressed by any tale that had no direct bearing on her own life. She was half Rackham's age, but the fullness of her figure, and her air of having withdrawn from life quietly and without fuss gave her the stamp of middle age.

Two or three times a week Sands crossed the concrete driveway, skirted the eugenia hedge, and pressed the Rackhams' door chime. He stayed for tea or for dinner, to play gin or Scrabble, or just to talk. 'That reminds me of a case I had in Toronto,' Sands would say, and Rackham would produce martinis and an expression of intense interest, and Alma would smile tolerantly, as if she didn't really believe a single thing Sands, or anyone else, ever said.

They made good neighbors: the Rackhams, Charles younger than his years, and Alma older than hers, and Sands who could be any age at all . . .

It was the last evening of August and through the open window of Sands's study came the scent of jasmine and the sound of a woman's harsh, wild weeping.

He thought at first that the Rackhams had a guest, a woman on a crying jag, perhaps, after a quarrel with her husband.

He went out into the front yard to listen, and Rackham came around the hedge, dressed in a bathrobe.

He said, sounding very surprised, 'Alma's crying.'

'I heard.'

'I asked her to stop. I begged her. She won't tell me what's the matter.'

'Women have cried before.'

'Not Alma.' Rackham stood on the damp grass, shivering, his forehead streaked with sweat. 'What do you think we should do about it?'

The *I* had become *we*, because they were good neighbors, and along with the games and the dinners and the scent of jasmine, they shared the sound of a woman's grief.

'Perhaps you could talk to her,' Rackham said.

'I'll try.'

'I don't think there is anything physically the matter with her. We both had a check-up at the Tracy clinic last week. George Tracy is a good friend of mine—he'd have told me if there was anything wrong.'

'I'm sure he would.'

'If anything ever happened to Alma I'd kill myself.'

Alma was crouched in a corner of the davenport in the living room, weeping rhythmically, methodically, as if she had accumulated a hoard of tears and must now spend them all in one night. Her fair skin was blotched with patches of red, like strawberry birthmarks, and her eyelids were blistered from the heat of her tears. She looked like a stranger to Sands, who had never seen her display any emotion stronger than ladylike distress over a broken teacup.

Rackham went over and stroked her hair. 'Alma, dear. What is the matter?'

'Nothing . . . nothing . . .'

'Mr Sands is here, Alma. I thought he might be able—we might be able—'

But no one was able. With a long shuddering sob, Alma got up and lurched across the room, hiding her blotched face with her hands. They heard her stumble up the stairs.

Sands said, 'I'd better be going.'

'No, please don't. I—the fact is, I'm scared. I'm scared stiff. Alma's always been so quiet.'

'I know that.'

'You don't suppose—there's no chance she's losing her mind?'

If they had not been good neighbors Sands might have remarked that Alma had little mind to lose. As it was, he said cautiously, 'She might have had bad news, family trouble of some kind.'

'She has no family except me.'

'If you're worried, perhaps you'd better call your doctor.'

'I think I will.'

George Tracy arrived within half an hour, a slight, fair-haired man in his early thirties, with a smooth unhurried manner that imparted confidence. He talked slowly, moved slowly, as if there was all the time in the world to minister to desperate women.

Rackham chafed with impatience while Tracy removed his coat, placed it carefully across the back of the chair, and discussed the weather with Sands.

'It's a beautiful evening,' Tracy said, and Alma's moans sliding down the stairs distorted his words, altered their meaning: *a terrible evening, an awful evening.* 'There's a touch of fall in the air. You live in these parts, Mr Sands?'

'Next door.'

'For heaven's sake, George,' Rackham said, 'will you hurry up? For all you know, Alma might be dying.'

'That I doubt. People don't die as easily as you might imagine. She's in her room?'

'Yes. Now will you *please*—'

'Take it easy, old man.'

Tracy picked up his medical bag and went towards the stairs, leisurely, benign.

'He's always like that.' Rackham turned to Sands, scowling. 'Exasperating son-of-a-gun. You can bet that if he had a wife in Alma's condition he'd be taking those steps three at a time.'

'Who knows?—perhaps he has.'

'*I* know,' Rackham said crisply. 'He's not even married. Never had time for it, he told me. He doesn't look it but he's very ambitious.'

'Most doctors are.'

'Tracy is, anyway.'

Rackham mixed a pitcher of martinis, and the two men sat in front of the unlit fire, waiting and listening. The noises from upstairs gradually ceased, and pretty soon the doctor came down again.

Rackham rushed across the room to meet him. 'How is she?'

'Sleeping. I gave her a hypo.'

'Did you talk to her? Did you ask her what was the matter?'

'She was in no condition to answer questions.'

'Did you find anything wrong with her?'

'Not physically. She's a healthy young woman.'

'Not *physically*. Does that mean—?'

'Take it easy, old man.'

Rackham was too concerned with Alma to notice Tracy's choice of words, but Sands noticed, and wondered if it had been conscious or unconscious: Alma's a healthy young woman ... Take it easy, old man.

'If she's still depressed in the morning,' Tracy said, 'bring her down to the clinic with you when you come in for your X-rays. We have a good neurologist on our staff.' He reached for his coat and hat. 'By the way, I hope you followed the instructions.'

Rackham looked at him stupidly. 'What instructions?'

'Before we can take specific X-rays, certain medication is necessary.'

'I don't know what you're talking about.'

'I made it very clear to Alma,' Tracy said, sounding annoyed. 'You were to take one ounce of sodium phosphate after dinner tonight, and report to the X-ray department at eight o'clock tomorrow morning without breakfast.'

'She didn't tell me.'

'Oh.'

'It must have slipped her mind.'

'Yes. Obviously. Well, it's too late now.' He put on his coat, moving quickly for the first time, as if he were in a rush to get away. The change made Sands curious. He wondered why Tracy was suddenly so anxious to leave, and whether there was any connection between Alma's hysteria and her lapse of memory about Rackham's X-rays. He looked at Rackham and guessed, from his pallor and his worried eyes, that Rackham had already made a connection in his mind.

'I understood', Rackham said carefully, 'that I was all through at the clinic. My heart, lungs, metabolism—everything fit as a fiddle.'

'People', Tracy said, 'are not fiddles. Their tone doesn't improve with age. I will make another appointment for you and send you specific instructions by mail. Is that all right with you?'

'I guess it will have to be.'

'Well, good night, Mr Sands, pleasant meeting you.' And to Rackham, 'Good night, old man.'

When he had gone, Rackham leaned against the wall, breathing hard. Sweat crawled down the sides of his face like worms and hid in the collar of his bathrobe. 'You'll have to forgive me, Sands. I feel—I'm not feeling very well.'

'Is there anything I can do?'

'Yes,' Rackham said. 'Turn back the clock.'

'Beyond my powers, I'm afraid.'

'Yes . . . Yes, I'm afraid.'

'Good night, Rackham.' *Good night, old man.*

'Good night, Sands.' *Good night old man to you, too.*

Sands shuffled across the concrete driveway, his head bent. It was a dark night, with no moon at all.

From his study Sands could see the lighted windows of Rackham's bedroom. Rackham's shadow moved back and forth behind the blinds as if seeking escape from the very light that gave it existence. Back and forth, in search of nirvana.

Sands read until far into the night. It was one of the solaces of growing old—if the hours were numbered, at least fewer of them need be wasted in sleep. When he went to bed, Rackham's bedroom light was still on.

They had become good neighbors by design; now, also by design, they became strangers. Whose design it was, Alma's or Rackham's, Sands didn't know.

There was no definite break, no unpleasantness. But the eugenia hedge seemed to have grown taller and thicker, and the concrete driveway a mile away. He saw the Rackhams occasionally; they waved or smiled or said, 'Lovely weather' over the backyard fence. But Rackham's smile was thin and painful, Alma waved with a leaden arm, and neither of them cared about the weather. They stayed indoors most of the time, and when they did come out they were always together, arm in arm, walking slowly and in step. It was impossible to tell whose step led, and whose followed.

At the end of the first week in September, Sands met Alma by accident in a drugstore downtown. It was the first time since the night of the doctor's visit that he'd seen either of the Rackhams alone.

She was waiting at the prescription counter wearing a flowery print dress that emphasized the fullness of her figure and the bovine expression of her face. A drugstore length away, she looked like a rather dull, badly dressed young woman with a passion for starchy foods, and it was hard to understand what Rackham had seen in her. But then Rackham had never stood a drugstore length away from Alma; he saw her only in close-up, the surprising, intense blue of her eyes, and the color and texture of her skin, like whipped cream. Sands wondered whether it was her skin and eyes, or her quality of serenity which had appealed most to Rackham, who was quick and nervous and excitable.

She said, placidly, 'Why, hello there.'

'Hello, Alma.'

'Lovely weather, isn't it?'

'Yes. . . . How is Charles?'

'You must come over for dinner one of these nights.'

'I'd like to.'

'Next week, perhaps. I'll give you a call—I must run now. Charles is waiting for me. See you next week.'

But she did not run, she walked; and Charles was not waiting for her, he was waiting for Sands. He had let himself into Sands's house and was pacing the floor of the study, smoking a cigarette. His color was bad, and he had lost weight, but he seemed to have acquired an inner calm. Sands could not tell whether it was the calm of a man who had come to an important decision, or that of a man who had reached the end of his rope and had stopped struggling.

They shook hands, firmly, pressing the past week back into shape. Rackham said, 'Nice to see you again, old man.'

'I've been here all along.'

'Yes. Yes, I know. . . . I had things to do, a lot of thinking to do.'

'Sit down. I'll make you a drink.'

'No, thanks. Alma will be home shortly, I must be there.'

Like a Siamese twin, Sands thought, *separated by a miracle, but returning voluntarily to the fusion—because the fusion was in a vital organ.*

'I understand,' Sands said.

Rackham shook his head. 'No one can understand, really, but you come very close sometimes, Sands. Very close.' His cheeks flushed, like a boy's. 'I'm not good at words or expressing my emotions, but I wanted to thank you before we leave, and tell you how much Alma and I have enjoyed your companionship.'

'You're taking a trip?'

'Yes. Quite a long one.'

'When are you leaving?'

'Today.'

'You must let me see you off at the station.'

'No, no,' Rackham said quickly. 'I couldn't think of it. I hate last-minute depot farewells. That's why I came over this afternoon to say good-bye.'

'Tell me something of your plans.'

'I would if I had any. Everything is rather indefinite. I'm not sure where we'll end up.'

'I'd like to hear from you now and then.'

'Oh, you'll hear from me, of course.' Rackham turned away with an impatient twitch of his shoulders as if he was anxious to leave, anxious to start the trip right now before anything happened to prevent it.

'I'll miss you both,' Sands said. 'We've had a lot of laughs together.'

Rackham scowled out of the window. 'Please, no farewell speeches. They might shake my decision. My mind is already made up, I want no second thoughts.'

'Very well.'

'I must go now. Alma will be wondering—'

'I saw Alma earlier this afternoon,' Sands said.

'Oh?'

'She invited me for dinner next week.'

Outside the open window two hummingbirds fought and fussed, darting with crazy accuracy in and out of the bougainvillea vine.

'Alma', Rackham said carefully, 'can be very forgetful sometimes.'

'Not that forgetful. She doesn't know about this trip you've planned, does she? . . . Does she, Rackham?'

'I wanted it to be a surprise. She's always had a desire to see the world. She's still young enough to believe that one place is different from any other place. . . . You and I know better.'

'Do we?'

'Goodbye, Sands.'

At the front door they shook hands again, and Rackham again promised to write, and Sands promised to answer his letters. Then Rackham crossed the lawn and the concrete driveway, head bent, shoulders hunched. He didn't look back as he turned the corner of the eugenia hedge.

Sands went over to his desk, looked up a number in the telephone directory, and dialed.

A girl's voice answered, 'Tracy clinic, X-ray department.'

'This is Charles Rackham,' Sands said.

'Yes, Mr Rackham.'

'I'm leaving town unexpectedly. If you'll tell me the amount of my bill I'll send you a check before I go.'

'The bill hasn't gone through, but the standard price for a lower gastrointestinal is twenty-five dollars.'

'Let's see, I had that done on the—'

'The fifth. Yesterday.'

'But my original appointment was for the first, wasn't it?'

The girl gave a does-it-really-matter sigh. 'Just a minute, sir, and I'll check.' Half a minute later she was back on the line. 'We have no record of an appointment for you on the first, sir.'

'You're sure of that?'

'Even without the record book, I'd be sure. The first was a Monday. We do only gall bladders on Monday.'

'Oh. Thank you.'

Sands went out and got into his car. Before he pulled away from the curb he looked over at Rackham's house and saw Rackham pacing up and down the verandah, waiting for Alma.

The Tracy clinic was less impressive than Sands had expected, a converted two-storey stucco house with a red tile roof. Some of the tiles were broken and the whole building needed paint, but the furnishings inside were smart and expensive.

At the reception desk a nurse wearing a crew cut and a professional smile told Sands that Dr Tracy was booked solid for the entire afternoon. The only chance of seeing him was to sit in the second-floor waiting-room and catch him between patients.

Sands went upstairs and took a chair in a little alcove at the end of the hall, near Tracy's door. He sat with his face half hidden behind an open magazine. After a while the door of Tracy's office opened and over the top of his magazine Sands saw a woman silhouetted in the door frame—a plump, fair-haired young woman in a flowery print dress.

Tracy followed her into the hall and the two of them stood looking at each other in silence. Then Alma turned and walked away, passing Sands without seeing him because her eyes were blind with tears.

Sands stood up. 'Dr Tracy?'

Tracy turned sharply, surprise and annoyance pinching the corners of his mouth. 'Well? Oh, it's Mr Sands.'

'May I see you a moment?'

'I have quite a full schedule this afternoon.'

'This is an emergency.'

'Very well. Come in.'

They sat facing each other across Tracy's desk.

'You look pretty fit,' Tracy said with a wry smile, 'for an emergency case.'

'The emergency is not mine. It may be yours.'

'If it's mine, I'll handle it alone, without the help of a poli—I'll handle it myself.'

Sands leaned forward. 'Alma has told you, then, that I used to be a policeman.'

'She mentioned it in passing.'

'I saw Alma leave a few minutes ago. . . . She'd be quite a nice-looking woman if she learned to dress properly.'

'Clothes are not important in a woman,' Tracy said, with a slight flush. 'Besides, I don't care to discuss my patients.'

'Alma is a patient of yours?'

'Yes.'

'Since the night Rackham called you when she was having hysterics?'
'Before then.'

Sands got up, went to the window, and looked down at the street.

People were passing, children were playing on the sidewalk, the sun shone, the palm trees rustled with wind—everything outside seemed normal and human and real. By contrast, the shape of the idea that was forming in the back of his mind was so grotesque and ugly that he wanted to run out of the office, to join the normal people passing on the street below. But he knew he could not escape by running. The idea would follow him, pursue him until he turned around and faced it.

It moved inside his brain like a vast wheel, and in the middle of the wheel, impassive, immobile, was Alma.

Tracy's harsh voice interrupted the turning of the wheel. 'Did you come here to inspect my view, Mr Sands?'

'Let's say, instead, your viewpoint.'

'I'm a busy man. You're wasting my time.'

'No. I'm giving you time.'

'To do what?'

'Think things over.'

'If you don't leave my office immediately, I'll have you thrown out.' Tracy glanced at the telephone but he didn't reach for it, and there was no conviction in his voice.

'Perhaps you shouldn't have let me in. Why did you?'

'I thought you might make a fuss if I didn't.'

'Fusses aren't in my line.' Sands turned from the window. 'Liars are, though.'

'What are you implying?'

'I've thought a great deal about that night you came to the Rackhams' house. In retrospect, the whole thing appeared too pat; too contrived: Alma had hysterics and you were called to treat her. Natural enough, so far.'

Tracy stirred but didn't speak.

'The interesting part came later. You mentioned casually to Rackham that he had an appointment for some X-rays to be taken the following day, September the first. It was assumed that Alma had forgotten to tell him. Only Alma *hadn't* forgotten. There was nothing to forget. I checked with your X-ray department half an hour ago. They have no record of any appointment for Rackham on September the first.

'Records get lost.'

'This record wasn't lost. It never existed. You lied to Rackham. The lie itself wasn't important, it was the *kind* of lie. I could have understood a lie of vanity, or one to avoid punishment or to gain profit. But this seemed such a silly, senseless, little lie. It worried me. I began to wonder about Alma's part in the scene that night. Her crying was most unusual for a woman of Alma's inert nature. What if her crying was also a lie? And what was to be gained by it?'

'Nothing,' Tracy said wearily. 'Nothing was gained.'

'But something was *intended*—and I think I know what it was. The scene was played to worry Rackham, to set him up for an even bigger scene. If that next scene has already been played, I am wasting my time here. Has it?'

'You have a vivid imagination.'

'No. The plan was yours—I only figured it out.'

'Very poor figuring, Mr Sands.' But Tracy's face was gray, as if mold had grown over his skin.

'I wish it were. I had become quite fond of the Rackhams.'

He looked down at the street again, seeing nothing but the wheel turning inside his head. Alma was no longer in the middle of the wheel, passive and immobile; she was revolving with the others—Alma and Tracy and Rackham, turning as the wheel turned, clinging to its perimeter.

Alma, devoted wife, a little on the dull side. . . . What sudden passion of hate or love had made her capable of such consummate deceit? Sands imagined the scene the morning after Tracy's visit to the house. Rackham, worried and exhausted after a sleepless night: '*Are you feeling better now, Alma?*'

'*Yes.*'

'*What made you cry like that?*'

'*I was worried.*'

'*About me?*'

'*Yes.*'

'*Why didn't you tell me about my X-ray appointment?*'

'*I couldn't. I was frightened. I was afraid they would discover something serious the matter with you.*'

'*Did Tracy give you any reason to think that?*'

'*He mentioned something about a blockage. Oh, Charles, I'm scared! If anything ever happened to you, I'd die. I couldn't live without you!*'

For an emotional and sensitive man like Rackham, it was a perfect set-up: his devoted wife was frightened to the point of hysterics, his good friend and physician had given her reason to be frightened. Rackham was ready for the next step. . . .

'According to the records in your X-ray department,' Sands said, 'Rackham had a lower gastrointestinal X-ray yesterday morning. What was the result?'

'Medical ethics forbid me to—'

'You can't hide behind a wall of medical ethics that's already full of holes. What was the result?'

There was a long silence before Tracy spoke. 'Nothing.'

'You found nothing the matter with him?'

'That's right.'

'Have you told Rackham that?'

'He came in earlier this afternoon, alone.'

'Why alone?'

'I didn't want Alma to hear what I had to say.'

'Very considerate of you.'

'No, it was not considerate,' Tracy said dully. 'I had decided to back out of our—our agreement—and I didn't want her to know just yet.'

'The agreement was to lie to Rackham, convince him that he had a fatal disease?'

'Yes.'

'Did you?'

'No. I showed him the X-rays, I made it clear that there was nothing wrong with him. . . . I tried. I tried my best. It was no use.'

'What do you mean?'

'He wouldn't believe me! He thought I was trying to keep the real truth from him.' Tracy drew in his breath sharply. 'It's funny, isn't it?— after days of indecision and torment I made up my mind to do the right thing. But it was too late. Alma had played her role too well. She's the only one Rackham will believe.'

The telephone on Tracy's desk began to ring but he made no move to answer it, and pretty soon the ringing stopped and the room was quiet again.

Sands said, 'Have you asked Alma to tell him the truth?'

'Yes, just before you came in.'

'She refused?'

Tracy didn't answer.

'She wants him to think he is fatally ill?'

'I—yes.'

'In the hope that he'll kill himself, perhaps?'

Once again Tracy was silent. But no reply was necessary.

'I think Alma miscalculated,' Sands said quietly. 'Instead of planning suicide, Rackham is planning a trip. But before he leaves, he's going to hear the truth—from you and from Alma.' Sands went towards the door. 'Come on, Tracy. You have a house call to make.'

'No. I can't.' Tracy grasped the desk with both hands, like a child resisting the physical force of removal by a parent. 'I won't go.'

'You have to.'

'No! Rackham will ruin me if he finds out. That's how this whole thing started. We were afraid, Alma and I, afraid of what Rackham would do if she asked him for a divorce. He's crazy in love with her, he's obsessed!'

'And so are you?'

'Not the way he is. Alma and I both want the same things—a little peace, a little quiet together. We are alike in many ways.'

'That I can believe,' Sands said grimly. 'You want the same things, a little peace, a little quiet—and a little of Rackham's money?'

'The money was secondary.'

'A very close second. How did you plan on getting it?'

Tracy shook his head from side to side, like an animal in pain. 'You keep referring to plans, ideas, schemes. We didn't start out with plans or schemes. We just fell in love. We've been in love for nearly a year, not daring to do anything about it because I knew how Rackham would react if we told him. I have worked hard to build up this clinic; Rackham could destroy it, and me, within a month.'

'That's a chance you'll have to take. Come on, Tracy.'

Sands opened the door and the two men walked down the hall, slowly and in step, as if they were handcuffed together.

A nurse in uniform met them at the top of the stairs. 'Dr Tracy, are you ready for your next——?'

'Cancel all my appointments, Miss Leroy.'

'But that's imposs——'

'I have a very important house call to make.'

'Will it take long?'

'I don't know.'

The two men went down the stairs, past the reception desk, and out into the summer afternoon. Before he got into Sands's car, Tracy looked back at the clinic, as if he never expected to see it again.

Sands turned on the ignition and the car sprang forward.

After a time Tracy said, 'Of all the people in the world who could have been at the Rackhams' that night, it had to be an ex-policeman.'

'It's lucky for you that I was.'

'Lucky.' Tracy let out a harsh little laugh. 'What's lucky about financial ruin?'

'It's better than some other kinds of ruin. If your plan had gone through, you could never have felt like a decent man again.'

'You think I will anyway?'

'Perhaps, as the years go by.'

'The years.' Tracy turned, with a sigh. 'What are you going to tell Rackham?'

'Nothing. You will tell him yourself.'

'I can't. You don't understand, I'm quite fond of Rackham, and so is Alma. We—it's hard to explain.'

'Even harder to understand.' Sands thought back to all the times he had seen the Rackhams together and envied their companionship, their mutual devotion. Never, by the slightest glance or gesture of impatience or slip of the tongue, had Alma indicated that she was passionately in love with another man. He recalled the games of Scrabble, the dinners, the endless conversations with Rackham, while Alma sat with her knitting, her face reposeful, content. Rackham would ask, 'Don't you want to play too, Alma?' And she would reply. 'No, thank you, dear, I'm quite happy with my thoughts.'

Alma, happy with her thoughts of violent delights and violent ends.

Sands said, 'Alma is equally in love with you?'

'Yes.' He sounded absolutely convinced. 'No matter what Rackham says or does, we intend to have each other.'

'I see.'

The blinds of the Rackham house were closed against the sun. Sands led the way up the verandah steps and pressed the door chime, while Tracy stood, stony-faced and erect, like a bill collector or a process server.

Sands could hear the chimes pealing inside the house and feel their vibrations beating under his feet.

He said, 'They may have gone already.'

'Gone where?'

'Rackham wouldn't tell me. He just said he was planning the trip as a surprise for Alma.'

'He can't take her away! He can't force her to leave if she doesn't want to go!'

Sands pressed the door chime again, and called out, 'Rackham? Alma?' But there was no response.

He wiped the sudden moisture off his forehead with his coat sleeve. 'I'm going in.'

'I'm coming with you.'

'No.'

The door was unlocked. He stepped into the empty hall and shouted up the staircase, 'Alma? Rackham? Are you there?'

The echo of his voice teased him from the dim corners.

Tracy had come into the hall. 'They've left, then?'

'Perhaps not. They might have just gone out for a drive. It's a nice day for a drive.'

'Is it?'

'Go around to the back and see if their car's in the garage.'

When Tracy had gone, Sands closed the door behind him and shot the bolt. He stood for a moment listening to Tracy's nervous footsteps on the concrete driveway. Then he turned and walked slowly into the living room, knowing the car would be in the garage, no matter how nice a day it was for a drive.

The drapes were pulled tight across the windows and the room was cool and dark, but alive with images and noisy with the past:

'*I wanted to thank you before we leave, Sands.*'

'*You're taking a trip?*'

'*Yes, quite a long one.*'

'*When are you leaving?*'

'*Today.*'

'*You must let me see you off at the station. . . .*'

But no station had been necessary for Rackham's trip. He lay in front of the fireplace in a pool of blood, and beside him was his companion on the journey, her left arm curving around his waist.

Rackham had kept his promise to write. The note was on the mantel, addressed not to Sands, but to Tracy.

Dear George:

You did your best to fool me but I got the truth from Alma. She could never hide anything from me, we are too close to each other. This is the easiest way out. I am sorry that I must take Alma along, but she has told me so often that she could not live without me. I cannot leave her behind to grieve.

Think of us now and then, and try not to judge me too harshly.

Charles Rackham

Sands put the note back on the mantel. He stood quietly, his heart pierced by the final splinter of irony: before Rackham had used the gun on himself, he had lain down on the floor beside Alma and placed her dead arm lovingly around his waist.

From outside came the sound of Tracy's footsteps and then the pounding of his fists on the front door.

'Sands, I'm locked out. Open the door. Let me in! Sands, do you hear me? Open this door!'

Sands went and opened the door.

8

LEIGH BRACKETT

So Pale, So Cold, So Fair

She was the last person in the world I expected to see. But she was there, in the moonlight, lying across the porch of my rented cabin.

She wore a black evening dress, and little sandals with very high heels. At her throat was a gleam of dim fire that even by moonlight you knew had to be made by nothing less than diamonds. She was very beautiful. Her name was Marjorie, and once upon a time, a thousand years ago, she had been engaged to me.

That was a thousand years ago. If you checked the calendar it would only say eight and a half, but it seemed like a thousand to me. She hadn't married me. She married Brian Ingraham, and she was still married to him, and I had to admit she had probably been right, because he could buy her the diamonds and I was still just a reporter for the Fordstown *Herald*.

I didn't know what Marjorie Ingraham was doing on my porch at two-thirty-five of a Sunday morning. I stood still on the graveled path and tried to figure it out.

The poker game was going strong in Dave Schuman's cabin next door. I had just left it. The cards had not been running my way, and the whiskey had, and about five minutes ago I had decided to call it a night. I had walked along the lake shore, looking with a sort of vague pleasure at the water and the sky, thinking that I still had eight whole days of vacation before I had to get back to my typewriter again.

And now here was Marjorie, lying across my porch.

I couldn't figure it out.

She had not moved. There was a heavy dew, and the drops glistened on her cheeks like tears. Her eyes were closed. She seemed to be sleeping.

'Marjorie?' I said. 'Marjorie—'

There wasn't any answer.

I went up to the low step and reached across it and touched her bare shoulder. It was not really cold. It only felt that way because of the dew that was on it.

I laid my fingers on her throat, above the diamonds. I waited and waited, but there was no pulse. Her throat was faintly warm, too. It felt like marble that has been for a time in the sun. I could see the two dark, curved lines of her brows and the shadows of her lashes. I could see her mouth, slightly parted. I held my hand over it and there was nothing, no slightest breath. All of her was still, as still and remote as the face of the moon.

She was not sleeping. She was dead.

I stood there, hanging onto the porch rail, feeling sick as the whiskey turned in me and the glow went out. A lot of thoughts went through my mind about Marjorie, and now suddenly she was gone, and I would not have believed it could hit me so hard. The night and the world rocked around me, and then, when they steadied down again, I began to feel another emotion.

Alarm.

Marjorie was dead. She was on my porch, laid out with her skirt neat and her eyes closed, and her hands folded across her waist. I didn't think it was likely she had come there by herself and then suddenly died in just that position. Someone had brought her and put her there, on purpose.

But who? And why?

I ran back to Dave Schuman's.

I must have looked like calamity, because the minute I came in the door they forgot the cards and stared at me, and Dave got up and said, 'Greg, what is it?'

'I think you better come with me,' I said, meaning all of them. 'I want witnesses.'

I told them why. Dave's face tightened, and he said, 'Marge Ingraham? My God.' Dave, who is in the circulation department of the *Herald*, went to school with me and Marjorie and knows the whole story.

He grabbed a flashlight and went out the door, and the local physician, our old poker pal Doc Evers, asked me, 'Are you sure she's dead?'

'I think so. But I want you to check it.'

He was already on his way. There were three other guys beside Dave Schuman and Doc Evers and me: another member of the *Herald* gang; Hughie Brown, who ran Brown's Boat Livery on the lake; and a young fellow who was a visiting relation or something of Hughie's. We hurried back along the lake shore and up the gravel path.

Marjorie had not gone away.

Somebody turned on the porch light. The hard, harsh glare beat down, more cruel but more honest than the moonlight.

Hughie Brown's young relative said, in a startled kind of way, 'But she can't be dead, look at the color in her skin.'

Doc Evers grunted and bent over her. 'She's dead, all right. At a rough guess, three or four hours.'

'How?' I asked.

'As the boy says, look at the color of her skin. That usually indicates carbon-monoxide poisoning.'

Dave said, in a curiously hesitant voice, 'Suicide?'

Doc Evers shrugged. 'It usually is.'

'It could have been accidental,' I said.

'Possibly.'

'Either way,' I said, 'She couldn't have died here.'

'No,' said Doc, 'hardly. Monoxide poisoning presupposes a closed space.'

'All right,' I said. 'Why was she brought here and left on my doorstep?'

Doc Evers said, 'Well, in any case, you're in the clear. You've been with us since before six last evening.'

Hughie Brown's young relative was staring at me. I realized what I was doing and shoved my hands in my pockets. I had been running my fingers over the scars that still show on my face, a nervous trick I haven't quite been able to shake.

'Sure,' said Dave. 'That's right. You're in the clear, Greg. No matter what.'

'That comforts me,' I said. 'But not greatly.'

I went back to fingering the scars.

I had enemies in Fordstown. I went out of my way to make them, with a batch of articles I was brainless enough to write about how things were being run in the city. The people involved had used a simple and direct method of convincing me that I had made a serious error in judgment. I turned again to look at poor Marjorie, and I wondered.

A man named Joe Justinian was my chief and unassailable enemy. Chief because he was the control center of Fordstown's considerable vice rackets, and unassailable because he owned the city administration, hoof, horns, and hide.

A uniformed cop and a city detective of the Fordstown force had stood by and watched while Justinian's boys had their fun, bouncing me up and down on the old brick paving of the alley where they cornered me. The detective had had to move his feet to keep from getting my blood on his shoes. Afterward neither he nor the cop could remember a single identifying feature about the men.

Justinian had two right-hand bowers. One was Eddie Sego, an alert and sprightly young hood who saw to it that everything ran smoothly. The other was Marjorie's husband—now widower—Brian Ingraham. Brian was the respectable one, the lawyer who maintained in the world the polite fiction that Mr Joseph Justinian was an honest businessman who operated a night club known as the Roman Garden, and who had various 'investments'.

Brian himself was one of Justinian's best investments. From a small lawyer with several clients he had become a big lawyer with one client.

And now his wife was dead on my doorstep.

Any way I looked at it, I couldn't see that this night was going to bring me anything but trouble.

Hughie Brown came back with a folded sheet fresh from the laundry. Doc Evers unfolded it, crisp and white, and that was the last I ever saw of Marjorie.

Doc said, 'Where's the nearest phone?'

On Monday afternoon I was in Fordstown, in the office of Wade Hickey, our current chief of police.

Brian Ingraham was there, too. He was sitting in the opposite corner, his head bowed, not looking at me or Hickey. He seemed all shrunken together and gray-faced, and his fingers twitched so that it was an effort to hold the cigarettes he was chainsmoking. I kept glancing at him, fascinated.

This was a new role for Brian. I had never seen him before when he didn't radiate perfect confidence in his ability to outsmart the whole world and everybody in it.

Hickey was speaking. He was a big, thick-necked man with curly gray hair and one of those coarse, ruddy, jovial faces that can fool some of the people all of the time, but others for only the first five minutes.

'The reports are all complete now,' he said, placing one large hand on a file folder in front of him on the desk. 'Poor Marjorie took her own life. What her reasons may have been are known only to herself and God—'

Suddenly, viciously, Ingraham said, 'You're not making a speech now, Wade. You don't have to ham it up.'

His face was drawn like something on a rack. Hickey gave him a pitying glance.

'I'm sorry, Brian,' he said, 'but these facts have to be made perfectly clear. Mr Carver is in a peculiar position here, and he has a right to know.' He turned to me and went on.

'Marjorie's car was found in a patch of woods off Beaver Run Road, maybe ten miles out of town. There's an old logging cut there, and she had driven in on it about a quarter of a mile, where she wasn't likely to be disturbed. As it happened, of course, somebody did find her, too late to be of any help—'

'Somebody', I said, 'with a fine sense of humor.'

'Or someone wanting to make trouble for you,' said Hickey. 'Let's not forget that possibility. You do have enemies, you know.'

'Yes,' I said. 'What a pity they were all complete strangers.'

Hickey's eyes got cold. 'Look, Carver,' he said, 'I'm trying to be decent about this. Don't make it hard for me.'

'It seems to me', I said, 'that I've been shamefully cooperative.'

'Cooperation', said Hickey, 'is how we all get along in this world. You oughtn't to be ashamed of it. Now then.' He turned a page over in the folder. 'Whoever found her and removed her body left the front door open, but all the windows were tight shut except the wind-wing on the right side. That was open sufficiently to admit a hose running from the exhaust pipe. The autopsy findings agree with the preliminary reports made by the doctor up at Lakelands—'

'Doctor Evers.'

'That's right, Doctor Evers—and the police doctor who accompanied the ambulance. Carbon-monoxide poisoning.' He closed the folder. 'There's only one possible conclusion.'

'Suicide,' I said.

Hickey spread his hands and nodded solemnly.

I looked at Brian Ingraham. 'You knew her better than anybody. What do you think?'

'What is there to think?' he said, in an old, dry, helpless voice that hardly carried across the room. 'She did it. That's all.' He ran the back of his hand across his eyes. He was crying.

'Now,' said Hickey, 'as to why her body was removed from the car, transported approximately twenty miles and left on your porch, Carver, I don't suppose we'll ever know. A ghoulish joke, an act of malice—a body can be an embarrassing thing to explain away—or simply the act of a nut, with no real motive behind it at all. Whatever the explanation, it isn't important. And we certainly can't connect you in any way with Marjorie's death. So if I were you, I'd go home and forget about it.'

'Yes,' I said. 'I guess that's the thing to do. Brian—'

'Yes.'

'Do you know of any reason? Was she sick, or unhappy?'

He looked at me, through me, beyond me, into some dark well of misery. 'No, I don't know of any reason. According to the autopsy she was in perfect health. As far as I knew'—he faltered, and then went on, in that curiously dead voice—'as far as I knew, she was happy.'

'It's always a cruel thing to accept,' said Hickey, 'when someone we love takes that way out. But we have to realize—'

'We,' said Ingraham, getting up. 'What the hell have you got to do with it, you greedy, grubbing, boot-licking slob? And how would you know, anyway? You've never loved anything but yourself and money since the day you were born.'

He went past me and out the door.

Hickey shook his fine, big, leonine head. 'Poor Brian. He's taking this mighty hard.'

'Yes,' I said.

'Well,' said Hickey, 'it's no wonder. Marjorie was a mighty fine girl.'

'Yes,' I said. I got up. 'I take it that's all?'

Hickey nodded. He picked up the file and shoved it in a drawer. He shut the drawer. Symbol of completion.

I went to the *Herald* and did a nice, neat, factual follow-up on the story I had already filed. Then I stopped at the State Store and picked up a bottle, and returned to the bachelor apartment I inhabit for fifty weeks of the year.

So I was home, as Hickey had recommended, but I did not forget it. I forgot to go out for food, and I forgot later to turn the lights on, but I couldn't forget Marjorie. I kept seeing her face turned toward me in the moonlight, with the dew on her cheeks and her lips parted. After a while it seemed to me that she had been trying to speak, to tell me something. And I got angry.

'That's just like you,' I said. 'Make a mess of things, and then come running to me for help. Well, this time I can't help you.'

I thought of her sitting all alone in her car in the old logging cut, listening to the motor throb, feeling death with every breath she breathed, and I wondered if she had thought that at the end. I wondered if she had thought of me at all.

'Such a waste, Marjorie. You could have left Brian. You could have done a million other things. Why did you have to go and kill yourself?'

It was hot and dark in the room. The Marjorie-image receded slowly into a thickening haze.

'That's it,' I said. 'Go away.'

The haze got thicker. It enveloped me, too. It was restful. Marjorie was gone. Everything was gone. It was very nice.

Then the noise began.

It was a sharp, insistent noise. A ringing. It had a definite significance, one I tried hard to ignore. But I couldn't, quite. It was the doorbell, and in the end I didn't have any choice. I fought my way partly out of the fog and answered it.

She was standing in the hall, looking in at me.

'Oh, God,' I said. 'No. I told you. You can't come back to me now. You're dead.'

Her voice reached me out of an enormous and terrible void.

'Please,' it said. 'Mr Carver, please! My name is Sheila Harding. I want to talk to you.'

She was shorter than Marjorie, and not so handsome. This girl's hair was brown and her eyes were blue.

I hung onto the door jamb. 'I don't know you,' I said, too far gone to be polite.

'I was a friend of Marjorie's.' She stepped forward. 'Please, I must talk to you.'

She pushed by me, and I let her. I switched the light on and closed the door. There was a chair beside the door. I sat in it.

She didn't look like her at all, really. She didn't move the same way, and the whole shape and outline of her was different. She kept glancing at me, and it dawned on me that she hadn't counted on finding me drunk.

'I can still hear you,' I said. 'What's on your mind?'

She hesitated. 'Maybe I'd better—'

'I plan to be drunk all the rest of this week. So unless it's something that can wait—'

'All right,' she said rather sharply. 'It's about Marjorie.'

I waited.

'She was a very unhappy person,' Sheila Harding said.

'That's not what Brian said. He said she was happy.'

'He knows better than that,' she said bitterly. 'He must know. He just doesn't want to admit it. Of course, I knew Marjorie quite a long while before I realized it, but that's different. We both belonged to the League.'

'Oh,' I said. 'You're one of those society dolls. Now wait.' The name Harding clicked over in my dim brain with a sound of falling coins. 'Gilbert Harding, Harding Steel, umpteen millions. I don't remember a daughter.'

'There wasn't one. I'm his niece.'

'Marjorie enjoyed belonging to the League,' I said. 'She was born and raised on the South Side, right where I was. Her biggest ambition was to grow up to be a snob.'

I was annoying Miss Harding, who said, 'That isn't important, Mr Carver. The important thing is that she needed a friend very badly, and for some reason she picked me.'

'You look the friendly type.'

Her mouth tightened another notch. But she went on. 'Marjorie was worried about Brian. About what he was doing, the people he was mixed up with.'

I laughed. I got up and went over to the window, in search of air. 'Brian was working for Justinian when she married him. She knew it. She thought it was just splendid of him to be so ambitious.'

'Nine years ago,' said Sheila quietly, 'Justinian was a lot more careful what he did.'

She sounded so sensible and so grim that I turned around and looked at her with considerably more interest.

'That's true,' I said. 'But I still think it was late in the day for Marjorie to get upset. I told her at the beginning just what the score was. She didn't give a damn, as long as it paid.'

'She did later. I told you she was an unhappy person. She had made some bad mistakes, and she knew it.'

'They weren't that bad,' I said. 'They weren't so bad she had to kill herself.'

Her eyes met mine, blue, compelling, strangely hard.

'Marjorie didn't kill herself,' she said.

I let that hang there in the hot, still air while I looked at it.

Marjorie didn't kill herself.

There were two sides to it. One: Of course she killed herself; the evidence is as clear as day. Two: I'm not surprised; I never thought she did.

I said carefully, 'I was in the office of the chief of police this afternoon. I heard all the evidence, the autopsy report, the works. Furthermore, I saw the body, and a doctor friend of mine saw it. Monoxide poisoning, self-administered, in her own car. Period.'

'I read the papers,' said Sheila. 'I know all about that. I know all about you, too.'

'Do you?'

'Marjorie told me.'

'Girlish confidences, eh?'

'Something a little more than that, Mr Carver. It was when you were beaten so badly, a year or so back, that Marjorie began to feel— well, to put it honestly—guilty.'

'I'm sorry. I'm not at my best tonight. Go on.'

'Then,' said Sheila, 'my brother was killed, just after New Year's.'

'Your brother?' I sat down again, this time on the edge of the bed, facing her.

'He was in the personnel department of Harding Steel, a very junior executive. He told me the numbers racket—the bug, he called it—was taking thousands of dollars out of the men's pay checks every month. I guess that goes on in all the mills, more or less.'

'Around here it does. And more, not less.'

'Well, Bill thought he'd found a way to catch the people who were doing it, and clean up Harding Steel. He was ambitious. He wanted to do something big and startling. He was all excited about it. And then a load of steel rods dropped on him, and that was that. Just a plant accident. Everybody was sorry.'

I remembered, now that she told me. I hadn't covered the story myself, and there was no reason in particular why it should stick in my mind. But there hadn't been any suspicion of foul play at the time. I said so.

'Of course not. They were very careful about it. But Bill had told me the night before that his life had been threatened. He almost bragged about it. He said they couldn't stop him now; he had the men he wanted—Justinian's men, naturally—right here.' She held out her hand and closed the fingers. 'He was murdered.'

'And you told this to Marjorie.'

'Yes. We were very good friends, Mr Carver. Very close. She didn't think I was hysterical. She knew Bill, and liked him. She became terribly angry and upset. She said she would find out everything she could, and if it was really murder she was going to make Brian quit Justinian.'

'Go on.'

'It took her a long time. But last Saturday afternoon, late, she stopped by. She said she was pretty sure she had the full story, and it was murder, and she was going to face Brian with it that night. I asked her for details. She wouldn't tell me anything because she didn't think Brian was personally involved, and she was in duty bound to give him his chance to get clear of Justinian before she told.

'Then she was going to give the whole story to my Uncle Gilbert. She said he was big enough to fight Justinian.'

And he was, plenty big enough. If he had even reasonable proof that his nephew had been murdered, he could go right over the heads of the local law, to where the Emperor Justinian of Fordstown had no influence at all. He could smash him into little pieces.

Reason enough for Justinian to silence Marjorie. Reason enough.

But . . .

Sheila was still talking. 'Marjorie did tell me one thing, Mr Carver.'

'What?'

'If Brian still insisted on sticking with Justinian, she was going to leave him. She said, "I'll go back to Greg, if he still wants me." '

That turned me cold all over. 'And she did. No, what am I saying? She didn't come, somebody brought her. Somebody. Who? Why?'

'Surely you must have guessed that by now, Mr Carver.'

'You tell me.'

'Who it was exactly, of course, I don't know. But it was somebody who knows Marjorie's suicide was a lie. It was somebody who liked her and wanted the truth known. Somebody who thought that if he brought her to you, you would understand and do something about it.'

Yes. I could see that.

'But why me? Why not lay her on Brian's doorstep? He was her husband.'

'They probably felt that he would be too shocked and grieved to understand. Or perhaps they didn't trust him to fight Justinian. You wouldn't be involved either way. And you already have a grudge against Justinian.'

Oh yes, I had a grudge, all right. But who was this thoughtful someone? One of the killers? An accidental witness? And why did he have to pass the thing along to anyone? Why didn't he just come out and tell the truth himself?

That last one was easy. He was afraid.

Well, so was I.

Sheila was waiting. She was looking at me, expectant, confident. She was a pretty girl. She seemed like a nice girl, a loyal friend, a loving sister. She had had her troubles. I hated to let her down.

I said, 'No sale. Marjorie killed herself. Let's just accept that and forget it.'

She stared at me with a slowly dawning astonishment. 'After what I've just told you—you can still say that?'

'Yes,' I said. 'I can. In the first place, how would Marjorie find it out even if your brother was really murdered? Eddie Sego plans those things, and Eddie is not the babbling type. Not to anybody, including the boss's lawyer's wife.'

'Eddie Sego had nothing to do with it. He was in the hospital then with a burst appendix. That's one thing that made it harder for Marjorie, because she didn't know where to start.' She added, with angry certainty, 'She did find out, somehow.'

'Okay then. She found out. Maybe she found out even more. Maybe she discovered that Brian was so deeply involved that she couldn't tell. Maybe she was in such a mess that there wasn't any other way out of it but suicide. You don't know what happened after she left you.' I got up and opened the door. 'Go home, Miss Harding. Forget about it. Lead a long and happy life.'

She didn't go. She continued to look at me. 'I understand,' she said. 'You're scared.'

'Miss Harding,' I said, 'have you ever been set upon by large men with brass knuckles? Have you ever spent weeks in a hospital getting your face put back together again?'

'No. But I imagine it wasn't pleasant. I imagine they warned you that the next time it would be worse.'

'A society doll with brains,' I said. 'You have the whole picture. Good night.'

'I don't think you have the whole picture yet, Mr Carver. If you could find the man who brought Marjorie's body to you, you would have a witness who could break Justinian.'

'All right,' I said, 'we'll get right down to bedrock. I don't like Justinian any better than you do, but it's going to take somebody or something bigger than me to break him. I tried to once, and he did the breaking. As far as I'm concerned, that's it.'

'I don't suppose', she said slowly, 'that I have any right to call you a coward.'

'No. You haven't.'

'Very well. I won't.'

And this time she went.

I closed the door and turned off the lights. Then I went to the window and looked down at the street, three floors below. I saw her come out of the building and get into a black-and-white convertible parked at the curb. She drove away. Before she was out of sight a man got out of a car across the street and then the car went off after her. The man who had been left behind loitered along the street, where he could watch the front of the building and my window.

Somebody was keeping tabs on what I did and who came to see me. Wade Hickey? Justinian? And why?

I began to think about Brian Ingraham, and wonder how deeply he might be involved. I began to think about Joe Justinian, and what might be done about him. The Marjorie-image came back into my mind, and it was smiling.

Then I thought of the brass knuckles and the taste of blood and oil on the old brick paving. I looked down at the loitering man. 'The hell with it,' I said, and I went and lay down on my bed.

But I couldn't sleep.

About midnight I quit trying. I smoked a couple of cigarettes, sitting by the window. I did not turn the lights on. I don't remember that I came to any conscious and reasoned decision, either. After a certain length of time I just got up and went.

I didn't go near my car. I knew they would be watching that, expecting me to use it. I slipped out the back entrance into the alley and across it to an areaway that ran alongside another apartment house to the next street. I was careful. I didn't see anybody. I didn't want anybody to see me. I still thought I could quit on this thing any time it got too risky.

At my age, and with my experience, I should have known better.

There were still honest cops on the force, plenty of them. It wasn't their fault if they were hamstrung. As things stood, they had two choices. They could resign and go to farming or selling shoes, or they could sweat it out, hoping for better days. One who was sweating it out was an old friend of mine, a detective named Carmen Prioletti.

His house was pitch-dark when I got to it, after a twenty-minute hike. I rang the bell, and pretty soon a light came on, and then Carmen, frowsy with sleep, stuck his head out the door and demanded to know what the hell.

'Oh,' he said. 'It's you.'

He let me in and we stood talking in low voices in the hall, so as not to wake the family.

'I want to borrow your car,' I said. 'No questions asked, and back in an hour. Okay?'

He looked at me narrowly. Then he said, 'Okay.' He got the keys and gave them to me.

'I'll need a flashlight, too,' I said.

'There's one in the car.' He added, 'I'll wait up.'

I drove through quiet streets to the northern edge of town, and beyond it, into the country, where the air was cool and the dark roads were overhung with trees, and the summer mist lay white and heavy in the bottoms. I drove fast until I came to Beaver Run Road, and then I went slower, looking for the logging cut. Beaver Run was a secondary road, unpaved, washboarded and full of potholes. Dust had coated the trees and brush on either side, so they showed up bleached and grayish.

I found the cut and turned into it, and stopped the motor. It became suddenly very still. I picked up the flashlight and got out. I walked down the rutted track.

They had taken Marjorie's car away, of course, and the comings and goings of men and tow trucks had pretty well flattened everything in sight. But I found where the car had been. I looked all around at the crushed brambles, the rank weeds and the Queen Anne's lace. Then I walked a little farther down the track where no one had been. I walked slowly, watching my feet. I circled around to the side of the track, as one would in walking around a car. My trouser legs were wet to the knees with dew. The briars caught in them and scratched my shins. I went back to Prioletti's car and sat sideways, with the door open, picking a batch of prickly green beggar's lice out of my socks. The socks, and my shoes, were wet.

I backed out of the cut and drove into town again, to Prioletti's.

He was waiting up for me, as he had promised. We sat in the kitchen, smoking, and all the time he watched me with his bright dark eyes.

'Carmen', I said, 'suppose you're a girl. You're wearing an evening dress, sheer stockings, high-heeled shoes. You decide to kill yourself.

You drive to a nice quiet spot, an old logging cut off a back road. You have brought a hose with you—'

Carmen's eyes were fairly glittering now, but wary. 'Continue.'

'You wish to attach that hose to the exhaust pipe, and then run it in through the front window. Now, to do this you have to get out of the car. You have to walk around it to the back, and then around it again to the front. Right?'

'Indubitably.'

'All right. There are briar thickets, weeds, beggar's lice, unavoidable, and all soaked with dew. What happens to your nylons and your fancy shoes?'

'They're pretty much of a wreck.'

'Hers were not.'

'I see,' said Carmen slowly. 'You're sure of that? Absolutely sure.'

'When I found her on my porch she was neat and pretty as a pin. Carmen, she never got out of that car until she was carried out, dead.'

I filled him in on Sheila Harding, and what she had told me. Then we were both through talking for awhile. The electric clock on the wall touched two and went past it. Carmen smoked and brooded.

'What did you have in mind?' he asked finally.

'That depends,' I said. 'How much are you willing to risk? The minute certain people around Headquarters realize you're suspicious, you'll be in trouble.'

'Leave that to me. I used to be proud of my job, Greg. Now I tell my kids I'm not really a cop, I play piano in a disorderly house.' He clenched his hands together on the table top, and shivered all over. 'This might be it. This might just by the grace of God be it.'

'You'll have to play it mighty close to the vest. Now, what I would like to know is whether the autopsy report mentioned any external marks, no matter how slight, around the wrists and ankles, and maybe the mouth. Or a bruise on the head, under the hair.'

'I'll see what I can find out. We'd better not be seen meeting. How about north of the lake in Mill Creek Park, around three?'

I nodded and got up.

I walked home. I didn't meet anyone along the way. When I got within a block or so of my apartment house I took extra pains to stay in the shadows. I figured to come in the way I had gone out, across the alley and through the back door. I figured the boys out front would never know I had been away.

I was happy in that thought right up to the minute I actually opened the door. Inside, in the narrow well of the service stairs, a dim light was burning, and I saw a man there. A large man, with a crushed hat pulled down over his eyes. I saw him in the act of leaping toward me, and I let go of the door and turned to run, and there was another man in back of me. He hit me as I turned, and then the man in the stairwell came out and banged me across the nape of the neck. I went down on my hands and knees in the alley, onto the uneven bricks, and there we were again. A visit with old friends. Justinian's boys.

One of them pulled me up and wrenched my head back, and the other one gave me a fast chop over the Adam's apple. That was to stop me yelling.

Then he said, 'Where were you?'

I coughed and choked. Nameless, who was holding my arm doubled up behind me, gave it an upward twist. I winced, and Faceless, who was in front of me, with his hat still pulled down so that nothing much showed in the dark of night, asked again, 'Where were you?'

I whispered, 'Out for a walk.'

'Yeah,' said Faceless, 'I know that. You didn't take your car. So where'd you walk to?'

'Around. No place.'

He hit me twice, once on the left cheekbone, once on the right.

'I'm asking you,' he said. 'Me. The dame came to see you, and right away you went sneaking out. I want to know why.'

'No connection,' I said. 'She just dropped by. And it wasn't right away. I was restless and couldn't sleep. I went for a walk. So sue me.'

Nameless said conversationally, 'I could break your arm.'

He showed me how easy it would be. I went down on my knees again. There was a taste of blood in my mouth. I thought my face was bleeding. I thought I could feel it running down my cheeks, hot and wet, to spatter on the bricks.

'If it hadn't been', said Faceless, 'that we could hear your phone ringing and ringing through the open window, and you didn't answer it, we wouldn't never have known you'd gone. Now, that kind of thing can lead to trouble.' He kicked me. 'Get up, buddy. I don't like to have to bend over when I'm talking.'

I got up. I couldn't stand the feeling of blood on my face. I got up fast. I threw myself backward, butting Nameless as hard as I could with my head. It must have been hard enough, because he grunted and let go. He fell, and I fell on top of him, whipped around with my feet under me, and went for Faceless. He looked very queer. He was cloud-shaped, huge and looming, and the alley and the building walls were all twisted and quivering as though I was seeing them through dark water. I hit him full on and he went over backward, floating, slow-motion, like something in a dream. The blood ran down my face, filling my eyes, my nose, my mouth. I thought, *This is what it feels like to be crazy.* I knocked his hat off and got hold of his head and beat it up and down, up and down, hard, hard on the alley bricks.

It was nice, but it didn't last long. It hardly lasted at all. Nameless got up. He was mad. He hit me with something much harder than a fist, and pretty soon Faceless got up, and he was mad, too. They let me know it. I heard one of them wanting to kill me right now, but the other one said, 'Not yet, not till we get the order.' He shook me. 'You get that, buddy? The order. It can come any minute. And when it does, you got nothing left to hope for.'

He threw me down and they went away, down a long black tunnel that lengthened until I got dizzy watching and shut my eyes. When I opened them again I was lying in the alley, alone. It was still dark. I wanted to go to my apartment. I know I started and I know I must have made it up two flights of the service stairs, because I was lying on the landing when Sheila found me . . .

'I'm sorry, I'm so sorry,' she said and helped me up, and we walked together up the rest of the steps and down the hall to the apartment. I told her to pull the blind shut.

'They're watching the place,' I said.

'I know it,' she said. 'Somebody followed me home.'

She took me into the bathroom and went to work.

'It's not bad at all,' she said. 'Just ordinary cuts and bruises. But why did they do this to you? What were you doing?'

'I went out on an errand,' I said. 'They'd never have known I was gone, but some clown had to call me on the telephone. They could hear it ringing and they knew I wasn't here. What's the matter?'

She was already pretty white and tense. Now she put her hand over her mouth and her eyes got big and full of tears.

'Oh Lord,' she said. 'Oh, Lord, that was me.'

'You?'

'I got to thinking after I got home. I didn't have any right to expect you to do anything. I didn't have any right to reproach you. I wanted to tell you that. And I thought I ought to warn you that you were being watched. So I called. When you didn't answer I thought at first you'd—'.

She hesitated, and I said, 'Passed out', and she nodded.

'Then I began to get really worried. I called again, and again, and then finally I had to come back to see if you were all right.' She began to cry. 'And it was my fault.'

'You didn't mean it,' I said. 'You were trying to help.' My first impulse was to kill her, but she looked so miserable. 'Please, stop crying.'

'I can't,' she whispered, and looked at the bloody washrag she had in her other hand. 'I think I'm going to faint.'

She looked as though she might. I put my arm around her and took her into the other room, and we sat together on the edge of the bed, with her face buried on my shoulder. I wound up kissing her.

I think both of us were surprised to find we liked it.

'You're a nice kid,' I said. 'If you weren't so rich—'

She said quickly, 'Didn't you know? My side of the family doesn't have a million to its name. We're the poor Hardings. That's one reason my brother was so anxious to show off.'

'You may be in danger yourself,' I said, suddenly alarmed for her. 'They're already curious about you.'

'Since you're not going to do anything about Marjorie, I can't see that it matters,' she said.

'Well—' I said.

'You *have* done something! What? Please tell me.'

'No. You're in trouble enough already. Anyway, it isn't much.' It wasn't, either, unless Prioletti could turn up something on that autopsy report. And even that would only be a first step, an opening wedge. 'One thing I'd give a lot to know', I told her, 'is where Brian Ingraham was the night his wife was killed.'

'You don't think', she said, her face reflecting horror, 'that Brian had anything to do with it.'

'He's Justinian's man. Body and bank account.'

'But his own wife!'

'This is a hard world we live in.'

She shivered. 'And Marjorie said she'd given the maid the night off, so they'd be alone, and she was going to make herself beautiful so Brian would have to choose her instead of Justinian. She was vain, poor Marjorie. I just can't believe—Well, it doesn't matter what I believe, does it? Anyway, I know where Brian was that night, or at least where Marjorie thought he was. She was going to have to wait until he got home to talk to him.'

'Go ahead,' I said. 'Where was he?'

'At the Roman Garden, with Justinian.'

Sin in a middle-western steel town is organized, functional, and realistic. It is not like in the movies. The necessary furniture is there, and nothing more. No velvet drapes, no gilt mirrors, no ultramodernistic salons, no unbelievably beautiful females. The houses are just houses, and the whores are just whores. Numbers slips can be bought in almost any dingy little sandwich shop, pool hall, or corner grocery, and anyone can play , even the kids with as little as a penny. The night clubs and gambling palaces, like the Roman Garden, are businesslike structures wasting no time on the fancy junk. There's a bar, and there are the gambling layouts, and that's that. Food, entertainment, and decor are haphazard. The bosses don't figure that's what you came for.

At nine o'clock on a hot morning the Roman Garden looked downright dreary. It was primarily a big, barny, old two-and-a-half-storey frame house, with a new front tacked on it, yellow glazed brick with glass-brick insets and a neon sign. There was a parking lot around back. A couple of cars were already in it. The sports car I knew was Eddie Sego's.

I went in through the back door. No one followed me. No one had followed me since the two musclemen left me in the alley. I had escorted Sheila to her apartment, making her promise that she would go to her uncle's first thing in the morning, and there had not been a sign of a tail, nor was there now. I wished I knew why.

I walked down the hall and pushed open the door that said OFFICE. A thoroughly respectable-looking middle-aged female was sitting at a desk, writing busily. I went past her to the door marked PRIVATE and went through it before she could do more than squawk.

Eddie Sego was in the inner office. He was busy, too. There's a lot of paper work in any business, and he had a stack of it. He was wearing a magnificent silk sports shirt, and a pair of horn-rimmed glasses. With his hairy forearms and thick, low-growing black hair, the glasses made him look like a studious gorilla.

He leaped up, startled. Then he saw who it was and sat down again, and swore. He took his glasses off.

'You ought to know better than that, Carver,' he said. 'Bursting in without warning. I might have thought it was a heist and shot you.' He looked at me with his head on one side. 'What are you doing here, anyway? And what hit you?'

'You know damn well what hit me,' I said. 'Eddie, it isn't fair. I've played ball. The Emperor wanted me to shut up, and I did. What more does he want?'

'Look,' said Eddie, 'I'm no mind reader. What's this all about?'

'Of course,' I said, 'you're not going to admit you know. Okay, I'll spell it out. Last night a girl came to visit me. A mutual friend just died, and she was looking for sympathetic conversation. Everything was going fine with us until she went home. Then I found out my place was being watched. A big goon followed her and scared the wits out of her, and then when I left my room for a breath of air two guys jumped me. They wanted to know where I was going and why, and then they threatened to kill me, when they got the order. And I haven't done a damned thing. Everybody's got a limit, even me. And I'm pretty close to it.'

'Are you?' said Eddie. He got up and came around the desk to me, he looked at me for a moment, close to. Then he hit me, fast as a coiled snake, in the pit of the belly. He watched me double up and move back, and his lip curled. He stood there with his hands at his sides, almost as though he was giving me an invitation.

I didn't take it, and Eddie said, 'Limit! You've got no limit. You haven't got anything.' He turned his back on me. 'You don't even have a reason to come whining to me. I didn't send anybody around. I don't care what dames you see, and I can't imagine Justinian does, either.'

He sounded as though he really had not sent anybody. In the small corner of my mind that was not concerned with the pain in my gut, I wondered if Justinian was playing this one over Eddie's head. It was possible.

I managed to say, 'They were his boys, just the same. The same two that beat me before.'

Eddie didn't even bother to answer that. He picked up the phone and dialed a number. I started to go, and he gave me a black look and said, 'Stick around.'

'Why? What are you doing?'

'I'm calling the cops.'

I stared at him, feeling my face go wide open and foolish. 'You're what?'

'Calling the cops. They're looking for you—didn't you know that? I got the word just a few minutes ago.'

I stopped holding my belly. I turned and went out of there, paying no attention to Eddie's shouts. I burned rubber going away.

So the cops were after me. This was a switch. This I had not looked for. I thought now that that was why the musclemen had been withdrawn. Justinian liked to keep his right hand and his left from getting tangled up. But I couldn't figure what possible charge they could have against me.

Of course, under the present setup, they didn't really need one . . .

I thought it was about time somebody did something about cleaning up this town.

I decided to go across the line into Pennsylvania for the rest of the day, until it was time to meet Prioletti. From Fordstown, Pennsylvania is less than thirty miles. I had a lot of time to kill, and nothing to do but hug my bruises and think. I thought of Marjorie, and of young Harding. I thought of the way Justinian's corporation was set up. Two main branches, gambling and prostitution, under separate heads, with separate organizations. Gambling subdivided into three—regular layouts like the Roman Garden, horse rooms, and the bug. The bug, day in and day out, probably brought in more money than all the rest put together. I thought of Eddie Sego, who was almost boss of all the gambling rackets, next under Justinian himself.

When it was time, I went back over the state line, using the farm roads, dusty and quiet in the heat of the afternoon. At three o'clock I was in Mill Creek Park, in a grove of trees north of the little lake with the swans on it. Prioletti was already there.

'I didn't know if you'd make it,' he said. He looked haggard and excited. 'You know I'm supposed to be looking for you?'

'Yeah,' I said. 'But what for?'

'Investigation. That's a big word. It can cover a lot of things. It can keep you out of circulation for a while, and it can demand answers to questions.'

He peered around nervously. 'I got a look at that report.'

'Any luck?'

'Minor contused area on the scalp, minor abrasions at the mouth corners and cuts on the inside of the lips. There were also bruises and other minor abrasions on both wrists. No explanation.'

'What would you say, Carmen?'

'Coupled with your other evidence, I would say it indicates that the girl was hit on the head, gagged and bound to prevent any outcry, and then driven to the logging cut, where her car was rigged for the fake suicide.'

I felt a qualm of sickness. I had known that was how it must have been, but put into words that way it sounded so much more brutal.

'Poor kid,' I said. 'I hope she never came to.'

'Yeah,' said Carmen. 'But we've almost got it, Greg. Brian Ingraham is the key. If he knew that Justinian—'

He broke off, looking over my shoulder. 'I was afraid of that,' he said. He reached out and grabbed me fiercely. 'Hit me. Hit me hard and then run. Hickey's cops.'

He said that as though it was a dirty word, and it was. I hit him, and he let go, and I ran. Hickey's cops ran after me, but they were still a long way back, and I knew the park intimately from boyhood days. They shouted and one of them fired a shot, but it was in the air. I guess the order hadn't come yet. Anyway, I shook them and got back to my car. For the second time that day I burned rubber, going away.

I headed for the Country Club section, and Brian Ingraham's home.

What Carmen had started to say was that if Brian, believing his wife a suicide, were to find out that Justinian had had her killed, he could be expected to turn on Justinian.

What Carmen had not said was that if Brian already knew it, and was co-operating with Justinian, his reaction would be quite different.

I went in the long drive to the house, set far back among trees. I rang the bell, and Brian opened the door, and I walked in after him down the hall.

Brian looked like a ghost. He seemed neither pleased nor displeased to see me. He didn't even ask me why I had come. He led me into the living room and then just stood there, as though he had already forgotten me.

'Brian, I've come about Marjorie.'

He looked at me, in the same queer, twisted, other-dimensional way he had in Hickey's office that day.

'You didn't have to,' he said. 'I know.'

And I thought, *Well, here it is, and I'm finished, and so is the case*. But something about his face made me ask him, 'What do you know?'

'Why she killed herself. It was me.' He said it simply, honestly, almost as though I was his conscience and he was trying to get straight with me. 'I said she was happy, but she wasn't. For a long time she wanted me to quit and go back into regular practice, but I wouldn't. I laughed at her. Kindly, Greg. Kindly, as you would laugh at a child. But she wasn't a child. She could see me quite clearly. As I have been seeing myself since Sunday morning.'

He paused. Then, still in that heartbreakingly simple way, he said, 'I loved her. And I killed her.'

He couldn't be lying. Not with that face and manner. It wasn't possible. I felt weak in the knees with relief.

'You had nothing to do with it,' I said. 'Justinian killed her, to save his neck.'

He stood still, and his eyes became very wide and strange. 'Justinian? Killed her?'

'Sit down,' I said, 'and I'll tell you how it was done.'

We sat in the quiet house, with the hot afternoon outside the French windows, and I talked. And Brian listened.

When I was all through he said, 'I see.' Then he was silent a long time. His face had altered, becoming stony and hard, and there was a dim, cold spark at the back of his eyes.

'I remember Sheila Harding. I didn't know about her brother. That side of Justinian's business is in Eddie Sego's hands, and Eddie is not talkative.'

'No,' I said. 'But Eddie was in the hospital then. Justinian had to attend to that emergency himself. And somehow Marjorie found out.'

'Marjorie was my wife,' said Brian softly. 'He had no right to touch her.' He stood up, and his voice became suddenly very loud. 'He had no right. Marjorie. My wife.'

I thought I heard a car, coming up the long drive and coming fast, but Brian was shouting so I couldn't be sure. I tried to shut him up, but he was coming apart at the seams in a way that couldn't be stopped. I couldn't blame him, but I wished he would make sense. I put my hands on his shoulders and shook him.

'For God's sake, Brian! We don't have all year——'

We didn't even have the rest of the afternoon. Two big men came in through the French windows, with guns in their hands. My old friends of the alley. Between them came a third man, with no gun. He never carried a gun. He didn't need one. He was Justinian, the Emperor of Fordstown.

Brian saw him. Instantly he became silent, poised, his eyes shining like the eyes of an animal I once saw, mangled by dogs and dying. He sprang at Justinian.

It was Eddie Sego, entering through the door behind us, who slugged Brian on the back of the head and put him down.

The long, full draperies were drawn across the French windows. The doors were locked. The cars, mine and Justinian's, had been taken around to the back, out of sight of any chance caller. The house itself stood in the middle of two wooded acres, and so did the houses on either side. In this section you paid for seclusion, and you got it.

Justinian was talking. He was a tall man, gray at the temples, distinguished-looking, dressed by the best tailors. He had immense charm. Women fell over fainting when he smiled at them, and then were always astonished to discover that the underlying ruthlessness in his steel-trap mouth and bird-of-prey eyes was the real Justinian.

He was not bothering now to be charming. He was entirely the business man, cerebral, efficient.

'It's a pity I didn't get here a little sooner,' he said. 'I might have stopped Carver. As it is—' He shrugged.

Brian looked up at him from the chair where he was sitting, with Eddie Sego behind him. 'Then you admit you killed Marjorie.'

Justinian shook his head. 'I haven't admitted anything, and I don't intend to. The thing is, you believe I killed her, or that I might have killed her. The doubt has been planted. I could go to a lot of trouble to convince you you're wrong, but I couldn't make you stop wondering. I could never trust you again, Brian, any more than you would trust me. So your usefulness to me is ended.'

He turned to glare at me. 'That's all *you've* accomplished, Carver.'

'Oh, I understand,' said Brian. 'I've understood all along. Why else was all the business done in your office, and all records kept in your safe? You wanted to be able to eliminate me at any time, with no danger of incriminating papers lying around where you couldn't get at them. So that angle is covered. But I'm a pretty important man, Joe. Won't there be some curiosity?'

'If the bereaved husband takes his own life? I don't think so.'

'I see,' said Brian. 'Just like Marjorie.'

'And what about me?' I asked.

Justinian shrugged. 'We planned that on the way. It will appear that Brian shot you first, before killing himself. You see? The old lover, accusing the husband of having driven his wife to . . .'

Brian whimpered and rose up, and Eddie Sego knocked him down again.

'All right,' Justinian said. 'He keeps his gun in the desk in the next room. Go get it.'

Eddie nodded. 'Cover him,' he said to Faceless. He went out.

I said, 'There's a couple of things wrong with your plan, Joe.'

'I'm listening.'

'Other people know the whole story. You can't kill off everybody in town.'

'If you mean Miss Harding, she doesn't know anything, not at first-

hand. Suspicions are a dime a dozen. If you mean Prioletti, he'll forget. He has a family to consider.'

'You're overlooking the most important person of all,' I said.

'Who's that?'

'The guy who brought me Marjorie's body. He knows.'

Justinian's face tightened ominously. 'A crank, that's all. Doesn't
mean a thing.'

Eddie Sego had come back from the next room. He was holding
Brian's gun. Brian was hunched over in his chair, but he was staring at
me intently. The two large men stood still and listened.

'You don't believe that, Joe,' I said. 'You're saying it because you
haven't been able to find out who the man is, and you don't want your
underlings to get panicky about it.'

'If he'd had anything to tell he'd have told it by now,' said Justinian.
'Anyway, I'll find him. One thing at a time.'

'You'd better find him fast, Joe,' I said, 'because he belongs to you.
You've got a traitor in your own camp.'

Justinian said, 'Hold it a minute, Eddie.' He moved a step or two
closer to me. 'That's an interesting thought. Go on with it.'

'Well,' I said, 'a casual crank would have had to just accidentally
stumble on the car with Marjorie's body in it. He would also have had
to know who she was, and that she had once been engaged to me. He
would have had to know I was on vacation, and where. Now, does all
that seem likely?'

He shook his head impatiently. 'Go on.'

'I'm just laying it out for you. Okay, we forget the crank. We say
instead it was somebody who was fond of Marjorie and wanted her
avenged, but was afraid to come out and tell the truth. So he figured that
handing me the body would sic me on to what really happened to her,'

'This sounds better.'

'But still not good enough. If he was just a friend of Marjorie's, how
did he know about the murder? Guess at it, stumble on it, happen to
follow the cars into the logging cut and then wait around unseen
while the thing was being done, when he could have been calling for
help? Not likely. If it was one of the killers suddenly getting con-
science-stricken, that fills all the requirements except one. Would he
deliberately sic someone onto himself, to get himself hanged?'

Very briefly, Justinian's eyes flicked from Nameless to Faceless and back again to me. 'No. This I can tell you.'

'So what does that leave? It leaves a man who knew about Marjorie's murder, but was personally clear of it. A man who was clear on the Harding murder, too—so clear he could afford to talk about it. A man who wanted the murderer brought to justice, but who didn't want to appear in the business himself. Too dangerous, if something went wrong. So he handed the job on to me. Not to Brian, because he was too close to it, but to me. See? If I got killed, he hadn't lost anything but this chance, and there'd be another some day. But if I succeeded in pulling you down, he——'

Nameless fired, past Justinian.

The noise was earsplitting. Justinian, with the instinct of an old campaigner, dropped flat on the floor. Eddie Sego, behind him and across the room, was already down and rolling for the shelter of a sofa. He wasn't hit. He did not intend to be hit, either.

'He was gonna shoot you in the back, Boss,' said Nameless, on a note of stunned surprise. 'He was gonna——'

I tipped my chair over onto him, and we went staggering down together, with my hands on his wrist. I wanted his gun. I wanted it bad.

He wasn't going to give it up without a struggle. We got tangled in the furniture and when I got a look around again I saw Justinian, kneeling behind a big armchair. He was paying no attention to us. He had bigger things on his mind, like the gun he was too proud to carry. Faceless was crouched over in an attitude of indecision, his gun wavering between me and Eddie Sego. He couldn't see Eddie, and he couldn't shoot me without very likely killing his friend. Eddie solved his problem for him. He fired from the opposite end of the sofa and Faceless fell over with a sort of heavy finality.

Brian Ingraham sat where he was, in the middle of it, watching with the blank gaze of a stupid child.

I saw a heavy glass ashtray on the floor where we had knocked it off an end table. I let go with one hand and grabbed it and hit Nameless with it. He relaxed, and then the gun was quite easy to take out of his fingers. I took it and whirled around.

Justinian was moving his armchair shield, inch by inch, toward the gun that Faceless had dropped.

I said, 'Hold it, Joe.'

He gave me a hot, blind look of feral rage, but he held it, and I picked up the gun. Justinian looked from me to where Eddie Sego was, and he cursed him in a short, violent burst, and then grew calm again.

'That was a crummy way to do it, Eddie. You didn't have guts enough to face up to me yourself.'

Eddie stood up now. He shrugged. 'Why should I commit suicide? I figured Carver ought to be mad enough to do something.' He glanced at me. 'I just about gave you up this morning. I was really going to turn you in.'

'How did you find out?' asked Justinian. 'I didn't tell you anything. The Harding job, yes. But about Marjorie. I didn't tell anybody.'

'A guy like me', said Eddie, 'can find out an awful lot if he sets his mind to it. Besides, I'd been feeding Marjorie what she wanted to know about Harding.'

'Sure,' I said. 'How else could she have found out? You've been taken, Joe. You're through.'

I motioned him to get up. And then Brian remembered who Justinian was, and what he had just admitted he had done, and he got up and rushed in between us and flung himself on Justinian, and I was helpless.

They rolled together, making ugly sounds. They rolled out from the shelter of the chair into the open center of the room. And I saw Eddie Sego raise his gun.

'Eddie,' I said. 'Let them alone.'

'What the hell,' he said, 'now he knows what I did I have to get him, or he'll drag me right along with him. I'm clean on those killings, but there's plenty else.'

'Eddie,' I said. 'No.'

He said, 'I can do without you, too,' and I saw the black, cold glitter come in his eyes.

I shot him in the right elbow.

He spun around and dropped the gun. He doubled up for a minute, and then he began to whimper and claw with his left hand for his own gun, in a holster under his left shoulder. I went closer to him and shot him again, carefully, through the left arm.

He crumbled down onto the floor and sat there, looking at me with big tears in his eyes. 'What did you have to do that for?' he said. 'You wanted him dead, too.'

'Not that way. And not Brian, too.'

'What do you care about Brian?' He rocked back and forth on the floor, hugging his arms against his sides and crying.

'You make me sick,' I said.

I went to where Justinian and Brian were in the center of the room, locked together, quiet now with deadly effort. I didn't look to see who was killing who. 'You make me sick,' I said. 'All of you make me sick.' I kicked them until they broke apart.

I felt sorry for Brian, but he still made me sick. 'Get up, Brian, you get on the phone and call the police. Prioletti and the decent cops, not Hickey's. They've been waiting a long time for this. Go on!'

He went, and I told Justinian to sit down, and he sat. He looked at Eddie Sego and laughed.

'Empires aren't so easy to inherit after all, are they, Eddie?' he said.

Eddie was still looking at me. 'I just don't see why you did it.'

'I'll tell you,' I said. 'Because I want to see you hang right along with the others. Did you think I was going to do your dirty work for you, for free?'

I turned to Justinian. 'How did you find out Marjorie was so close to you on the Harding thing?'

'Why,' he said, 'I guess it was a remark Eddie made that got me worried.'

'A remark that got Marjorie killed. But you didn't care, did you, Eddie? What's another life, more or less, to you?'

His face had turned white, with fear instead of pain. Justinian was looking at me with a sort of astonishment. And then Brian came and took my arm, and I stepped back and shook my head, and we sat down and waited until Prioletti came.

When they were all gone and the house was empty and quiet again, I stood for a minute looking around at all the things that had been Marjorie's, and there was a peacefulness about them now. I went out softly and closed the door, and drove away down the long drive.

9

WILLIAM CAMPBELL GAULT

Take Care of Yourself

I finally caught up to her around eleven o'clock in a bar just off Windward Avenue. Windward Avenue is in Venice and Venice is not what you would call the high-rent district in the Los Angeles area.

A juke box was doling out the nasal complaints of a hillbilly songstress and most of the men at the bar looked like they worked with their hands. At the far end of the bar from the doorway, Angela Ladugo was sitting in front of what appeared to be a double martini.

The Ladugo name is a big one in this county, going way back to the Spanish land grants. Angela seemed to have inherited her looks from mama's side of the family, which was mostly English.

I paused for a moment in the doorway and she looked up and her gaze met mine and I thought for a moment she smiled. But I could have been wrong her face was stiff and her eyes were glazed.

The bartender, a big and ugly man, looked at me appraisingly and then his gaze shifted to Miss Ladugo and he frowned. A couple of the workingmen looked over at me and back at their glasses of beer.

There was an empty stool next to Angela; I headed toward it. The bartender watched me every step of the way and when I finally parked, he was standing at our end, studying me carefully.

I met his gaze blandly. 'Bourbon and water.'

'Sure thing,' he said.

'New around here, are you?'

'Where's *here*—Venice?'

'Right.'

Before I could answer, Angela said, 'Don't hit him yet, Bugsy. Maybe he's a customer.'

I looked over at her, but she was looking straight ahead. I looked back at the bartender. 'I'm not following the plot. Is this a private bar?'

He shook his head. 'Are you a private cop?'

I nodded.

He nodded, too, toward the door. 'Beat it.'

'Easy now,' I said. 'I'm not just *any* private cop. You could phone Sergeant Nystrom over at the Venice Station. Do you know him?'

'I know him.'

'Ask him about me, about Joe Puma. He'll give you a good word on me.'

'Beat it,' he said again.

Angela Ladugo sighed heavily. 'Relax, Bugsy. Papa would only send another one. At least this one looks—washed.'

The big man looked between us and went over to get my whiskey. I brought out a package of cigarettes and offered her one.

'No, thank you,' she said in the deliberate, carefully enunciated speech of the civilized drunk on the brink of the pit.

'Do you come here for color, Miss Ladugo?' I asked quietly, casually.

She frowned and said distinctly, 'No. For sanctuary.'

The bartender brought my bourbon and water. 'That'll be two bucks.'

He was beginning to annoy me. I said, 'Kind of steep here, aren't you?'

'I guess. Two bucks, *cash.*'

'Drink it yourself,' I told him. 'Ready to go, Miss Ladugo?'

'No.' she said. 'Bugsy, you're being difficult. The man's only doing his job.'

'What kind of men do that kind of job?' he asked contemptuously.

A silence. Briefly, I considered my professional decorum. And then I gave Bugsy my blankest stare and said evenly, 'Maybe you've got some kind of local reputation as a tough guy, mister, but frankly I never heard of you. And I don't like your insolence.'

The men along the bar were giving us their attention now. A bleached blonde in one of the booths started to giggle nervously. The juke box gave us *Sixteen Tons.*

Angela sighed again and said quietly, 'I'm ready to go. I'll see you later, Bugsy. I'll be back.'

'Don't go if you don't want to,' he said.

She put a hand carefully on the bar and even more carefully slid off the stool. 'Let's go, Mr—'

'Puma,' I supplied. 'My arm, Miss Ladugo?'

'Thank you, no. I can manage.'

She was close enough for me to smell her perfume, for me to see that her transparently fair skin and fine hair were flawless. She couldn't have been on the booze for long.

Outside, the night air was chilly and damp.

'Now, I'll take your arm,' she said. 'Where's your car?'

'This way. About a block. Are you all right?'

A wino came lurching across the street, narrowly missed being hit by a passing car. From the bar behind us, came the shrill lament of another ridge-running canary.

'I'm all right,' Miss Ladugo said. 'I'm—navigable.'

'You're not going to be sick, are you?'

'Not if you don't talk about it, I'm not. Where did Papa find you?'

'I was recommended by a mutual acquaintance. Would you like some coffee?'

'If we can go to a place that isn't too clattery. Isn't Bugsy wonderful? He's so loyal.'

'Most merchants are loyal to good accounts, Miss Ladugo. Just another half block, now.'

She stopped walking. 'Don't patronize me. I'm *not* an alcoholic, Mr—Panther, or whatever it is.'

'Puma,' I said. 'I didn't mean to sound condescending, but you must admit you're very drunk.'

'Puma,' she said. 'That's a strange name. What kind of name is that?'

'Italian,' I told her. 'Just a little bit, now, just a few steps.'

'You're simpering, Mr Puma. Don't simper.'

I opened the door of my car on the curb side and helped her in. The flivver started with a cough and I swung in a U turn, heading for Santa Monica.

Nothing from her. In a few minutes I smelled tobacco and looked over to see her smoking. I asked, 'Zuky's joint all right?'

'I suppose.' A pause. 'No. Take me home. I'll send someone for my car.'

'Your car—' I said. 'I didn't think about that. I should have left mine and driven yours. I guess I live closer to Venice than you do.'

'In that case, why don't we go to *your* house for a cup of coffee?'

'It isn't a house; it's an apartment, Miss Ladugo. And my landlord frowns on my bringing beautiful women there.'

'Am I beautiful?'

I thought she moved closer. 'You know you are,' I said. 'All beautiful women know it.'

Now, I felt her move closer. I said, 'And you're drunk and you don't want to hate yourself in the morning. So why don't you open that window on your side and get some cold, fresh air?'

A chuckle and her voice was husky. 'You mustn't give me a rejection complex.' Another pause. 'You—'

'Quit it,' I shot back at her.

Her breathing was suddenly harsh. 'You bastard. I'm *Spanish*, understand. Spanish and English. And the Spanish goes back to before this was even a state.'

'I know,' I said. 'I just don't like to be sworn at. Are you sure you don't want to go to Zuky's?'

Her voice was soft again. 'I'll go to Zuky's. I—I didn't mean what I said. I—In bars like Bugsy's, a lady can pick up some—some unladylike attitudes.'

'Sure,' I said. 'What's the attraction there? Bugsy?'

'It's a friendly place,' she said slowly. 'It's warm and plain and nobody tries to be anything they aren't.' She opened the window on her side and threw her cigarette out.

I said, 'You try to be something you aren't when you go there. Those aren't your kind of people.'

'How do you know? What do you know about me?'

'I know you're rich and those people weren't. I can guess you're educated and I'm sure they aren't. Have any of them invited you to their homes?'

'Just the single ones,' she said. 'Are you lecturing me, Mr Puma?'

'I'll quit it. It's only that I hate to see—oh, I'm sorry.' I stopped for the light at Olympic, and looked over at her.

She was facing my way. 'Go on. You hate to see what?'

'I hate to see quality degenerate.'

166

The chuckle again. 'How naive. Are you confusing quality with wealth, Mr Puma?'

'Maybe.' The light changed and I drove on toward Wilshire.

Two blocks this side of it, she asked, 'Who recommended you to Dad?'

'Anthony Ellers, the attorney. I've done some work for him.'

She was silent until I pulled the car into the lot behind Zuky's. Then she asked, 'Don't you ever drink, Mr Puma?'

'Frequently. But I don't *have* to.'

She sighed. 'Oh God, a moralist! Tony Ellers certainly picks them.'

I smiled at her. 'My credit rating's good, too. How about a sandwich with your coffee? It all goes on the expense account.'

She studied me in the dimness of the car and then she smiled, too. 'All right, all right. Get around here now and open the door for me like a gentleman.'

Zuky's was filled with the wonderful smells of fine kosher food. From a booth on the mezzanine, Jean Hartley waved and made a circle with his thumb and forefinger. I ignored him.

We took a booth near the counter. Almost all the seats at the counter were taken, as were most of the booths. I said, 'This is a warm and plain and friendly place and the food is good. Why not here instead of Bugsy's?'

Her gaze was candid. 'You tell me.'

I shook my head. 'Unless you have some compulsion to degrade yourself. Cheap bars are for people who can't afford good bars. And all bars are for people who haven't any really interesting places to go. With your kind of money, there must be a million places more fun than Bugsy's.'

Her smile was cool. 'Like?'

'Oh, Switzerland or Sun Valley or Bermuda or the Los Angeles Country Club.'

'I've been to all those places,' she said. 'They're no better.'

The waitress came and we ordered corned beef sandwiches and coffee.

Jean Hartley materialized and said, 'Joe, Joe old boy, gee it's great to see you.'

'It's been nice seeing you, Jean,' I said. 'So long.'

My welcome didn't dim his smile. 'Joe boy, you're being difficult.'

'Go, Jean,' I said. 'This isn't the *Palladium*.'

He looked from me to Miss Ladugo and back to me. He shook his head. 'I don't blame you,' he said, and went away.

'Handsome man,' Angela said.

I shrugged.

'Tell me,' she asked, 'are you really as square as you sound?'

I shrugged again.

'That man wanted to meet me, didn't he? And he didn't know I'm rich, either, did he?'

'He probably does,' I said. 'He's worked his way into better fields since he milked the lonely hearts club racket dry.'

'Oh? Is he what's called a confidence man?'

'No. They work on different principles. Jean trades on people's loneliness, on widows and spinsters, all the drab and gullible people who want to be told they're interesting.'

Angela Ladugo smiled. 'He seemed very charming. I suppose that's one of his weapons.'

'I suppose. I never found him very charming.'

'You're stuffy,' she said. 'You're—'

The waitress came with our orders and Angela stopped. The waitress went away, and I said, 'I'm a private investigator. Decorum is part of what I sell.'

She looked around and back at me. 'Are you sexless, too?'

'I've never been accused of it before. I've never taken advantage of a drunken woman, if that's what you mean.'

'I'm not drunk. I was, but I'm not now.'

'Eat,' I said. 'Drink your coffee.'

There was no further dialogue of any importance. She ate all of her sandwich and drank two cups of coffee. And then I drove her back to Beverly Hills and up the long, winding driveway that kept the Ladugo mansion out of view from the lower-class drivers on Sunset Boulevard.

A day's work at my usual rates and it never occurred to me to be suspicious of the Buick four-door hardtop that seemed to have followed us from Santa Monica.

I billed Mr Ladugo for mileage and the sandwiches and coffee and fifty dollars for my labor and got a check almost immediately. I had done what I was trained to do; the girl needed a psychiatrist more than a bodyguard.

I worked half a week on some hotel skips and a day on a character check on a rich girl's suitor. Friday afternoon, Mr Ladugo called me.

What kind of man, he wanted to know, was Jean Hartley?

'He's never been convicted,' I said. 'Is it facts you want, sir, or my opinion of the man?'

'Your opinion might be interesting, considering that you introduced him to my daughter.'

'I didn't introduce him to your daughter, Mr Ladugo. Whoever told you that, lied.'

'My daughter told me that. Could I have your version of how they happened to meet?'

I told him about Zuky's and the short conversation I'd had with Jean Hartley. And I asked, 'Do you happen to know what kind of car Mr Hartley drives?'

'It's red, I know that. Fairly big car. Why?'

I told him about the Buick that had followed us from Santa Monica. That had been a red car.

'I see,' he said, and there was a long silence. Finally, 'Are you busy now?'

'I'll be through with my present assignment at four o'clock. I'll be free after that.' I was through right then, but I didn't want the carriage trade to think I might possibly be hungry.

'I'd like you to keep an eye on her,' he said. 'Have you enough help to do that around the clock?'

'I can arrange for it. Why don't I just go to this Jean Hartley and lean on him a little?'

'Are you—qualified to do that?'

'Not legally,' I answered. 'But physically, I am.'

'No,' he said, 'nothing like that. I can't—afford anything like that. Angela's shopping now, but she should be home by five.'

I phoned Barney Allison and he wasn't busy. I told him it would be the sleep watch for him; I could probably handle the rest of the day.

'It's your client,' he said. 'I figured to get the dirty end of the stick.'

'If you don't need the business, Barney—'

'I do, I do.' he said. 'Command me.'

Then I looked for Jean Hartley in the phone book, but he wasn't in it. He undoubtedly had an unlisted number. I phoned Sam Heller of the bunko squad, but Sam had no recent address of Jean's.

At four-thirty, I was parked on Sunset, about a block from the Ladugo driveway. At four-fifty, a Lincoln Continental turned in and it looked like Angela was behind the wheel.

I'd brought a couple sandwiches and a vacuum bottle of coffee; at six, I ate. At six-thirty, I was enjoying a cigarette and a disk jockey when a Beverly Hills prowl car pulled up behind my flivver.

The one who came around to my side of the car was young and healthy and looked pugnacious. He asked cheerfully if I was having car trouble.

I told him I wasn't.

'Noticed you first almost two hours ago,' he went on. 'You live in the neighborhood, do you?'

'About seven miles from here.' I pulled out the photostat of my license to show him.

He frowned and looked at the other cop, who was standing on the curb. 'Private man.'

The other man said nothing nor did his expression change. It was a bored expression.

'Waiting for someone?' the younger one asked me.

I nodded. 'If you're worried about me, boys, you could go up to the house and talk to Mr Ladugo. But don't let his daughter see you. She's the one I'm waiting for and Mr Ladugo is paying me to wait.'

'Ladugo,' the young man said. 'Oh, yes. Ladugo. Well, good luck, Mr Puma.'

They went away.

Even in Beverly Hills, that name meant something. Puma, now, there was a name you had to look up, but not Ladugo. Why was that? I gave it some thought while I waited and decided it was because he was older, and therefore richer. But he wasn't as old as my dad, and my dad had just finished paying the mortgage on a seven thousand dollar home. He'd been paying on it for twenty years. I must learn to save my money, cut down on cigarettes, or something. Or get into another line of work, like Jean Hartley.

At seven-thirty, the Continental came gliding out of the Ladugo driveway, making all the Cadillacs on Sunset look like 1927 Flints. I gave her a couple of blocks and followed in the Continental's little sister.

There was a guilty knowledge gnawing at me. If we hadn't gone to Zuky's, she wouldn't have met Jean Hartley. And I wouldn't have been hired to follow her.

At a road leading off to the right, just beyond the UCLA campus, the Continental turned and began climbing into the hills. It was a private road, serving a quartette of estates, and I didn't follow immediately. If it dead-ended up above, Angela and I would eventually come nose to nose.

I waited on Sunset for five minutes and then turned in the road. The houses were above the road and four mailboxes were set into a field-stone pillar at the first driveway. Atop the pillar were four names cut out of wrought iron and one of the names was Ladugo. Her trip seemed innocent enough; I drove out again to wait on Sunset.

It was dark, now, and the headlights of the heavy traffic heading toward town came barreling around the curve in a steady stream of light. My radio gave me the day's news and some comments on the news and then a succession of platters.

A little before ten o'clock, the Continental came out on Sunset again and headed west. I gave it a three block lead.

It went through Santa Monica at a speed that invited arrest, but she was lucky, tonight. On Lincoln Avenue, she swung toward Venice.

Not back to Bugsy's, I thought. *Not back to that rendezvous of the literate and the witty, that charming salon of the sophisticated.* A block from Windward, she parked. I was parking a half block behind that when she went through the doorway.

I got out and walked across the street before going down that way. When I came abreast of the bar, I could see her sitting next to a man whose back was to me. I walked down another half block and saw the red Buick four-door Riviera. The registration slip on the steering column informed me that this was the car of Jean Hartley. His address was there, too, and I copied it.

Then I went back to wait.

I didn't have long. In about ten minutes, both of them came out of Bugsy's. For a few moments, they talked and then separated and headed for their cars.

I followed Angela's, though the Buick seemed to be going to the same place. Both of them turned right on Wilshire and headed back toward Westwood.

Westwood was the address on Jean Hartley's steering column. And that's where they finally stopped, in front of a sixteen unit apartment building of fieldstone and cerise stucco, built around a sixty foot swimming pool.

I waited until they had walked out of sight and then came back to the floodlighted patio next to the pool. A list of the tenants was on a board here and one of the tenants was *Hartley Associates*.

Some associates he'd have. With numbers under their pictures. But who could guess that by looking at him? I went sniffing around until I found his door.

There was an el in the hallway at this point, undoubtedly formed by the fireplace in the apartment. It afforded me enough cover.

Hartley Associates. What could that mean? Phoney stock? I heard music and I heard laughter. The music was Chopin's and the laughter was Angela's. Even in the better California apartment houses, the walls are thin.

Some boys certainly do make out.

I heard a thud that sounded like a refrigerator door closing.

I wanted to smoke, but smoke would reveal me to others who might pass along the hall. Chopin changed to Debussy and I thought I heard the tinkle of ice in glasses. Light music, cool drinks and a dark night—while I stood in the hall, hating them both.

Time dragged along on its belly.

And then, right after eleven o'clock, I thought I heard a whimper. There had been silence for minutes and this whimper was of the complaining type. I was moving toward the door, where I could hear better, when I heard the scream.

I tried the knob and the door was locked. I stepped back and put a foot into the panel next to the knob and the door came open on the second kick.

Light from the hall poured into the dark apartment and I could see

Angela Ladugo, up against a wall, the palms of her hands pressed against the wall, her staring eyes frightened.

She was wearing nothing but that almost translucent skin and her fair hair. I took one step into the room and found a light switch next to the door.

When the lights went on, I could see Hartley sitting on a davenport near the fireplace and I headed his way. I never got there.

As unconsciousness poured into my reverberating skull, I remembered that the sign downstairs had warned me he had associates.

I came to on the floor. Hartley sat on the davenport, smoking. There was no sign of Angela Ladugo or anyone else.

I asked, 'Where is she?'

'Miss Ladugo? She's gone home. Why?'

'Why? She screamed, didn't she? What the hell were you doing to her?'

He frowned. 'I didn't hear any scream. Are you sure it was in this apartment?'

'You know it was. Who hit me?'

Hartley pointed at an ottoman. 'Nobody hit you. You stumbled over that.'

I put a hand on the floor and got slowly to my feet. The pain in my skull seemed to pulse with my heartbeat.

Hartley said, 'I haven't called the police—yet. I thought perhaps you had a reason for breaking into my apartment.'

'Call 'em,' I said. 'Or I will.'

He pointed toward a hallway. 'There's the phone. You're free to use it.'

I came over to stand in front of him. 'Maybe I ought to work you over first. They might be easier on you than I'd be.'

He looked at me without fear. 'Suit yourself. That would add assault to the rap.'

I had nothing and he knew it. I wasn't about to throw the important name of Angela Ladugo to a scandal-hungry press. I was being paid to protect her, not publicize her. I studied him for seconds, while reason fought the rage in me.

Finally, I asked, 'What's the racket this time, Jean?'

He smiled. 'Don't be that way, Joe. So the girl likes me. That's a crime? She was a little high and noisy, but you can bet she's been that way before. Did she hang around? If she'd been in trouble, wouldn't she have stayed around to see that you were all right?'

'How do I know what happened to her?' I asked.

He looked at his watch. 'She should be phoning any minute, from home. I'll let you talk to her if you want.'

I sat down on the davenport. 'I'll wait.'

He leaned back and studied the end of his cigarette. 'What were you doing out there, Joe? Are you working for her father?'

'No. I felt responsible for her meeting you. I'm working for myself.'

He smiled. 'I'll bet. I can just see Joe Puma making this big noble gesture. Don't kid me.'

I said slowly, 'This isn't the right town to buck anyone named Ladugo, Jean. He could really railroad you.'

'Maybe. I can't help it if the girl likes me.'

'That girl's sick,' I said. 'She has some compulsion to debase herself. Is that the soft spot you're working?'

'She likes me,' he said for the third time. 'Does there have to be a dollar in it? She's a beautiful girl.'

'For you,' I said, 'there has to be a dollar in it. And I intend to see you don't ever latch onto it. I've got friends in the Department, Jean.'

He sighed. 'And all I've got is the love of this poor woman.'

The phone rang, and he went over to it. I came right along.

He said, 'Hello,' and handed me the phone.

I heard Angela say, 'Jean? Is everything all right? There won't be any trouble, will there?'

'None,' I said. 'Are you home?'

'I'm home. Jean—is that you—?'

I gave him the phone and went into the kitchen to get a drink of water. The lump on the back of my head was sore, but the rattles were diminishing in my brain.

If she was home, she was now under the eye of Barney Allison. I could use some rest.

I went out without saying any more to Jean, but I didn't go right home. I drove back to Venice.

The big man behind the bar greeted me with a frown when I came in. I said, 'I'd like to talk to you.'

'It's not mutual.'

'I'd like to talk about Angela Ladugo. I'm being paid to see that she doesn't get into trouble.'

He looked down at the bar to where a man was nursing a beer. He looked back at me. 'Keep your voice low. I don't want any of these slobs to know her name.'

I nodded. 'The man who met her here tonight can do her more harm than any of your customers are likely to. His name is Jean Hartley. Have you ever heard of him?'

'I've heard of him.' His eyes were bleak.

I said, 'I'll have a beer if it's less than two dollars.'

He drew one from the tap. 'On the house. What's Hartley's pitch?'

'I don't know. What's *your* attraction, Bugsy?'

He looked at me suspiciously. 'I knew her mother. Way, way back, when we were both punks. I was just a preliminary boy and her mother danced at the *Blue Garter*. I guess you're too young to remember the *Blue Garter*.'

'Burlesque?'

'Something like that. A cafe. But Angela Walker was no tramp—don't get that idea. Her folks back in England were solid middle-class people.'

'I see. And that's where Ladugo met her, at the *Blue Garter*?'

'I don't know. She was dancing there when she met him.'

'And you kept up the acquaintanceship through the years?'

He colored slightly. 'No. Not that she was a snob. But Venice is a hell of a long ways from Beverly Hills.'

'She's dead now?'

'Almost three years.'

'And Angela has renewed the friendship. Her mother must have talked about you.'

'I guess she did. What's it to you, Mac?'

'Nothing, I guess. I'm just looking for a pattern.'

'We don't sell 'em, here. I thought you were watching the girl.'

'She's home,' I said. 'Another man will watch her until I go back to work in the morning. This is pretty good beer.'

'For twenty cents, you can have another one.'

I put two dimes on the counter, and said, 'Hartley scares me. He's tricky and handsome and completely unscrupulous.'

He put a fresh glass of beer in front of me. 'I wouldn't call him handsome.'

'Angela did. She went up to his apartment tonight. I broke in and somebody clobbered me. When I came to, she was gone. But she phoned him from home while I was still there.'

Bugsy looked at me evenly. 'Maybe the old man should have hired somebody who knew his business.'

'You might have a point there. I'll go when I finish the beer.'

He went down to serve the man at the other end of the bar. He came back to say, 'I always mixed Angela's drinks real, real weak. She's got no tolerance for alcohol.'

I said nothing, nursing the beer.

Bugsy said, 'Can't you muscle this Hartley a little? He didn't look like much to me.'

'He's a citizen,' I said, 'just like you. And the Department is full of boys who hate private operatives, just like you do.'

'Maybe I resented the old man sending you down here to drag her home. Some of the joints she's been in, this could be a church.'

'He didn't send me down *here*. I wound up here because she did. I don't think he knows where she goes.'

Bugsy drew himself a small beer. He looked at it as he said, 'And maybe he doesn't care. Maybe he just hired you to keep the Ladugo name out of the papers.'

'That could be,' I said, and finished my beer. 'Goodnight, Bugsy.'

He nodded.

At home, I took a warm shower and set the alarm for seven o'clock. I wanted to write my reports of the two days before going over to relieve Barney.

I'd finished them by eight, and a little before nine, I drove up in front of the Ladugo driveway. There was no sign of Barney Allison.

He wouldn't desert a post; I figured Angela must have already left the house. I drove to the office. If Barney had a chance to leave a message, he would have left it with my phone-answering service.

Barney's Chev was parked about four doors from the entrance to my office. Angela wasn't in sight; I went over to the Chev.

Barney said, 'She went through that doorway about fifteen minutes ago. Maybe she's waiting for you.'

'Maybe. Okay, Barney, I'll take it from here.'

He yawned and nodded and drove away.

Angela Ladugo was waiting in the first floor lobby, sitting on a rattan love seat. Her gaze didn't quite meet mine as I walked over.

When I was standing in front of her, she looked at the floor. Her voice was very low, 'What—happened last night?'

'You tell me. Do you want to go up to the office?'

She shook her head. 'It's quiet enough here.' She looked up. 'I—can't drink very well. You might think that's absurd, but it's—I mean, I really don't know what happened last night. I wasn't really—conscious.'

'Didn't you drive home?'

She shook her head. 'I'm almost sure I didn't. I think someone drove me home in my car. Was it Jean?'

'You don't need to lie to me, Miss Ladugo,' I said gently. 'I'm on your side.'

'I'm not lying.'

I said, 'You phoned Hartley when you got home. You didn't sound drunk to me then. You just sounded scared.' Her eyes were blank. 'You were there?'

'That's right. You're not going to see Hartley again, are you?'

She shook her head. 'Of course not. Are you—still going to follow me?'

'Shouldn't I?'

She took a deep breath that sounded like relief. 'I don't know. Are you going to tell my dad about—last night?'

'Most of it is in the report I wrote. *Most* of it. I'm not sure where the line of ethics would be. It isn't my intention to shock your father or—hurt you.'

She looked at the floor again. 'Thank you.'

The downcast eyes bit was right out of the Brontës; I hoped she didn't think I was falling for her delicate lady routine.

She looked up with a smile. 'As long as you're going to be following me, why don't we go together?' Charm she had, even though I knew it was premeditated.

'Fine,' I said. 'It'll save gas.'

We went to some shops I had never seen before—on the inside, that is. Like her poorer sisters, she shopped without buying. We went to *Roland's* for lunch.

There, under the impulse of a martini, I asked her, 'Were you and your mother closer than you are with your father?'

She nodded, her eyes searching my face.

'You don't—resent your father?'

'I love him. Can't we talk about something else?'

We tried. We discussed some movies we'd both seen and one book we'd both read. Her thoughts were banal; her opinions adolescent. We ran out of words, with the arrival of the coffee.

Then, as we finished, she said, 'Why don't we go home and talk to my father? I'm sure I don't need to be watched anymore.'

'Might look bad for me,' I said. 'So far as he knows, you're not aware I'm following you.'

Some of her geniality was gone. 'I'll phone him.'

Which she did, right there at the table. And after a few moments of sweet talk, she handed the phone to me.

Her father said, 'Pretend I'm taking you off the job. But keep an eye on her.'

'All right, sir,' I said, and handed the phone back to her.

When she'd finished talking, she smiled at me. 'You can put the check on the expense account, I'm sure. Good luck, Mr Puma.'

'Thank you,' I said.

We both rose and then she paused, to suddenly stare at me. 'I haven't annoyed you, have I? I mean, that report about last night—this doesn't mean you'll—make it more complete?'

I shook my head. 'And I hope you won't betray your father's trust.'

The smile came back. 'Of course I won't.'

I asked, 'How do I get back to my car?'

'You can get a cab, I'm sure,' she said. 'I'd drop you, but I have so much more shopping to do.'

She had me. I couldn't follow her in a cab and I couldn't admit I was going to follow her. I nodded goodbye to her and signaled for the check.

I got a cab in five minutes and was back to my car in ten more. And, on a hunch, I drove right over to Westwood.

I came up Hartley's street just as the Continental disappeared around the corner. A truck came backing out of a driveway, and, by the time I got started again, she must have made another turn. Because the big black car was nowhere in sight.

I drove back to Hartley's apartment building. There was an off chance he was home and she had arranged to meet him somewhere. I parked in front.

Ten minutes of waiting, and I went up to his door. I could hear a record player giving out with Brahms. I rang the bell. No answer. I knocked. No answer.

The music stopped and in a few seconds started over again. Hartley could be asleep or out, or maybe he liked the record. I tried the door; it was locked.

Was there another door? Not in the hallway, but perhaps there was one opening on the balconies overlooking the pool.

I found that there was a small sun-deck right off Hartley's door. The door was locked but I could see into his living room through a window opening onto the sun-deck. I could see Hartley.

He was on the floor, his face and forehead covered with dark blood. I didn't know if he was dead, but he wasn't moving.

I went along the balcony to the first neighbor's door and rang the bell. A Negro woman in a maid's uniform opened it and I told her, 'The tenant in Apartment 22 has been seriously hurt. Would you phone the police and tell them to bring a doctor along? It's Mr Hartley and he's on the floor in his living room. They'll have to break in, unless the manager's around.'

'I'll phone the manager, too,' she said.

I went to the nearest pay phone and called Mr Ladugo. He wasn't home. I phoned Barney Allison and told him what had happened.

'And you didn't wait for the police to arrive? You're in trouble, Joe.'

'Maybe. What I want you to do is keep phoning Mr Ladugo. When you get him, tell him what happened. And tell him his daughter was just leaving the place as I drove up.'

'Man, we could *both* lose our licenses.'

'You couldn't. Do as I say now.'

'All right. But I'm not identifying myself. And when the law nabs you, you'd better not tell them you told me about this.'

'I won't. Get going, man!'

From there, I drove to Santa Monica, to one of the modest sections of that snug, smug suburb where one of my older lady friends lived. She was well past seventy, and retired. But for forty years, she had handled the society page for Los Angeles' biggest newspaper.

She was out in front, pruning her roses. She smiled at me. 'Hello, stranger. If it's money you want, I'm broke. If it's a drink, you know where the liquor is.'

'Just information, Frances,' I said. 'I want to know all you know about the Ladugos.'

'A fascinating story,' she said. 'Come on in; I'll have a drink with you.'

She told me what she knew plus the gossip.

Then I said, 'Because Ladugo's wife was messing around with this other man, it doesn't necessarily follow that Ladugo wasn't the child's father. She and the other man could have been enjoying a perfectly platonic friendship.'

'They might have been. But I don't think so. And neither did any of their friends at that time. I mean her good friends, not the catty ones. They were frankly scandalized by her behavior.'

'All right,' I said. 'Your gossip has usually proven more accurate than some supposedly factual stories. May I use your phone?'

She nodded.

I phoned Barney Allison and he told me I could reach Mr Ladugo at home. I phoned Mr Ladugo.

He said, 'My daughter's here now, Mr Puma. She tells me that she never went into Mr Hartley's apartment. She stayed there quite awhile, ringing his bell, because she could hear music inside and she thought he must be home.'

'She told me this morning,' I said, 'that she was never going to see him again. She could be lying now, too.'

A pause. 'I—don't think she is. She's very frightened.' Another pause. 'How about Hartley? Is he dead?'

'I don't know. Did Hartley try to blackmail you, Mr Ladugo?'

'Blackmail me? Why? How?'

'Let me talk to Miss Ladugo, please,' I said.

His voice was harsh. 'Is something going on I don't know about?'

'Could be. But I don't know about it either. Could I speak with Miss Ladugo?'

Another pause and then, 'Just a moment.'

The soft and humble voice of Angela Ladugo, 'What is it you want, Mr Puma?'

'The truth, if it's in you. Was Hartley blackmailing you? What was it, pictures?'

'I don't know what you're talking about, Mr Puma.'

'Okay,' I said. 'I'm supposed to be working for your father. But I'm not going to lose my license over a job. I'm going to the police now.'

Silence for a few seconds, and then, 'That would be stupid. That would be extremely poor business. Wait, here's Father.'

After an interval Mr Ladugo got on the wire. His voice was almost a whisper. 'Will you come over here, first, Mr Puma? And would you bring your reports along?'

'I'll be there in less than an hour,' I said.

As I hung up, Frances said, 'Scandal, eh? And do I get let in on it? No, no. I tell you all and you tell me nothing.'

'Honey,' I said, 'you're a reporter. Telling all is your business. But *privacy* is what I sell.'

'I'm not a reporter any more, Wop. I'm a lonely old woman looking for gossip to warm my heart over. Don't hurry back, you slob.'

'I love you, Frances,' I said. 'I love you all the ways there are. And I'll be back with the gossip.'

I didn't stop for the reports. I went over to the office for that purpose, but I saw the Department car in front and kept going. Sergeant Sam Heller would remember that I was asking about Jean Hartley the other day and that's why the law was waiting in front of my office. This would indicate that Hartley was either dead or unconscious, or the law would be parked somewhere else.

In the Ladugo home, Papa was waiting for me with Angela in his library. He sat in a leather chair behind his desk; Angela stood near the sliding glass doors that led to the pool and patio.

I said, 'I couldn't get the reports. The police were waiting for me at my office, so I kept moving.'

He nodded. 'Somebody must have recognized you.'

'I guess.'

He looked at his daughter's back and again at me. 'Why did you mention blackmail?'

'You tell me,' I said. 'Has it happened before?'

He colored. Angela turned. Her voice was ice. 'What kind of remark was that, Mr Puma?'

I looked at her coolly. 'Blackmail could be a good way to milk your dad. Especially, if you worked with Hartley.'

'And why should I cheat my own father? I'm his only child, Mr Puma.'

'Maybe,' I suggested, 'you get everything you want—except money. I don't know, of course, but that's one thought.'

Ladugo said, 'Aren't you being insolent, Mr Puma?'

'I guess I am,' I said. 'Your daughter brings out the worst in me, sir.' I took a deep breath and looked at him quietly.

He was rolling a pencil on this desk with the flat of his hand. 'When you finally talk to the police, it wouldn't be necessary to tell them *why* you were at Hartley's apartment, would it.'

'I'm afraid it would. If he's dead, I'm sure it would.'

He continued to roll the pencil and now he was looking at it, absorbed in the wonder of his moving hand. 'You'd have to tell them the truth? I mean, there could be other reasons why you were over there, couldn't there?'

I smiled. 'For how much?'

He looked up hopefully. 'For—a thousand dollars?'

I shook my head. 'Not even for a million.'

He was beet red and there was hate in his eyes. 'Then why did you mention money?'

'Because I wanted you to come right out with a bribe offer. I don't like pussy-footing.'

I looked over at his daughter and thought I saw a smile on that sly face. I looked back at Mr Ladugo and was ashamed of myself. He was thoroughly humiliated. His hands were on top of the desk now and he was staring at them.

I said, 'I'm sorry. Now that the damage is done, I'm sorry. But there has been such a mess of deception in this business, I was getting sick. Believe me, Mr Ladugo, if I'm not forced to mention your name, I won't. Tell me honestly, though, have you been blackmailed before?'

He looked at his daughter and back at the desk. He nodded.

10

DAVID ELY

The Sailing Club

Of all the important social clubs in the city, the most exclusive was also the most casual and the least known to outsiders. This was a small group of venerable origin but without formal organization. Indeed, it was without a name, although it was generally referred to as the Sailing Club, for its sole apparent activity was a short sailing cruise each summer. There were no meetings, no banquets, no other functions—in fact, no club building existed, so that it was difficult even to classify it as a club.

Nevertheless, the Sailing Club represented the zenith of a successful businessman's social ambitions, for its handful of members included the most influential men in the city, and many a top executive would have traded all of his other hard-won attainments for an opportunity to join. Even those who had no interest in sailing would willingly have sweated through long practice hours to learn, if the Club had beckoned. Few were invited, however. The Club held its membership to the minimum necessary for the operation of its schooner, and not until death or debility created a vacancy was a new man admitted.

Who were the members of this select group? It was almost impossible to be absolutely certain. For one thing, since the Club had no legal existence, the members did not list it in their *Who's Who* paragraphs or in any other catalogue of their honors. Furthermore, they appeared reluctant to discuss it in public. At luncheons or parties, for example, the Club might be mentioned, but those who brought up the name did not seem to be members, and as for those distinguished gentlemen who carefully refrained at such times from commenting on the subject—who could tell? They might be members, or they might deliberately be assuming an air of significant detachment in the hope of being mistaken for members.

Naturally, the hint of secrecy which was thus attached to the Sailing Club made it all the more desirable in the eyes of the rising business leaders who yearned for the day when they might be tapped for membership. They realized that the goal was remote and their chances not too likely, but each still treasured in his heart the hope that in time this greatest of all distinctions would reward a lifetime of struggle and success.

One of these executives, a man named John Goforth, could without immodesty consider himself unusually eligible for the Club. He was, first of all, a brilliant success in the business world. Although he was not yet fifty, he was president of a dynamic corporation which had become preeminent in several fields through a series of mergers he himself had expertly negotiated. Each year, under his ambitious direction, the corporation expanded into new areas, snapping up less nimble competitors and spurring the others into furious battles for survival.

Early in his career Goforth had been cautious, even anxious, but year by year his confidence had increased, so that now he welcomed new responsibilities, just as he welcomed the recurrent business crises where one serious mistake in judgment might cause a large enterprise to founder and to sink. His quick rise had not dulled this sense of excitement, but rather had sharpened it. More and more, he put routine matters into the hands of subordinates, while he zestfully attacked those special problems that forced from him the full measure of daring and skill. He found himself not merely successful, but powerful, a man whose passage through the halls of a club left a wake of murmurs, admiring and envious.

This was the life he loved, and his mastery of it was his chief claim to recognition by the most influential social group of all, the Sailing Club. There was another factor which he thought might count in his favor: his lifelong attachment to the sea and to sailing.

As a boy, he had stood in fascination at the ocean's edge, staring out beyond the breakers to the distant sails, sometimes imagining himself to be the captain of a great ship; at those times, the toy bucket in his hand had become a long spyglass, or a pirate's cutlass, and the strip of reed that fluttered from his fingers had been transformed into a gallant pennant, or a black and wicked skull-and-bones. At the age of ten, he had been taught to sail at his family's summer place on the shore; later, he was allowed to take his father's boat out alone—and later still, when he was almost of college age, he was chosen for the crew of one of the yacht-club entries in the big regatta. By that time, he had come to regard the sea as a resourceful antagonist in a struggle all the more absorbing because of the danger, and a danger that was far from theoretical, for every summer at least one venturesome sailor would be lost forever, far from land, and even a sizable boat might fail to return from some holiday excursion.

Now, in his middle years, John Goforth knew the sea as something more than an invigorating physical challenge. It was that still, but he recognized that it was also an inexhaustible source of renewal for him. The harsh sting of blown spray was a climate in which he thrived, and the erratic thrusts of strength that swayed his little boat evoked a passionate response of answering strength within himself. In those moments—like the supreme moments of business crisis—he felt almost godlike, limitless, as he shared the ocean's solitude, its fierce and fitful communion with the wind, the sun and the sky.

As time passed, membership in the Sailing Club became the single remaining honor which Goforth coveted but did not have. He told himself: not a member—no, not yet! But of course he realized that this prize would not necessarily fall to him at all, despite his most strenuous efforts to seize it. He sought to put the matter out of his mind; then, failing that, he decided to learn more about the Club, to satisfy his curiosity, at least.

It was no easy task. But he was a resourceful and determined man, and before long he had obtained a fairly accurate idea of the real membership of the Sailing Club. All of these men were prominent in business or financial circles, but Goforth found it strange that they seemed to lack any other common characteristic of background or attainments. Most were university men, but a few were not. There was, similarly, a variety of ethnic strains represented among them. Some were foreign-born, even, and one or two were still foreign citizens. Moreover, while some members had a long association with sailing, others seemed to have no interest whatever in the sea.

Yet just as Goforth was prepared to shrug away the matter and conclude that there was no unifying element among the members of the Sailing Club, he became aware of some subtle element that resisted analysis. Did it actually exist, or did he merely imagine it? He studied the features of the supposed Club members more closely. They were casual, yes, and somewhat aloof—even bored, it seemed. And yet there was something else, something buried: a kind of suppressed exhilaration that winked out briefly, at odd moments, as though they shared some monumental private joke.

As his perplexing survey of the Club members continued, Goforth became conscious of a quite different sensation. He could not be sure, but he began to suspect that while he was quietly inspecting them, they in turn were examining him.

The most suggestive indication was his recent friendship with an older man named Marshall, who was almost certainly a Club member. Marshall, the chairman of a giant corporation, had taken the lead in their acquaintanceship, which had developed to the point where they lunched together at least once a week. Their conversation was ordinary enough—of business matters, usually, and sometimes of sailing, for both were ardent seamen—but each time, Goforth had a stronger impression that he was undergoing some delicate kind of interrogation which was connected with the Sailing Club.

He sought to subdue his excitement. But he often found that his palms were moist and, as he wiped them, he disciplined his nervousness, telling himself angrily that he was reacting like a college freshman being examined by the president of some desirable fraternity.

At first he tried to moderate his personality, as well. He sensed that his aggressive attitude toward his work, for example, was not in harmony with the blasé manner of the Club members. He attempted a show of nonchalance, of indifference—and all at once he became annoyed. He had nothing to be ashamed of. Why should he try to imitate what was false to his nature? He was *not* bored or indifferent, he was *not* disengaged from the competitive battle of life, and he would not pretend otherwise. The Club could elect him or not, as it chose.

At his next session with Marshall, he went out of his way to make clear how fully he enjoyed the daily combat of business. He spoke, in fact, more emphatically than he had intended to, for he was irritated by what seemed to be the other man's ironic amusement.

Once Marshall broke in, wryly: 'So you really find the press of business life to be thoroughly satisfying and exciting?'

'Yes, I do,' said Goforth. He repressed the desire to add: 'And don't you, too?' He decided that if the Sailing Club was nothing but a refuge for burned-out men, bored by life and by themselves, then he wanted no part of it.

At the same time, he was disturbed by the thought that he had failed. The Sailing Club might be a worthless objective for a man of his temperament—still he did not like to feel that it might be beyond his grasp.

After he had parted none too cordially from Marshall, he paced along the narrow streets toward the harbor, hoping that the ocean winds would blow away his discontent. As he reached the water's edge, he saw a customs launch bounce by across the widening wake of a huge liner. A veil of spray blew softly toward him. Greedily he awaited the familiar reassurance of its bitter scent. But when it came, it was not quite what he had expected. He frowned out at the water. No, it was not at all the same.

That winter, Goforth became ill for the first time in years. It was influenza, and not a serious case, but the convalescent period stretched on and on, and before he was well enough to do any work, it was spring.

His troubles dated from that illness, he decided; not business troubles, for he had a fine executive staff, and the company did not suffer. The troubles were within himself. First, he went through a mild depression (the doctors had of course cautioned him of this as an after-effect), and then an uncharacteristic lassitude, broken by intermittent self-doubts. He noted, for example, that his executive vice-president was doing a good job of filling in the presidency—and then subsequently realized that this fact had no particular meaning for him. He became uneasy. He should have felt impatient to get back in harness, to show them that old Goforth still was on top.

But he had felt no emotion. It was this that disturbed him. Was it simply a delayed result of illness, or was it some inevitable process of aging which the illness had accelerated? He tested himself grimly. He made an analysis of a stock program proposal worked out by one of the economists. He did a masterly job; he knew it himself, with a rush of familiar pride. In its way, his study was as good as anything he had ever done. No, he was not growing feeble—not yet. The malaise that possessed him was something else, undoubtedly not permanent.

That summer he spent with his family at their place on the shore. He did not feel up to sailing; he watched others sail as he lay on the beach, and was again mildly surprised by his reaction. He did not envy them at all.

In the fall he was back at his desk, in full charge once more. But he was careful to follow the advice of the doctors and the urgings of his wife, and kept his schedule light. He avoided the rush-hour trains by going to work late and leaving early, and two or three times a month he remained at home, resting. He knew that he once would have chafed impatiently at such a regimen, but now he thought it sensible and had no sensation of loss. As always, he passed the routine problems down to his staff; but now, it seemed, so many things appeared routine that there was not much left on his desk. The shock came late in winter, when he realized that he had actually turned over to his staff a question of vital importance. It had been well-handled, true enough, and he had kept in touch with its progress, but he should have attended to it personally. Why hadn't he? Was he going through some kind of metamorphosis that would end by his becoming a semi-active chairman of the board? Perhaps he should consider early retirement. . . .

It was in his new condition of uncertainty that he had another encounter with Marshall, this time at a private university club to which they both belonged. Marshall offered to stand him a drink, and commented that he seemed to have recovered splendidly from his illness.

Goforth glanced at him, suspecting irony. He felt fully Marshall's age now, and looked, he thought, even older. But he accepted the drink, and they began to talk.

As they chatted, it occurred to him that he had nothing to lose by speaking frankly of his present perplexities. Marshall *was* older, in point of fact; possibly the man could offer some advice.

And so Goforth spoke of his illness, his slow convalescence, his disinclination to resume his old working pace, even his unthinkable transfer of responsibility to his staff—and strangest of all, his own feeling that it did not really matter, none of it.

Marshall listened attentively, nodding his head in quiet understanding, as if he had heard scores of similar accounts.

At length, Goforth's voice trailed off. He glanced at Marshall in mild embarrassment.

'So,' said Marshall calmly, 'you don't find business life so exciting any more?'

Goforth stirred in irritation at this echo of their previous conversation. 'No,' he replied, shortly.

Marshall gave him a sharp, amused look. He seemed almost triumphant, and Goforth was sorry he had spoken at all. Then Marshall leaned forward and said:

'What would you say to an invitation to join the Sailing Club?'

Goforth stared at him. 'Are you serious?'

'Quite so.'

It was Goforth's turn to be amused. 'You know, if you'd suggested this two years ago, I'd have jumped at the chance. But now—'

'Yes?' Marshall seemed not at all taken aback.

'But now, it seems of little importance. No offense, mind you.'

'I completely understand.'

'To put it with absolute frankness, I don't honestly care.'

Marshall smiled. 'Excellent!' he declared. 'That's precisely what makes you eligible!' He winked at Goforth in a conspiratorial way. 'We're all of that frame of mind, my friend. We're all suffering from that same disease——'

'But I'm well now.'

Marshall chuckled. 'So the doctors may say. But you know otherwise, eh?' He laughed. 'The only cure, my friend, is to cast your lot with fellow sufferers—the Sailing Club!'

He continued with the same heartiness to speak of the Club. Most of it Goforth already had heard. There were sixteen members, enough to provide the entire crew for the Club's schooner during its annual summer cruise. One of the sixteen had recently died, and Goforth would be nominated immediately to fill the vacancy; one word of assent from him would be enough to assure his election.

Goforth listened politely; but he had reservations. Marshall did not say exactly what the Club did on its cruises, and Goforth moodily assumed it was not worth mentioning. Probably the members simply drank too much and sang old college songs—hardly an enviable prospect.

Marshall interrupted his musing. 'I promise you one thing,' he said, more seriously. 'You won't be bored.'

There was a peculiar intensity in the way he spoke; Goforth wondered at it, then gave up and shrugged his shoulders. Why not? He sighed and smiled: 'All right. Of course. I'm honored, Marshall.'

The cruise was scheduled to begin on the last day of July. The evening before, Goforth was driven by Marshall far out along the shore to the estate of another member, who kept the schooner at his private dock. By the time they arrived, all of the others were there, and Goforth was duly introduced as the new crewman.

He knew them already, either as acquaintances or by reputation. They included men so eminent that they were better known than the companies or banking houses they headed. There were a few less prominent, but none below Goforth's own rank, and certainly none was in any sense obscure. He was glad to note that all of them had fought their way through the hard competitive years, just as he had done, and then in the course of the evening he slowly came to realize a further fact—that not one of these men had achieved any major triumph in recent years. He took some comfort from this. If he had fallen into a strange lassitude, then so perhaps had they. Marshall had evidently been right. He was among 'fellow sufferers'. This thought cheered him, and he moved more easily from group to group, chatting with as much self-possession as if he had been a member of the Club for years.

He had already been told that the ship was in full readiness and that the group was to sail before dawn, and so he was not surprised when the host, a gigantic old man named Teacher, suggested at nine o'clock that they all retire.

'Has the new member signed on?' someone inquired.

'Not yet,' said Teacher. He beckoned to Goforth with one huge hairless hand. 'This way, my friend,' he said. He led Goforth into an adjoining room, with several of the others following and, after unlocking a wall safe, withdrew a large black volume so worn with age that bits of the binding flaked off in his fingers.

He laid it on a table, thumbed through its pages and at length called Goforth over and handed him a pen. Goforth noticed that the old man had covered the top portion of the page with a blank sheet of paper; all that showed beneath were signatures, those of the other members.

'Sign the articles, seaman,' said Teacher gruffly, in imitation of an old-time sea captain.

Goforth grinned and bent over the page, although at the same time he felt a constitutional reluctance to sign something he could not first examine. He glanced at the faces surrounding him. Someone chuckled, and a voice in the background said: 'You can read the whole thing, if you like—after the cruise.'

There was nothing to do but sign, so he signed boldly, with a flourish, and then turned to shake the hands thrust out to him. 'Well done!' someone exclaimed. They all crowded around then to initial his signature as witnesses, and Teacher insisted that they toast the new member with brandy, which they did cheerfully enough, and then went off to bed. Goforth told himself that the ceremony had been a juvenile bit of foolishness, but somehow it had warmed him with the feeling of fellowship.

His sense of well-being persisted the next morning, when in the predawn darkness he was awakened and hurriedly got dressed to join the others for breakfast.

It was still dark when they went down to the ship, each man carrying his seabag. As he climbed aboard, Goforth was just able to make out the name painted in white letters on the bow: *Freedom IV*.

Since he was experienced, he was assigned a deckhand's job, and as he worked alongside the others to ready the sails for hoisting, he sensed a marked change in the attitude of the men.

The Club had its reputation for being casual, and certainly the night before the members had seemed relaxed to the point of indolence, but there was a difference now. Each man carried out his tasks swiftly, in dead seriousness and without wasted motion, so that in a short time, the *Freedom IV* was skimming eastward along the Sound toward the heart of the red rising sun. Goforth was surprised and pleased. There was seamanship and discipline and sober purpose on this ship, and he gladly discarded his earlier notion that they would wallow about with no program beyond liquor and cards.

With satisfaction, he made a leisurely tour of the ship. Everything was smart and sharp, on deck and below, in the sleeping quarters and galley. Teacher, who seemed to be the captain, had a small cabin forward and it, too, was a model of neatness. Goforth poked his head inside to admire it further. Teacher was not there, but in a moment the old man stepped through a narrow door on the opposite bulkhead, leading to some compartment beneath the bow, followed by two other members. They greeted Goforth pleasantly, but closed and locked the door behind them, and did not offer to show him the compartment. He, for his part, refrained from asking, but later in the day he inspected the deck above it and saw that what had seemed earlier to be merely a somewhat unorthodox arrangement of crisscross deck planking was actually a hatchway, cleverly concealed. He crouched and ran his fingers along the hidden edges of the hatch, then glanced up guiltily to meet Marshall's eyes. Marshall seemed amused, but all he said was: 'Ready for chow?'

In the next few days, Goforth occasionally wondered what the forward compartment contained. Then he all but forgot about it, for his enjoyment of the voyage was too deep-felt to permit even the smallest question to trouble him. He was more content now than he had been in many months. It was not because he was sailing again, but rather, he believed, because he was actively sharing with others like himself a vigorous and demanding experience. It seemed, indeed, that they formed a little corporation there on the *Freedom IV*—and what a corporation! Goforth's companion on the dogwatch, who wore a huge red bandanna around his head, was an international banker who treated with the chiefs of foreign governments on a basis of equality, and even the member who occupied the lowly post of cook's helper was a man accustomed to deal in terms of millions.

Yes, what a crew it was! Now Goforth began to understand the suppressed excitement he had long ago detected as a subtle mark identifying members of the Sailing Club. Theirs was no ordinary cruise, but a grand exercise of seamanship, as if they had decided to pit their collective will against the force and cunning of the ocean, to retrieve through a challenge to that most brutal of antagonists the sense of daring which they once had found in their work.

They were searching for something. For a week they had sailed a zigzag course, always out of sight of land, but Goforth had not the faintest notion of their whereabouts, nor did he judge that it would be proper for him to inquire. Were they pursuing a storm to provide them with some ultimate test with the sea? He could not be sure. And yet he was quite willing to wait, for there was happiness enough in each waking moment aboard the *Freedom IV*.

On the eighth day, he perceived an abrupt change. There was an almost tangible mood of expectancy among the members, a quickening of pace and movement, a tightening of smiles and laughter that reminded him oddly of the atmosphere in a corporation board room, when the final crisis of some serious negotiation approaches. He guessed that some word had been passed among the crew, save for himself, the neophyte.

The men were tense, but it was the invigorating tensity of trained athletes waiting in confidence for a test worthy of their skills. The mood was infectious; without having any idea of what lay ahead, Goforth began to share the exhilaration of his shipmates and to scan the horizon eagerly.

For what? He did not care now. Whatever it might be, he felt an elemental stirring of pride and strength and knew that he would meet whatever ultimate trial impended with all the nerve and daring that his life had stamped into his being.

The *Freedom IV* changed course and plunged due east toward a haze that lay beneath heavier clouds. Goforth thought perhaps the storm lay that way and keenly watched for its signs. There was none, but he took some heart at the sight of another yacht coming toward them, and hopefully imagined that it was retreating from the combat which the *Freedom IV* seemed so ardently to seek.

He studied the sky. The clouds drifted aimlessly, then broke apart for a moment to disclose a regular expanse of blue. He sighed as he saw it, and glanced around at the other crewmen to share his feeling of frustration.

But there was no disappointment on those faces. Instead, the mood of tension seemed heightened to an almost unbearable degree. The men stood strained and stiff, their features set rigidly, their eyes quick and piercing as they stared across the water. He searched their faces desperately for comprehension, and as it slowly came to him—when at last he *knew*—he felt the revelation grip him physically with a wild penetrating excitement.

He *knew*, and so he watched with fierce absorption but without surprise as the forward hatch swung open to permit what was beneath to rise to the surface of the deck, and watched still more intently as the crew leaped smartly forward to prepare it with the speed born of long hours of practice. He stood aside then, for he knew he would need training, too, before he could learn his part, but after the first shot from the sleek little cannon had smashed a great hole in the side of the other yacht, he sprang forward as readily as the others to seize the rifles which were being passed around; and as the *Freedom IV* swooped swiftly in toward the floundering survivors, his cries of delight were mixed with those of his comrades, and their weapons cracked out sharply, gaily, across the wild echoing sea.

11

EDWARD D. HOCH

The Oblong Room

It was Fletcher's case from the beginning, but Captain Leopold rode along with him when the original call came in. The thing seemed open and shut, with the only suspect found literally standing over his victim, and on a dull day Leopold thought that a ride out to the University might be pleasant.

Here, along the river, the October color was already in the trees, and through the park a slight haze of burning leaves clouded the road in spots. It was a warm day for autumn, a sunny day. Not really a day for murder.

'The University hasn't changed much,' Leopold commented, as they turned into the narrow street that led past the fraternity houses to the library tower. 'A few new dorms, and a new stadium. That's about all.'

'We haven't had a case here since that bombing four or five years back.' Fletcher said. 'This one looks to be a lot easier, though. They've got the guy already. Stabbed his room-mate and then stayed right there with the body.'

Leopold was silent. They'd pulled up before one of the big new dormitories that towered toward the sky like some middle-income housing project, all brick and concrete and right now surrounded by milling students. Leopold pinned on his badge and led the way.

The room was on the fourth floor, facing the river. It seemed to be identical to all the others—a depressing oblong with bunk beds, twin study desks, wardrobes, and a large picture window opposite the door. The Medical Examiner was already there, and he looked up as Leopold and Fletcher entered. 'We're ready to move him. All right with you, Captain?'

'The boys get their pictures? Then it's fine with me. Fletcher, find out what you can.' Then, to the Medical Examiner, 'What killed him?'

'A couple of stab wounds. I'll do an autopsy, but there's not much doubt.'

'How long dead?'

'A day or so.'

'A day!'

Fletcher had been making notes as he questioned the others. 'The precinct men have it pretty well wrapped up for us, Captain. The dead boy is Ralph Rollings, a sophomore. His room-mate admits to being here with the body for maybe twenty hours before they were discovered. Room-mate's name is Tom McBern. They've got him in the next room.'

Leopold nodded and went through the connecting door. Tom McBern was tall and slender, and handsome in a dark, collegiate sort of way. 'Have you warned him of his rights?' Leopold asked a patrolman.

'Yes sir.'

'All right.' Leopold sat down on the bed opposite McBern. 'What have you got to say, son?'

The deep brown eyes came up to meet Leopold's. 'Nothing, sir. I think I want a lawyer.'

'That's your privilege, of course. You don't wish to make any statement about how your room-mate met his death, or why you remained in the room with him for several hours without reporting it?'

'No, sir.' He turned away and stared out the window.

'You understand we'll have to book you on suspicion of homicide.'

The boy said nothing more, and after a few moments Leopold left him alone with the officer. He went back to Fletcher and watched while the body was covered and carried away. 'He's not talking. Wants a lawyer. Where are we?'

Sergeant Fletcher shrugged. 'All we need is motive. They probably had the same girl or something.'

'Find out.'

They went to talk with the boy who occupied the adjoining room, the one who'd found the body. He was sandy-haired and handsome, with the look of an athlete, and his name was Bill Smith.

'Tell us how it was, Bill,' Leopold said.

'There's not much to tell. I knew Ralph and Tom slightly during my freshman year, but never really well. They stuck pretty much together. This year I got the room next to them, but the connecting door was always locked. Anyway, yesterday neither one of them showed up at class. When I came back yesterday afternoon I knocked at the door and asked if anything was wrong. Tom called out that they were sick. He wouldn't open the door. I went into my own room and didn't think much about it. Then, this morning, I knocked to see how they were. Tom's voice sounded so . . . strange.'

'Where was your own room-mate all this time?'

'He's away. His father died and he went home for the funeral.' Smith's hands were nervous, busy with a shredded piece of paper. Leopold offered him a cigarette and he took it. 'Anyway, when he wouldn't open the door I became quite concerned and told him I was going for help. He opened it then—and I saw Ralph stretched out on the bed, all bloody and . . . dead.'

Leopold nodded and went to stand by the window. From here he could see the trees down along the river, blazing gold and amber and scarlet as the October sun passed across them. 'Had you heard any sounds the previous day? Any argument?'

'No. Nothing. Nothing at all.'

'Had they disagreed in the past about anything?'

'Not that I knew of. If they didn't get along, they hardly would have asked to room together again this year.'

'How about girls?' Leopold asked.

'They both dated occasionally, I think.'

'No special one? One they both liked?'

Bill Smith was silent for a fraction too long. 'No.'

'You're sure?'

'I told you I didn't know them very well.'

'This is murder, Bill. It's not a sophomore dance or class day games.'

'Tom killed him. What more do you need?'

'What's her name, Bill?'

He stubbed out the cigarette and looked away. Then finally he answered. 'Stella Banting. She's a junior.'

'Which one did she go with?'

'I don't know. She was friendly with both of them. I think she went out with Ralph a few times around last Christmas, but I'd seen her with Tom lately.'

'She's older than them?'

'No. They're all twenty. She's just a year ahead.'

'All right,' Leopold said. 'Sergeant Fletcher will want to question you further.'

He left Smith's room and went out in the hall with Fletcher. 'It's your case, Sergeant. About time I gave it to you.'

'Thanks for the help, Captain.'

'Let him talk to a lawyer and then see if he has a story. If he still won't make a statement, book him on suspicion. I don't think there's any doubt we can get an indictment.'

'You going to talk to that girl?'

Leopold smiled. 'I just might. Smith seemed a bit shy about her. Might be a motive there. Let me know as soon as the medical examiner has something more definite about the time of death.'

'Right, Captain.'

Leopold went downstairs, pushing his way through the students and faculty members still crowding the halls and stairways. Outside he unpinned the badge and put it away. The air was fresh and crisp as he strolled across the campus to the administration building.

Stella Banting lived in the largest sorority house on campus, a great columned building of ivy and red brick. But when Captain Leopold found her she was on her way back from the drug store, carrying a carton of cigarettes and a bottle of shampoo. Stella was a tall girl with firm, angular lines and a face that might have been beautiful if she ever smiled.

'Stella Banting?'

'Yes?'

'I'm Captain Leopold. I wanted to talk to you about the tragedy over at the men's dorm. I trust you've heard about it?'

She blinked her eyes and said, 'Yes. I've heard.'

'Could we go somewhere and talk?'

'I'll drop these at the house and we can walk if you'd like. I don't want to talk there.'

She was wearing faded bermuda shorts and a bulky sweatshirt, and walking with her made Leopold feel young again. If only she smiled occasionally—but perhaps this was not a day for smiling. They headed away from the main campus, out toward the silent oval of the athletic field and sports stadium. 'You didn't come over to the dorm,' he said to her finally, breaking the silence of their walk.

'Should I have?'

'I understood you were friendly with them—that you dated the dead boy last Christmas and Tom McBern more recently.'

'A few times. Ralph wasn't the sort anyone ever got to know very well.'

'And what about Tom?'

'He was a nice fellow.'

'*Was?*'

'It's hard to explain. Ralph did things to people, to everyone around him. When I felt it happening to me, I broke away.'

'What sort of things?'

'He had a power—a power you wouldn't believe any twenty-year-old capable of.'

'You sound as if you've known a lot of them.'

'I have. This is my third year at the University. I've grown up a lot in that time. I think I have, anyway.'

'And what about Tom McBern?'

'I dated him a few times recently just to confirm for myself how bad things were. He was completely under Ralph's thumb. He lived for no one but Ralph.'

'Homosexual?' Leopold asked.

'No, I don't think it was anything as blatant as that. It was more the relationship of teacher and pupil, leader and follower.'

'Master and slave?'

She turned to smile at him. 'You do seem intent on midnight orgies, don't you?'

'The boy is dead, after all.'

'Yes. Yes, he is.' She stared down at the ground, kicking randomly at the little clusters of fallen leaves. 'But you see what I mean? Ralph was always the leader, the teacher—for Tom, almost the messiah.'

'Then why would he have killed him?' Leopold asked.

'That's just it—he wouldn't! Whatever happened in that room, I can't imagine Tom McBern ever bringing himself to kill Ralph.'

'There is one possibility, Miss Banting. Could Ralph Rollings have made a disparaging remark about you? Something about when he was dating you?'

'I never slept with Ralph, if that's what you're trying to ask me. With either of them, for that matter.'

'I didn't mean it that way.'

'It happened just the way I've told you. If anything, I was afraid of Ralph. I didn't want him getting that sort of hold over me.'

Somehow he knew they'd reached the end of their stroll, even though they were still in the middle of the campus quadrangle, some distance from the sports arena. 'Thank you for your help, Miss Banting. I may want to call on you again.'

He left her there and headed back toward the men's dorm, knowing that she would watch him until he was out of sight.

Sergeant Fletcher found Leopold in his office early the following morning, reading the daily reports of the night's activities. 'Don't you ever sleep, Captain?' he asked, pulling up the faded leather chair that served for infrequent visitors.

'I'll have enough time for sleeping when I'm dead. What have you got on McBern?'

'His lawyer says he refuses to make a statement, but I gather they'd like to plead him not guilty by reason of insanity.'

'What's the medical examiner say?'

Fletcher read from a typed sheet. 'Two stab wounds, both in the area of the heart. He apparently was stretched out on the bed when he got it.'

'How long before they found him?'

'He'd eaten breakfast maybe an hour or so before he died, and from our questioning that places the time of death at about ten o'clock. Bill Smith went to the door and got McBern to open it at about eight the following morning. Since we know McBern was in the room the previous evening when Smith spoke to him through the door, we can assume he was alone with the body for approximately twenty-two hours.'

Leopold was staring out the window, mentally comparing the city's autumn gloom with the colors of the countryside that he'd witnessed the previous day. Everything dies, only it dies a little sooner, a bit more drably, in the city. 'What else?' he asked Fletcher, because there obviously was something else.

'In one of the desk drawers,' Fletcher said, producing a little evidence envelope. 'Six sugar cubes, saturated with LSD.'

'All right.' Leopold stared down at them. 'I guess that's not too unusual on campuses these days. Has there ever been a murder committed by anyone under the influence of LSD?'

'A case out west somewhere. And I think another one over in England.'

'Can we get a conviction, or is this the basis of the insanity plea?'

'I'll check on it, Captain.'

'And one more thing—get that fellow Smith in here. I want to talk with him again.'

Later, alone, Leopold felt profoundly depressed. The case bothered him. McBern had stayed with Rollings' body for twenty-two hours. Anybody that could last that long would have to be crazy. He was crazy and he was a killer and that was all there was to it.

When Fletcher ushered Bill Smith into the office an hour later, Leopold was staring out the window. He turned and motioned the young man to a chair. 'I have some further questions, Bill.'

'Yes?'

'Tell me about the LSD.'

'What?'

Leopold walked over and sat on the edge of the desk. 'Don't pretend you never heard of it. Rollings and McBern had some in their room.'

Bill Smith looked away. 'I didn't know. There were rumors.'

'Nothing else? No noise through that connecting door?'

'Noise, yes. Sometimes it was . . . .'

Leopold waited for him to continue, and when he did not, said, 'This is a murder investigation, Bill.'

'Rollings . . . he deserved to die, that's all. He was the most completely evil person I ever knew. The things he did to poor Tom . . .'

'Stella Banting says Tom almost worshipped him.'

'He did, and that's what made it all the more terrible.'

Leopold leaned back and lit a cigarette. 'If they were both high on LSD, almost anyone could have entered that room and stabbed Ralph.'

But Bill Smith shook his head. 'I doubt it. They wouldn't have dared unlock the door while they were turned on. Besides, Tom would have protected him with his own life.'

'And yet we're to believe that Tom killed him? That he stabbed him to death and then spent a day and a night alone with the body? Doing what, Bill? Doing what?'

'I don't know.'

'Do you think Tom McBern is insane?'

'No, not really. Not legally.' He glanced away. 'But on the subject of Rollings, he was pretty far gone. Once, when we were still friendly, he told me he'd do anything for Rollings—even trust him with his life. And he did, one time. It was during the spring weekend and everybody had been drinking a lot. Tom hung upside down out of the dorm window with Rollings holding his ankles. That's how much he trusted him.'

'I think I'll have to talk with Tom McBern again,' Leopold said. 'At the scene of the crime.'

Fletcher brought Tom McBern out to the campus in handcuffs, and Captain Leopold was waiting for them in the oblong room on the fourth floor. 'All right, Fletcher,' Leopold said. 'You can leave us alone. Wait outside.'

McBern had lost a good deal of his previous composure, and now he faced Leopold with red-ringed eyes and a lip that trembled when he spoke. 'What . . . what did you want to ask me?'

'A great many things, son. All the questions in the world.' Leopold sighed and offered the boy a cigarette. 'You and Rollings were taking LSD, weren't you?'

'We took it, yes.'

'Why? For kicks?'

'Not for kicks. You don't understand about Ralph.'

'I understand that you killed him. What more is there to understand? You stabbed him to death right over there on that bed.'

Tom McBern took a deep breath. 'We didn't take LSD for kicks,' he repeated. 'It was more to heighten the sense of religious experience—a sort of mystical involvement that is the whole meaning of life.'

Leopold frowned down at the boy. 'I'm only a detective, son. You and Rollings were strangers to me until yesterday, and I guess now he'll always be a stranger to me. That's one of the troubles with my job. I don't get to meet people until it's too late, until the damage'—he gestured toward the empty bed—'is already done. But I want to know what happened in this room, between you two. I don't want to hear about mysticism or religious experience. I want to hear what happened—why you killed him and why you sat here with the body for twenty-two hours.'

Tom McBern looked up at the walls, seeing them perhaps for the first and thousandth time. 'Did you ever think about this room? About the shape of it? Ralph used to say it reminded him of a story by Poe, *The Oblong Box*. Remember that story? The box was on board a ship, and of course it contained a body. Like Queequeg's coffin which rose from the sea to rescue Ishmael.'

'And this room was Ralph's coffin?' Leopold asked quietly.

'Yes.' McBern stared down at his handcuffed wrists. 'His tomb.'

'You killed him, didn't you?'

'Yes.'

Leopold looked away. 'Do you want your lawyer?'

'No. Nothing.'

'My God! Twenty-two hours!'

'I was . . .'

'I know what you were doing. But I don't think you'll ever tell it to a judge and jury.'

'I'll tell you, because maybe you can understand.' And he began to talk in a slow, quiet voice, and Leopold listened because that was his job.

Toward evening, when Tom McBern had been returned to his cell and Fletcher sat alone with Leopold, he said, 'I've called the District Attorney, Captain. What are you going to tell him?'

'The facts, I suppose. McBern will sign a confession of just how it happened. The rest is out of our hands.'

'Do you want to tell me about it, Captain?'

'I don't think I want to tell anyone about it. But I suppose I have to. I guess it was all that talk of religious experience and coffins rising from the ocean that tipped me off. You know, that Rollings pictured their room as a sort of tomb.'

'For him it was.'

'I wish I'd known him, Fletcher. I only wish I'd known him in time.'

'What would you have done?'

'Perhaps only listened and tried to understand him.'

'McBern admitted killing him?'

Leopold nodded. 'It seems that Rollings asked him to, and Tom McBern trusted him more than life itself.'

'Rollings asked to be stabbed through the heart?'

'Yes.'

'Then why did McBern stay with the body so long? For a whole day and night?'

'He was waiting,' Leopold said quietly, looking at nothing at all. 'He was waiting for Rollings to rise from the dead.'

12

TONY HILLERMAN

First Lead Gasser

John Hardin walked into the bureau, glanced at the wall clock (which told him it was 12:22 a.m.), laid his overcoat over a chair, flicked the switch on the teletype to ON, tapped on the button marked BELL, and then punched on the keys with a stiff forefinger:

ALBUQUERQUE . . . YOU TURNED ON? . . . SANTA FE

He leaned heavily on the casing of the machine, waiting, feeling the coolness under his palms, noticing the glass panel was dusty, and hearing the words again and that high, soft voice. Then the teletype bumped tentatively and said:

SANTA FE . . . AYE AYE GO WITH IT . . . ALBUQUERQUE

And John Hardin punched:

ALBUQUERQUE . . . WILL FILE LEAD SUBBING OUT GASSER ITEM IN MINUTE. PLEASE SEND SCHEDULE FOR 300 WORDS TO DENVER . . . SANTA FE

The teletype was silent as Hardin removed the cover from the typewriter (dropping it to the floor). Then the teletype carriage bumped twice and said:

SANTA FE . . . NO RUSH DENVER UNTHINKS GASSER WORTH FILING ON NATIONAL TRUNK DIXIE TORNADOES JAMMING WIRE AND HAVE DANDY HOTEL FIRE AT CHICAGO FOLKS OUTJUMPING WINDOWS ETC HOWEVER STATE OVERNIGHT FILE LUKS LIKE HOTBED OF TRANQUILITY CAN USE LOTS OF GORY DETAILS THERE . . . ALBUQUERQUE

Their footsteps had echoed down the long concrete tube, passed the dark barred mouths of cell blocks, and Thompson had said, 'Is it always this goddam quiet?' and the warden said, 'The cons are always quiet on one of these nights.'

Hardin sighed and said something under his breath and punched:

ALBUQUERQUE . . . REMIND DENVER NITESIDE THAT DENVER DAYSIDE HAS REQUEST FOR 300 WORDS TO BE FILED FOR OHIO PM POINTS . . . S F

He turned his back on the machine, put a carbon book in the typewriter, hit the carriage return twice, and stared at the clock, which now reported the time to be 12:26. While he stared, the second hand made the laborious climb toward 12 and something clicked and the clock said it was 12:27.

Hardin started typing, rapidly:

First Lead Gasser
Santa Fe, N.M., March 28—(UPI)—George Tobias Small, 38, slayer of a young Ohio couple who sought to befriend him, died a minute after midnight today in the gas chamber at the New Mexico State Penitentiary.

He examined the paragraph, pulled the paper from the typewriter, and dropped it. It slid from the top of the desk and planed to the floor, spilling its carbon insert. On a fresh carbon book Hardin typed:

First Lead Gasser
Santa Fe, N.M., March 28—(UPI)—George Tobias Small, 38, who clubbed to death two young Ohio newlyweds last July 4, paid for his crime with his life early today in the New Mexico State Penitentiary gas chamber.

The hulking killer smiled nervously at execution witnesses as three guards pushed three unmarked buttons, one of which dropped cyanide pills into a container of acid under the chair in which he was strapped.

Hulking? Maybe tall, stooped killer: maybe gangling. Not really nervously. Better timidly: smiled timidly. But actually it was an embarrassed smile. Shy. Stepping from the elevator into that too-bright basement room, Small had blinked against the glare and squinted at them lined by the railing—the press corps and the official creeps in the role of 'official witnesses'. He looked surprised and then embarrassed and looked away, then down at his feet. The warden had one hand on his arm: the two of them walking fast toward the front of the chamber, hurrying, while a guard held the steel door open. Above their heads, cell block eight was utterly silent.

Hardin hit the carriage return.

The end came quickly for Small. He appeared to hold his breath for a moment and then breathed deeply of the deadly fumes. His head fell forward and his body slumped in death.

The room had been hot. Stuffy. Smelling of cleaning fluid. But under his hand, the steel railing was cold. 'Looks like a big incinerator,' Thompson said. 'Or like one of those old wood stoves with the chimney out the top.' And the man from the *Albuquerque Journal* said, 'The cons call it the space capsule. Wonder why they put windows in it. There's not much to see.' And Thompson said, with a sort of laugh, that it was the world's longest view. Then it was quiet. Father McKibbon had looked at them a long time when they came in, unsmiling, studying them. Then he had stood stiffly by the open hatch, looking at the floor.

Small, who said he had come to New Mexico from Colorado in search of work, was sentenced to death last November after a district court jury at Raton found him guilty of murder in the deaths of Mr and Mrs Robert M. Martin of Cleveland. The couple had been married only two days earlier and was en route to California on a honeymoon trip.

You could see Father McKibbon saying something to Small—talking rapidly—and Small nodded and then nodded again, and then the warden said something and Small looked up and licked his lips. Then he stepped through the hatch. He tripped on the sill, but McKibbon caught his arm and helped him sit in the little chair, and Small looked up at the priest. And smiled. How would you describe it? Shy, maybe, or grateful. Or maybe sick. Then the guard was reaching in, doing something out of sight. Buckling the straps probably, buckling leather around a warm ankle and a warm forearm which had MOTHER tattooed on it, inside a heart.

Small had served two previous prison terms. He had compiled a police record beginning with a Utah car theft when he was fifteen. Arresting officers testified that he confessed killing the two with a jack handle after Martin resisted Small's attempt at robbery. They said Small admitted flagging down the couple's car after raising the hood on his old-model truck to give the impression he was having trouble.

Should it be flagging down or just flagging? The wall clock inhaled electricity above Hardin's head with a brief buzzing sigh and said 12:32. How long had Small been dead now? Thirty minutes, probably, if cyanide worked as fast as they said. And how long had it been since yesterday, when he had stood outside Small's cell in death row? It was late afternoon, then. You could see the sunlight far down the corridor, slanting in and striped by the bars. Small had said, 'How much time have I got left?' and Thompson looked at his watch and said, 'Four-fifteen from midnight leaves seven hours and forty-five minutes', and Small's bony hands clenched and unclenched on the bars. Then he said, 'Seven hours and forty-five minutes now', and Thompson said, 'Well, my watch might be off a little.'

Behind Hardin the teletype said *ding, ding, ding, dingding.*

SANTA FE . . . DENVER NOW SEZ WILL CALL IN 300 FOR OHIO PM WIRE
SHORTLY. HOW BOUT LEADING SAD SLAYER SAMMY SMALL TODAY GRIMLY
GULPED GAS. OR SOME SUCH???? . . . ALBUQUERQUE

The teletype lapsed into expectant silence, its electric motor purring. Outside, a car drove by with a rush of sound.

Hardin typed:

Small refuted the confession at his trial. He claimed that after Martin stopped to assist him the two men argued and that Martin struck him. He said he then 'blacked out' and could remember nothing more of the incident. Small was arrested when two state policemen who happened by stopped to investigate the parked vehicles.

'The warden told me you was the two that work for the outfits that put things in the papers all over, and I thought maybe you could put something in about finding . . . about maybe . . . something about needing to know where my mother is. You know, so they can get the word to her.' He walked back to his bunk, back into the darkness, and sat down and then got up again and walked back to the barred door, three steps. 'It's about getting buried. I need someplace for that.' And Thompson said, 'What's her name?' and Small looked down at the floor. 'That's part of the trouble. You see, this man she was living with when we were there in Salt Lake, well, she and him . . .'

Arresting officers and other witnesses testified there was nothing mechanically wrong with Small's truck, that there was no mark on Small to indicate he had been struck by Martin, and that Martin had been slain by repeated blows on the back of his head.

Small was standing by the bars now, gripping them so that the stub showed where the end of his ring finger had been cut off. Flexing his hands, talking fast. 'The warden, well, he told me they'd send me wherever I said after it's over, back home, he said. They'd pay for it. But I won't know where to tell them unless somebody can find Mama. There was a place we stayed for a long time before we went to San Diego, and I went to school there some but I don't remember the name of it, and then we moved someplace up the coast where they grow figs and like that, and then I think it was Oregon next, and then I believe it was we moved on out to Salt Lake.' Small stopped talking then, and let his hands rest while he looked at them, at Thompson and him, and said, 'But I bet Mama would remember where I'm supposed to go.'

Mrs Martin's body was found in a field about forty yards from the highway. Officers said the pretty bride had apparently attempted to flee, had tripped and injured an ankle, and had then been beaten to death by Small.

Subject: George Tobias Small, alias Toby Small, alias G. T. Small. White male, about 38 (birth date, place unknown); weight, 188, height 6'4"; eyes, brown; complexion, ruddy; distinguishing characteristics: noticeable stoop, carries right shoulder higher than left. Last two joints missing from left ring finger, deep scar on left upper lip, tattoo of heart with word MOTHER on inner right forearm.

Charge: Violation Section 12-2(3) Criminal Code.

Disposition: Guilty of Murder, Colfax County District Court.

Sentence: Death.

Previous Record: July 28, 1941, sentenced Utah State Reformatory, car theft. April 7, 1943, returned Utah State Reformatory, B&E and parole violation. February 14, 1945, B&E, resisting arrest. Classified juvenile incorrigible. August 3, 1949, armed robbery, 5–7 years at . . .

Small had been in trouble with the law since boyhood, starting his career with a car theft at twelve and then violating reformatory parole with a burglary. Before his twenty-first birthday he was serving the first of three prison terms.

Small had rested his hands on the brace between the bars, but they wouldn't rest. The fingers twisted tirelessly among themselves. Blind snakes, even the stub of the missing finger moving restlessly. 'Rock fell on it when I was little. Think it was that. The warden said he sent the word around about Mama, but I guess nobody found her yet. Put it down that she might be living in Los Angeles. That man with us there in Salt Lake, he wanted to go out to the coast and maybe that's where they went.'

It was then Thompson stopped him. 'Wait a minute,' Thompson said. 'Where was she from, your mother? Why not . . .'

'I don't remember that,' Small said. He was looking down at the floor.

And Thompson asked, 'Didn't she tell you?' and Small said, still not looking at us, 'Sure, but I was little.'

'You don't remember the town or anything? How little were you?' And Small sort of laughed and said, 'Just exactly twelve,' and laughed again, and said, 'That's why I thought maybe I could come home, it was my birthday. We was living in a house trailer then, and Mama's man had been drinking. Her too. When he did that, he'd whip me and run me off. So I'd been staying with a boy I knew there at school, in the garage, but his folks said I couldn't stay anymore and it was my birthday, so I thought I'd go by, maybe it would be all right.'

Small had taken his hands off the bars then. He walked back to the bunk and sat down. And when he started talking again it was almost too low to hear it all.

'They was gone. The trailer was gone. The man at the office said they'd just took off in the night. Owed him rent, I guess,' Small said. He was quiet again.

Thompson said, 'Well,' and then he cleared his throat, said, 'Leave you a note or anything?'

And Small said, 'No, sir. No note.'

'That's when you stole the car, I guess,' Thompson said. 'The car theft you went to the reformatory for.'

'Yes, sir,' Small said. 'I thought I'd go to California and find her. I thought she was going to Los Angeles, but I never knowed no place to write. You could write all the letters you wanted there at the reformatory, but I never knowed the place to send it to.'

Thompson said, 'Oh,' and Small got up and came up to the bars and grabbed them.

'How much time have I got now?'

Small stepped through the oval hatch in the front of the gas chamber at two minutes before midnight, and the steel door was sealed behind him to prevent seepage of the deadly gas. The prison doctor said the first whiff of the cyanide fumes would render a human unconscious almost instantly.

'We believe Mr Small's death will be almost painless,' he said.

'The warden said they can keep my body a couple days but then they'll just have to go on ahead and bury me here at the pen unless somebody claims it. They don't have no place cold to keep it from spoiling on 'em. Anyway, I think a man oughta be put down around his kin if he has any. That's the way I feel about it.'

And Thompson started to say something and cleared his throat and said, 'How does it feel to—I mean, about tonight?' and Small's hands tightened on the bars. 'Oh, I won't say I'm not scared. I never said that but they say it don't hurt but I been hurt before, cut and all, and I never been scared of that so much.'

Small's words stopped coming and then they came loud, and the guard reading at the door in the corridor looked around and then back at his book. 'It's the not knowing,' he said, and his hands disappeared from the bars and he walked back to the dark end of the cell and sat on the bunk and got up again and walked and said, 'Oh, God, it's not knowing.'

Small cooperated with his executioners. While the eight witnesses required by law watched, the slayer appeared to be helping a guard attach the straps which held his legs in place in the gas chamber. He leaned back while his forearms were strapped to the chair.

The clock clicked and sighed and the minute hand pointed at the eight partly hidden behind a tear-shaped dribble of paint on the glass, and the teletype, stirred by this, said *ding, ding, ding*.

SANTA FE . . . DENVER WILL INCALL GASSER AFTER SPORTS ROUNDUP NOW MOVING. YOU BOUT GOT SMALL WRAPPED UP? . . . ALBUQUERQUE

Hardin pulled the carbon book from the typewriter and marked out 'down' after the verb 'flagging'. He penciled a line through 'give the impression he was' and wrote in 'simulate'. He clipped the copy to the holder above the teletype keyboard, folding it to prevent obscuring the glass panel, switched the key from KEYBOARD to TAPE, and began punching. The thin yellow strip, lacy with perforations, looped downward toward the floor and built rapidly there into a loopy pile.

He had seen Small wiping the back of his hand across his face. When he came back to the bars he had looked away.

'The padre's been talking to me about it every morning,' Small had said. 'That's Father McKibbon. He told me a lot I never knew before, mostly about Jesus, and I'd heard about that, of course. It was back when I was in that place at Logan, that chaplain there, he talked about Jesus some, and I remembered some of it. But that one there at Logan, he talked mostly about sin and about hell and things like that, and this McKibbon, the padre here, well, he talked different.' Small's hands had been busy on the bars again and then Small had looked directly at him, directly into his face, and then at Thompson. He remembered the tense heavy face, sweaty, and the words and the voice too soft and high for the size of the man.

'I wanted to ask you to do what you could about finding my mama. I looked for her all the time. When they'd turn me loose, I'd hunt for her. But maybe you could find her. With the newspapers and all. And I want to hear what you think about it all,' Small said. 'About what happens to me after they take me out of that gas chamber. I wanted to see what you say about that.' And then Small said into the long silence, 'Well, whatever it's going to be, it won't be any worse than it's been.' And he paused again, and looked back into the cell as if he expected to see someone there, and then back at us.

'But when I walk around in here and my foot hits the floor I feel it, you know, and I think that's Toby Small I'm feeling there with his foot on the cement. It's *me*. And I guess that don't sound like much, but after tonight I guess there won't be that for one thing. And I hope there's somebody there waiting for me. I hope there's not just me.' And he sat down on the bunk.

'I was wondering what you thought about this Jesus and what McKibbon has been telling me.' He had his head between his hands now, looking at the floor, and it made his voice muffled. 'You reckon he was lying about it? I don't see any cause for it, but how can a man know all that and be sure about it?'

The clatter of the transmission box joined the chatter of the perforator. Hardin marked his place in the copy and leaned over to fish a cigarette out of his overcoat. He lit it, took it out of his mouth, and turned back to the keyboard. Above him, above the duet chatter of tape and keyboard, he heard the clock strike again, and click, and when he looked up it was 12:46.

McKibbon had his hand on Small's elbow, crushing the pressed prison jacket, talking to him, his face fierce and intent. And Small was listening, intent. Then he nodded and nodded again and when he stepped through the hatch he bumped his head on the steel hard enough so you could hear it back at the railing, and then Hardin could see his face through the round glass and it looked numb and pained.

McKibbon had stepped back, and while the guard was working with the straps, he began reading from a book. Loud, wanting Small to hear. Maybe wanting all of them to hear.

'Have mercy on me, O Lord; for unto thee have I cried all the day, for thou, O Lord, art sweet and mild: and plenteous in mercy unto all that call upon thee. Incline thine ear, O Lord, and hear me: for I am needy and poor. Preserve my soul; for I am holy: O thou my God, save thy servant that trusteth in thee.'

The pile of tape on the floor diminished and the final single loop climbed toward the stop bar and the machine was silent. Hardin looked through the dusty glass, reading the last paragraph for errors.

There was his face, there through the round window, and his brown eyes unnaturally wide, looking at something or looking for something. And then the pump made a sucking noise and the warden came over and said, 'Well, I guess we can all go home now.'

He switched the machine back from TAPE to KEYBOARD and punched:

SMALL'S BODY WILL BE HELD UNTIL THURSDAY, THE WARDEN SAID, IN THE EVENT THE SLAYER'S MOTHER CAN BE LOCATED TO CLAIM IT. IF NOT, IT WILL BE BURIED IN THE PRISON LOT.

He switched off the machine. And in the room the only sound was the clock, which was buzzing again and saying it was 12:49.

First Lead Gasser

AUTHOR'S NOTE: Whatever the merits of 'First Lead Gasser' as a short story, it is important to me. The incident it concerns happened (with 'only the names changed to protect the innocent'), and it caused me to think seriously for the first time about writing fiction. The Thompson of the short story was the late John Curtis of the Associated Press. I was Hardin, then New Mexico manager of the now defunct United Press. Toby Small, under another name but guilty of the same crime, did in fact inhale cyanide fumes at midnight in the basement gas chamber of the New Mexico State Prison. Thus 'First Lead Gasser' is more or less autobiographical. That alone is scant reason to present it to a magazine whose readers have come to expect mystery short stories.

What makes it important to me, and perhaps of some interest to you, are two facts. First, my inability to deal with the 'truth' of the Toby Small tragedy in the three hundred words allotted me by journalism stuck in my mind. How could one report the true meaning of that execution while sticking to objective facts? I played with it, and a sort of nonfiction short story evolved. Second, Toby Small's hands on the bars, Toby Small's shy smile through the gas chamber window, and the story Toby Small told Curtis and me became part of those memories a reporter can't shake.

Those of you who have read *People of Darkness* met Toby Small under the name of Colton Wolf, reincarnated as he might have evolved if fate had allowed him to live a few murders longer. The plot required a professional hit man. Since it seems incredible to me that anyone would kill for hire, I was finding it hard to conceive the character. Then the old memory of Small's yearning for his mother came to my rescue. I think I did a better job of communicating the tragedy of Small in the book than in the short story. A quarter century of additional practice should teach one something. But I'm still not skilled enough to do justice to that sad afternoon, listening to a damaged man wondering what he would find when he came out of the gas chamber.

BIOGRAPHICAL NOTES

1

Edgar Allan Poe (1809–49) led a short and tragic life oppressed by poverty, complicated by alcohol abuse, and shadowed by deaths of those he loved. Born in Boston, Poe was orphaned as a toddler, educated briefly in England, and later expelled from West Point. He married a 13-year-old cousin who died a decade later. Never employed for long in one place, he served as editor and literary critic on several important magazines while turning out essays, poetry, and short stories at a feverish pace. First published in *Godey's Lady's Book* in November 1846, 'The Cask of Amontillado' is a link between Poe's ratiocinative work, which established his reputation as the father of the modern detective story, and his tales of horror, in which a threatening, brooding atmosphere instils awe in the reader.

2

Ellis Parker Butler (1869–1937) was born in Muscatine, Iowa, the eldest of eight children. When his father and grandfather's pork-packing business went bust, failing family finances caused Butler to be housed with his Aunt Lizzie, a cultured spinster who encouraged her nephew's love of literature. Forced to quit high school by the family's financial needs, Butler pursued a variety of jobs before founding *Decorative Furnisher* magazine in New York in 1899. His runaway success was the farcical *Pigs Is Pigs* (1906) a slim volume about a bureaucratic slip-up that leads to an overabundance of guinea pigs in a consignment office. Butler also authored *Perkins of Portland: Perkins the Great* (1906), which includes some crime stories, and *Philo Gubb, Correspondence School Detective* (1919), featuring an hilariously hapless sleuth. First printed under the title 'Our First Burglar' in *Everybody's Magazine* in 1909, 'The Silver Protector' proves that burglary prevention can be a crime.

3

Susan Glaspell (1882–1948) graduated from Drake University in Des Moines, Iowa, and became a reporter for the *Des Moines Daily News*, before drawing upon her home-town experience in Davenport, Iowa, to become an important local-colour writer. After marrying George Cram Cook, a rebel against small-town pretensions, Glaspell incorporated literary realism into her fiction. She left Davenport for New York City's Greenwich Village, and Cape Cod, Massachusetts, where she founded, with Eugene O'Neill, the Provincetown Players. She became a novelist and Pulitzer Prize-winning playwright. The short story 'A Jury of Her Peers' was originally a one-act play based on a case of spousal abuse that Glaspell covered as a reporter. This classic of realism was first published in *Every Week* magazine on 5 March 1917.

4

Carter Dickson is a pseudonym adopted by John Dickson Carr (1906–77), a writer acknowledged as the unsurpassed master of the locked room mystery or impossible crime. The son of a Pennsylvania congressman, Carr was educated at Haverford College and in Paris. Upon his marriage to an Englishwoman he moved to Great Britain, where he lived for most of the rest of his life, turning out seventy novels over his lifetime and scripting radio dramas for the BBC. Carr/Dickson's famous series characters include the Parisian Henri Bencolin; the omniscient Dr Gideon Fell; Sir Henry Merrivale; and Colonel March of The Department of Queer Complaints. In 'The Other Hangman', which was first published in the 1935 anthology *A Century of Detective Stories*, the author ventures into the realm of the crime story, where psychology rather than detection drives the action.

5

Cornell (George Hopley-) Woolrich (1903–68) led as dark an existence as do the characters in his fiction. Born in New York City to parents who were already estranged, Woolrich spent part of his childhood in Latin America with his civil engineer father and the rest residing in New York hotels with his socialite mother. He started writing during an illness-induced absence from Columbia University, producing romantic novels. He went to Hollywood in 1929 but, after his wife of three weeks left him, Woolrich returned to share New York hotel digs with his mother, where he obsessively penned prose packed with suspense and paranoia, publishing some work under the pseudonyms William Irish and George Hopley. First published in *Dime Detective* in August 1937, 'Murder at the Automat' demonstrates how a miser's desire for the cheapest sandwich in the place does him in.

6

Raymond Chandler (1888–1959) was born in Chicago and educated in England, where he later worked as a freelance writer. During the First World War, Chandler served with Canadian forces before transferring to the Royal Flying Corps (RAF). Upon his return to the United States in 1919, he directed various companies until his drinking habits and the Great Depression combined to end his career in business. Chandler was 45 years old when he began to write for *Black Mask* magazine in 1933. Six years later he published his first novel, *The Big Sleep*. His series private eye is Philip Marlowe, a loner whose personal code of honour makes him a wisecracking, modern knight errant in a world seen as decadent and corrupt. Marlowe meets trouble—and the hot Santa Ana wind—head-on in 'Red Wind', first published in *Dime Detective* in January 1938.

7

Margaret (Ellis Sturm) Millar (1915–94) was born in Ontario, Canada, and educated in Canada before she met and married Kenneth Millar. Although the two were both published as teens in the same magazine, and her husband published four novels under the Millar name, she was initially the better known of the two to write under the Millar name, which she used throughout her career, while her husband gained literary fame under the pseudonym Ross Macdonald. Millar wrote her first mystery novel, *The Invisible Worm*, in 1941 while convalescing from a heart ailment. Using various series characters, she was known for her psychological exploration of character combined with a talent to evoke uneasiness, as typified in her 1960 novel, *A Stranger in My Grave*, and in 'The Couple Next Door', first published in *Ellery Queen's Mystery Magazine* in July 1954.

8

Leigh Brackett (1915–78), best known as a science fiction writer, was also an important early female practitioner of hardboiled fiction. Her first full-length novel, *No Good from a Corpse* (1944), was a private-eye tale set in California, written in a Chandleresque style. In 1946 Brackett, who admired Raymond Chandler, collaborated with William Faulkner and Jules Furthman on the screenplay for Chandler's *The Big Sleep* and later wrote the 1973 screenplay for *The Long Goodbye*. She also penned three suspense novels. Two of them were published in 1957, the same year that the men's magazine *Argosy* printed 'So Pale, So Cold, So Fair', a noir piece in which a 'society doll with brains' helps a journalist to discover the truth behind the apparent suicide of the love of his life.

9

William Campbell Gault (1910–1985) was a Milwaukee-born writer of juvenile fiction, private eye novels, and short stories published in the pulp magazines. Gault's particular talent as a crime writer was to express a wry, hardboiled outlook on human nature and contrast it with the behaviour of his thoroughly decent heroes including Joe Puma and Brock 'The Rock' Callahan. The Mystery Writers of America awarded his novel *Don't Cry For Me* (1952) an Edgar award for best first novel and critics lauded Gault's private eye prose. None the less, he found better commercial success in writing boys' sports novels. He turned his talents to that market for two decades, beginning in the 1960s, and was a septuagenarian when he made an award-winning comeback in the crime genre. 'Take Care of Yourself' was first published in *Murder* in July 1957.

10

David Ely is the pseudonym of David Eli Lilienthal (1927–   ), a writer of male action fiction. Born in Chicago, Ely attended the University of North Carolina for a year before completing his bachelor's degree at Harvard University. He was then awarded a Fulbright Scholarship to Oxford University, following which he served in the US Navy from 1945–1946 and then the US Army from 1950–1952. He worked as a reporter for the *St Louis Post-Dispatch* between his military services. Ely was then employed by the Development and Resources Corporation in New York, before he turned to writing full-time. Ely demonstrated his fascination with the male urge to succeed at all costs in six novels and his 1968 volume of short stories, *Time Out*. First published in *Cosmopolitan* magazine in 1962, 'The Sailing Club' is a tale of male competitiveness taken to the ultimate extreme.

11

Edward D(entinger) Hoch (1930–) has written five novels and established himself as a highly respected editor of anthologies, but his great achievement is to have made a living largely from the writing of short fiction. This native of Rochester, New York, began writing detective stories when he was a teenager and continued throughout his studies at the University of Rochester, two years in the US Army, and jobs in the Rochester Public Library, with Pocket Books in New York City, and in advertising and public relations in Rochester. Hoch's perseverance led him to break into print at age 25, and he has published nearly 800 short stories since then. 'The Oblong Room' was first published in *The Saint* in July 1967. When Hoch won an Edgar Allan Poe Award for it, he decided to turn to writing full-time.

12

Tony Hillerman (1925–) is the best-known living writer of American regional mysteries. Born in the dust-bowl village of Sacred Heart, Oklahoma, Hillerman attended a boarding-school for Potawatomie Indian girls and dreamed of becoming a chemical engineer. His college career was interrupted by military service in the US Army infantry in the Second World War. After the war, Hillerman studied journalism at the University of Oklahoma, became a journalist for seventeen years, and then a professor of journalism at the University of New Mexico for five years before becoming a full-time writer. While most of his work features the Native American Navajo Tribal police officers Joe Leaphorn and Jim Chee, Hillerman used his experience of the world of journalism in two novels and in 'First Lead Gasser', a story first published in *Ellery Queen's Mystery Magazine* in April 1993.

SOURCE ACKNOWLEDGEMENTS

Carter Dickson, *The Other Hangman*, first published in *A Century of Detective Stories*, edited Anon (Hutchinson, 1935), US Copyright. Reprinted by permission of Harold Ober Associates Incorporated, Copyright © 1935 by John Dickson Carr. UK Copyright © David Higham Associates.

Cornell Woolrich, *Murder at the Automat*, first published in *Dime Detective*, August 1937, reprinted by permission of the author's estate.

Raymond Chandler, *Red Wind*, first published in *Dime Detective*, January 1938, reprinted in *Trouble is My Business*, Raymond Chandler (Vintage Crime/Black Lizard, Vintage Books, Division of Random House, New York, 1992), US Copyright © Houghton Mifflin Company, New York; UK Copyright © Hamish Hamilton Ltd., London.

Margaret Millar, *The Couple Next Door*, first published in *Ellery Queen's Mystery Magazine*, July 1954, reprinted by permission of Margaret Millar and David Higham Associates.

Leigh Brackett, *So Pale, So Cold, So Fair*, first published in *Argosy*, 1957, reprinted in *Hard-Boiled: An Anthology of American Crime Stories*, edited by Bill Pronzini and Jack Adrian (Oxford University Press, 1995), reprinted by permission of Spectrum Literary Agency on behalf of the Estate of Leigh Brackett Hamilton, published by permission of The Estate of Leigh Brackett, c/o Ralph M. Vicinanza Ltd., New York.

William Campbell Gault, *Take Care of Yourself*, first published in *Murder* in July 1957, reprinted by permission of the author's estate.

David Ely, *The Sailing Club*, first published in *Cosmopolitan*, 1962, reprinted by permission of the author and Roberta Pryor Inc., New York.

Edward D. Hoch, *The Oblong Room*, first published in *The Saint*, July 1967, © 1967 by Fiction Publishing Company, renewed by the author.

Tony Hillerman, *First Lead Gasser*, published in *The Tony Hillerman Companion*, Tony Hillerman (HarperCollins, 1994), reprinted by permission of Curtis Brown Ltd. Copyright © 1994 by Tony Hillerman.

OXFORD

MORE OXFORD PAPERBACKS

This book is just one of nearly 1000 Oxford Paperbacks currently in print. If you would like details of other Oxford Paperbacks, including titles in the World's Classics, Oxford Reference, Oxford Books, OPUS, Past Masters, Oxford Authors, and Oxford Shakespeare series, please write to:

UK and Europe: Oxford Paperbacks Publicity Manager, Arts and Reference Publicity Department, Oxford University Press, Walton Street, Oxford OX2 6DP.

Customers in UK and Europe will find Oxford Paperbacks available in all good bookshops. But in case of difficulty please send orders to the Cash-with-Order Department, Oxford University Press Distribution Services, Saxon Way West, Corby, Northants NN18 9ES. Tel: 01536 741519; Fax: 01536 746337. Please send a cheque for the total cost of the books, plus £1.75 postage and packing for orders under £20; £2.75 for orders over £20. Customers outside the UK should add 10% of the cost of the books for postage and packing.

USA: Oxford Paperbacks Marketing Manager, Oxford University Press, Inc., 200 Madison Avenue, New York, N.Y. 10016.

Canada: Trade Department, Oxford University Press, 70 Wynford Drive, Don Mills, Ontario M3C 1J9.

Australia: Trade Marketing Manager, Oxford University Press, G.P.O. Box 2784Y, Melbourne 3001, Victoria.

South Africa: Oxford University Press, P.O. Box 1141, Cape Town 8000.

ILLUSTRATED HISTORIES IN OXFORD PAPERBACKS

THE OXFORD ILLUSTRATED HISTORY OF ENGLISH LITERATURE

Edited by Pat Rogers

Britain possesses a literary heritage which is almost unrivalled in the Western world. In this volume, the richness, diversity, and continuity of that tradition are explored by a group of Britain's foremost literary scholars.

Chapter by chapter the authors trace the history of English literature, from its first stirrings in Anglo-Saxon poetry to the present day. At its heart towers the figure of Shakespeare, who is accorded a special chapter to himself. Other major figures such as Chaucer, Milton, Donne, Wordsworth, Dickens, Eliot, and Auden are treated in depth, and the story is brought up to date with discussion of living authors such as Seamus Heaney and Edward Bond.

'[a] lovely volume . . . put in your thumb and pull out plums' Michael Foot

'scholarly and enthusiastic people have written inspiring essays that induce an eagerness in their readers to return to the writers they admire' *Economist*

Oxford Paperback Reference

OXFORD PAPERBACK REFERENCE

From *Art and Artists* to *Zoology*, the Oxford Paperback Reference series offers the very best subject reference books at the most affordable prices.

Authoritative, accessible, and up to date, the series features dictionaries in key student areas, as well as a range of fascinating books for a general readership. Included are such well-established titles as Fowler's *Modern English Usage*, Margaret Drabble's *Concise Companion to English Literature*, and the bestselling science and medical dictionaries.

The series has now been relaunched in handsome new covers. Highlights include new editions of some of the most popular titles, as well as brand new paperback reference books on *Politics*, *Philosophy*, and *Twentieth-Century Poetry*.

With new titles being constantly added, and existing titles regularly updated, Oxford Paperback Reference is unrivalled in its breadth of coverage and expansive publishing programme. New dictionaries of *Film*, *Economics*, *Linguistics*, *Architecture*, *Archaeology*, *Astronomy*, and *The Bible* are just a few of those coming in the future.

PAST MASTERS

A wide range of unique, short, clear introductions to the lives and work of the world's most influential thinkers. Written by experts, they cover the history of ideas from Aristotle to Wittgenstein. Readers need no previous knowledge of the subject, so they are ideal for students and general readers alike.

Each book takes as its main focus the thought and work of its subject. There is a short section on the life and a final chapter on the legacy and influence of the thinker. A section of further reading helps in further research.

The series continues to grow, and future Past Masters will include **Owen Gingerich** on *Copernicus*, **R G Frey** on *Joseph Butler*, **Bhiku Parekh** on *Gandhi*, **Christopher Taylor** on *Socrates*, **Michael Inwood** on *Heidegger*, and **Peter Ghosh** on *Weber*.